D1605825

SECOND COMES WAR

PROMISED IN BLOOD, 2

LILITH VINCENT

First I bled. Then I fought. Now, it's war.

Fate turned on me, chewed me up and spat me out. I've been dragged down into the depths of hell until my lungs are burning and the light of day has turned blood red.

But I'm still breathing.

Fate turned on them, as well. The devil princes who rule this city, and who dare try and rule me. I might not have their muscle or brutality, but I possess the ultimate power.

Their hearts.

Why settle for pieces of shattered souls when I can have everything? I'm the Princess of Coldlake, and when war is declared and the battle lines are drawn, this city is going to burn.

This city will be ours.

Author's note: Second Comes War is the second book in the Promised in Blood series and ends on a cliffhanger. These books contain dark themes, violence, and a Why Choose romance with ruthlessly possessive men. The story is dark, dirty, and delicious, so please read at your discretion.

SECOND COMES WAR (PROMISED IN BLOOD, 2) by LILITH VINCENT

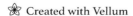 Created with Vellum

1

Chiara

"Dance with me, baby."

Mom's face swims into focus. Her smiling, beautiful face.

"Mom!" Happiness bursts through me. The happiness of a child, and when I look at my hands stretching toward her, I see that I am a child. A little girl with chubby fingers and dimples in her knuckles.

Mom picks me up and twirls me in her arms. When she sets me on my feet, she starts to dance. She's dressed in one of her neat two-piece wool suits and she's taken off her high heels. A record spins on the old record player, and a mournful tune twines through the air.

"Come on, baby. Dance with me."

I'm rooted to the spot in front of her, gazing up with wide open eyes. "I...don't know how."

She gives a musical laugh. "But everyone knows how to dance. Just move your feet, baby. Side to side, like this." In her stockinged feet, she treads the carpet. Her fingers tickle my palms, urging me to give it a try.

"I...can't. I must have forgotten how when I died."

The smile fades from Mom's face. Her feet drag on the carpet and come to a stop. She cups my cheeks, and yet it feels like someone's pinching my nose. Hard.

"Ow. You're hurting me."

"Baby. Wake up."

"I am awake."

"You have to wake up," she whispers.

I stare into Mom's eyes, too afraid to blink in case she disappears. If I leave her, I won't see her again for a long, long time. A sob rises in my throat. "But I don't want to go. I want to stay here with you."

Her eyes are filled with despair, but she pushes me away. "You've got to baby. You've got to."

My heart contracts, my lungs spasm, and it all comes rushing back. Every hateful piece of it.

Life.

Sorrow.

Pain.

"MOM, no. I don't want to go. *Please.*"

Someone captures my flailing hands. A car engine roars.

"She's coming around." A large hand slaps my cheek

gently. "*Bambina*, open your eyes for me." A deep voice, richly accented. Sometimes severe, sometimes comforting, but always commanding.

Cassius Ferragamo.

"She didn't do it. Fuck. *Fuck*." A voice tightly coiled with venom. There's a muted thump like whoever it is has hit the steering wheel with the heel of his hand.

Lorenzo Scava.

"It doesn't matter that she didn't do it. It matters that she had the choice." A cunning, intense voice that he can use like a weapon to get what he wants.

Vinicius Angeli.

"We'll take comfort in that when the mayor slits her fucking throat," Lorenzo snarls.

But wasn't there a fourth voice? An arrogant, autocratic one that's by turns charming and despicable.

Salvatore lifting the gun. A sharp crack, and then a bullet hitting my stomach with the force of a battering ram.

I'm laying on my back, and I raise my head and stare at my midsection. The front of my wedding gown is a shocking mess of blood and torn fabric. I don't feel anything but cold, and that's a bad sign, isn't it? That's the worst sign.

"Am I dying?" I whisper.

Cassius is hovering over me on the back seat, his heavy brows drawn together and his brown eyes stormy. He grasps the neckline of my wedding gown and rips it open. The strapless gown rends right down the middle, exposing my breasts in their white lace bra. I squeeze my eyes shut for a second, bracing for the sight of torn flesh.

And then open my eyes and look at the damage.

In wonder, I touch the smooth skin of my stomach. It's

reddened and mottled, but there's no bullet wound, and the blood doesn't seem to be...mine?

"A shame. It was a nice dress," Cassis says, picking at the bodice of the garment with a thumb and forefinger. It's thick. Reinforced with more than fabric. "You must feel like you've been punched in the guts, *bambina*. Don't worry. This blood is synthetic."

A bulletproof bodice. Fake blood. A pretend wedding.

But a very real bullet.

"You guessed Salvatore might try to kill me," I say, struggling to sit up. How did I even get here?

My lungs are burning. My stomach is burning. Cassius forbade me from saying his former friend's name, but I don't care. I need answers.

Vinicius turns around in the passenger seat. His breathtakingly handsome face is creased in sympathy, and he reaches out and touches my cheek. "We suspected your father would want you dead if you wouldn't obey him. I'm sorry, kitten."

Hot tears crowd the back of my throat as I picture Dad's disgust as he turned away from me, his only child, falling into the swimming pool. Salvatore's expression of disdain replays vividly in my mind as he pointed the gun at me. I knew he could be ruthless, but there were times when I genuinely cared for him, and I thought he cared for me.

What a brutal life this is. The one who kisses you and promises you forever one moment is the one firing bullets at you the next. He was my first kiss. The first one to touch me. The first man to take my heart and cradle it in his wicked, undeserving hands.

I gaze down at the vicious impact welt on my stomach. And the first man to break me open with despair.

The tatters of my wedding dress fall around me on the leather seat. I meet Lorenzo's glacial blue eyes in the rearview mirror, so pale they're nearly colorless and as unnerving as the honed edge of a blade.

"There's a hoodie in the back," he says, and turns his attention to the road. His tattooed fingers grip the steering wheel as he drives.

Cassius reaches over the back seat and grabs an over-sized black sweatshirt. Oversized on me, anyway. The garment would fit perfectly on Lorenzo's muscled shoulders, but I'm swimming in it as I pull it over my body like a dress.

It smells like him. Lorenzo. His rich, overpowering masculine scent that invaded my head as he invaded my body at gunpoint. I stare at the black fabric, feeling like its warmth is Lorenzo's warmth. I'm as conflicted as ever by the man's merciless, unpredictable cruelty and the way he manages to make me genuinely feel like the sarcastic pet name he calls me.

Princess.

I rub my hands over my face. Being Coldlake's princess is what got me into this mess. Naïve. Sheltered. Oblivious to what was going on in my own home. The huge, expensive home that was paid for, not by my father's salary as mayor, but by corrupt deals with criminals.

Three of them are in the car with me right this second. All of them I've had sex with, and I loved every terrifying, delicious second of feeling their skin against my skin, their mouths against my lips, my throat, my pussy.

They helped me take revenge against the man who murdered my mother in cold blood, and what did I do?

I.

Fucked.

It.

Up.

I groan and press the sleeves of the hoodie over my face. I feel like my head's going to explode at the lightning pace my thoughts are going. I thought I was prepared to face my father, but I didn't understand that what I really wanted from him wasn't his death.

I've seen their wedding photos from when they were both twenty and deeply in love. Over the years I saw the adoration in Dad's face as Mom gave speeches on stage at campaign rallies. He loved her just as much in recent years as he did when they were first married. Or I thought he did.

I wanted his sorrow.

I wanted his pain.

I wanted to see that the man who brought me into this world still had some humanity left, despite trying to sell me off to the highest bidder.

A strong hand reaches back and clasps mine, and a voice roughened with emotion says, "Kitten, it will be okay."

I open my eyes, and there's heartfelt sincerity in Vinicius' golden-hazel gaze.

"You don't know that."

I tried to kill the Mayor of Coldlake.

I'm a dead woman.

"*Bambina*, come here." Cassius tries to pull me into his arms, but I put my palm against his chest and resist him.

"Stop. I don't understand." They're all taking my near-death experience in stride. What happened to the furious, obsessive over-protectiveness they've all shown for me the past year? Merely sitting in a car with a Geak was enough to propel them all into a frenzied car chase that ended with the boy being beaten to a pulp and killed.

Salvatore just *shot* me. They should be baying for his blood, and yet we're calmly driving through the city. Am I nothing to these men now?

Fine. That's absolutely fine with me because Coldlake is the last place I want to be when Dad finds out I'm not dead. I reach for the door handle. "Just pull over and let me out."

Lorenzo gives one short, humorless bark of laughter and keeps driving.

"I said let me *out*."

"And where would you go?" Vinicius challenges me. "Right now, the mayor thinks you're dead, and you need to keep it that way."

I glance at the diamond sparkling on my left hand. I still have my insanely expensive engagement ring. I'll leave the city, or better yet, leave the country. It's what I wanted to do in the first place.

"Anywhere but Coldlake."

"Ah, princess," Lorenzo says, "Don't you want us anymore?"

The line between captors and lovers has become blurred lately, but no man is going to shrug off my attempted murder and then try to touch me, whether he's keeping me captive or not.

"Salvatore shot me and you're all acting like it's no big deal."

Lorenzo sneers at the road ahead. "No big deal? Oh,

princess, how wrong you are. We've got unfinished business with Salvatore Fiore."

"Lots of unfinished business," Cassius echoes, his eyes narrowed with dark intent.

In the front seat, Vinicius cracks his knuckles.

A vivid picture flashes in my mind of the three of them beating Salvatore to death.

Lorenzo twists the wheel of the car. We pull into a side street and Lorenzo slams on the brakes. It's a rundown part of the city, not unlike the area Griffin took me when he attempted to deliver me to the Geak leader, Jax. Streets so uncaring that you could beat someone to death here and no one would take a second glance.

The passenger door next to me opens. The sunshine is so bright that I can't make out the face of the person standing outside. I see a white shirt fitted to powerful shoulders. Light brown hair that's glistening in the sun. A winning smile and row of neat, white teeth.

I blink several times, and he comes into focus.

Salvatore.

The man I was promised to.

The man who just tried to kill me.

He steps up onto the running board and swings into the back seat beside me. His damp shirt sticks to his chest. There are droplets of pool water in his hair. His tanned features are glowing as he gazes down at me with unguarded love and affection.

"I missed you, baby," he breathes.

He takes my face in his hands and slants his mouth over mine. It feels like the very first kiss he gave me, and every kiss after that.

Overwhelming.

Devastating.

The sweetness of heaven and the burning fires of hell.

Lorenzo's snarl cuts through my shock. "Kiss her later, Salvatore. We need to get moving."

Salvatore turns around and slams the door, and I'm pinned between him on one side and Cassius on the other.

"Fuck, I've missed you guys, too." Salvatore says, grinning at the others and running his fingers through his wet hair. Vinicius reaches back with his fist and Salvatore bumps it with his own. Cassius grasps his shoulder with brotherly affection.

This can't be happening, and yet Lorenzo has pulled back onto the street, and neither Vinicius nor Cassius are trying to get their hands around Salvatore's neck.

What the *hell*?

"Come here. We've got some catching up to do." Salvatore pulls me into his arms and tries to kiss me again. I gather my senses at the last second and turn my face away.

Salvatore's eyes narrow and he growls, "I told you never to do that again."

Nearly a year ago he came to my house and sat at dinner with me and Dad, smirking and devouring me with his eyes. I was bewildered and afraid, but I was ready for him when he cornered me in the hall after dinner, turning my face away when he tried to take more than I was willing to give.

That's the last time you refuse me anything. Next time, I'll fucking make you.

"And? You're going to make me?" I challenge him.

Salvatore's jaw tightens and his hands grip my wrists.

Cassius gives Salvatore a warning look and a tiny shake of his head.

A *warning look*? Not a fist to the face for betraying the three of them and then trying to murder me?

I glare around at the men in the car. "I've got news for all of you. No one's kissing me until I understand what's going on. And not even then," I add quickly, as Salvatore cups my face in his hand, smiling that breath-taking smile once more.

"Baby, look at you. You're magnificent."

I don't feel magnificent. My heart is racing beneath Lorenzo's hoodie and I've broken out in a cold sweat.

"I knew that they'd all see what I saw in you," Salvatore says, "but this plan has been a nightmare of waiting."

I stare around the car. Lorenzo's eyes are narrowed at the road ahead and his grin is devilish. Vinicius stretches his arms over his head and rolls his shoulders luxuriously. On my other side, Cassius has relaxed back in his seat and he's smiling to himself as he gazes at Salvatore with his arms around me. Like I'm right where I belong.

With them.

All of them.

"Is someone going to tell me what's going on?"

Salvatore grins at me lazily, looking every inch the dangerous mafia prince that he is. "I guess we can tell her now."

In the driver's seat, Lorenzo bares his teeth at the road ahead. "Welcome to the party, princess. Buckle the fuck in."

2

Salvatore

Four weeks earlier

"Change of plans. We want her."

I breathe in sharply at the sound of Cassius' voice on the other end of the line. There's no need for me to ask who he means by *her* and which plans he's talking about changing.

But this doesn't make sense. The wedding is in a week's time. Everything's already been decided. I'm marrying Chiara, and then we're going to use the mayor to get what we want.

I open my mouth to ask what the fuck has changed, but instead I tell him, "I'm coming over."

"The others are already here," he replies, and hangs up.

Two minutes later, I'm leaving the casino in my gray Maserati and driving the seven blocks to Cassius' skyscraper.

As the elevator doors slide open to the penthouse, the three of them are right there waiting for me. Cassius is in a white button-down shirt, scowling over a glass of vodka and ice. Vinicius is lounging on the sofa with one long leg crossed over the other. He's dressed in a designer suit and his blond hair is rumpled like he's been running agitated fingers through it. Lorenzo is wearing a bloodstained T-shirt with a hungry expression in his eyes.

We all stare at each other.

And then I break into a grin and spread my arms. "You fuckers. It's been too long."

Cassius passes me a glass of vodka and clinks his against mine. "*Saluti*. We need to talk. This is an unprecedented situation."

We've been careful not to be in the same room since Chiara Romano's seventeenth birthday. You never know what spies the mayor has. "What's happened?"

Cassius pushes his hand into his pocket and brings out the enormous emerald-cut diamond engagement ring on the tip of his finger.

My mouth falls open. I come forward and take it from him. It's the same ring. The four million dollar engagement ring I purchased for my promised bride. "How the hell did you get this? I only put it on Chiara's finger a few hours ago."

Vinicius smirks up at me from the sofa. "She proposed. Your bride wants us."

Just a few hours ago, I had Chiara on her knees and I was laying down the law. Instead of obeying me, she ducked under my arm and ran to Cassius.

"Disobedient little brat," I murmur.

Vinicius laughs. "You told her what the Fiore's expect from their brides and she didn't listen, is that it?"

"She never fucking listens," I shoot back.

"If she's got the audacity to stand up to you, I wonder how she'd handle all four of us," Cassius muses.

I pass the ring back to him. "Alluring idea. But you realize what we'd be giving up?"

"Of course," Vinicius says quietly.

"You were ready to give it up ten months ago," Cassius says. "Do you still feel the same way?"

Ten months ago, on the night I sat in my car listening to her scream while her father had her chipped. She turned to me to save her, but I couldn't risk angering the mayor.

It was the first time I thought, *Fuck this plan.* I wanted her more than I wanted the plan to succeed.

I still do. I just didn't expect the others would agree with me.

I called Cassius from my car and he reminded me that we couldn't sacrifice one plan for another. I tried to think of a way to make both those things fit together—to possess Chiara the way we wanted and to have the mayor under our thumb—but it was impossible.

Lorenzo regards me with narrowed eyes and his head tilted to one side. "Did you fuck her tonight?"

I shake my head. "What can I say? I'm old-fashioned."

Vinicius laughs. What we're contemplating is anything but old-fashioned. The four of us with one woman at our heart. One woman who trusts us completely. Not a pawn.

A queen.

"She gets so fucking wet—"

"I remember," Lorenzo says, his eyes alight with interest. "I'm glad you haven't fucked her. I'll be the first."

Cassius shakes his head. "You? She's terrified of you, Scava."

He bares his teeth. "All the better."

Vinicius sits forward. "How about we make this interesting. A bet. The first one to win her trust gets to take her to bed."

"How do we know when we have her trust?" Cassius asks.

Vinicius thinks about this for a second. "She asks for your protection, your help, or makes a move on you."

I expect Lorenzo to protest that the odds are stacked against him. Nothing about him inspires trust in a woman.

Lorenzo considers this, his eyes narrowed. "If she asks for help...Sure. I'll play, but don't be sore losers when I win and I'm balls deep in Chiara while she moans my name."

"Our sheltered, Catholic schoolgirl virgin turning to you for help?" replies Vinicius. "If you wanted to win, you shouldn't have ripped her panties off the first chance you got. This is going to be a race between me and Cassius."

"Whatever," Lorenzo replies, but the gauntlet has been thrown down and his eyes are glittering.

"No fair. I don't get to play," I say, reaching for the vodka bottle to top off my glass.

Lorenzo holds out his empty glass, and I pour in a double. "You've had her to yourself all year, asshole. Now it's our turn to get to know the Princess of Coldlake."

"This is about more than who gets to fuck her first. She's not a sex toy. She's our..." Cassius struggles to find the right word, but simply finishes, "Ours."

My heart gives an excited double thump at that word. *Ours*. We're really going to try this. Our insane plan to secure a few glittering shards of happiness in a brutal world.

"We hope so," says Vinicius. "She may not like one of us. Or any of us."

"She may never forgive you for lying to her all this time," Cassius says, looking at me. "What are we going to tell her?"

"Don't say a word. Keep up the charade for now. Take her..." I pause and then smile. "Take her on our wedding day. Kidnap her at the altar, in front of the whole of Coldlake. Keep her here and see if the three of you can bond with her. If a couple of weeks go by and it's not working, I'll pretend to snatch her back from you and we'll go ahead with the original plan like nothing happened."

I can tell what the three of them are thinking. Can they even bond with Chiara after kidnapping her?

"You know her best," Vinicius says. "What do you think? Can we make it work?"

I take a mouthful of vodka and feel it burn down my throat. "She's got a good heart. But it's bruised and bleeding."

We all are. That's the only reason why this might work. That, and the fact that we're all fiercely attracted to the beautiful little blonde. Whether she likes it or even admits it to herself, she's just as entranced by us.

"Think about it this way," I add. "Whichever way things go, we'll win in the end."

I see the truth of this burning in all their faces.

We'll win.

We always win.

I turn to go. As the elevator doors slide closed I call to my friends, "See you on my wedding day."

I wish I could be with them after they take her and witness for myself how she'll stand up to all of them.

Oh, baby. What a wedding day you're going to have.

Kick, bite, scratch, fight, scheme, do whatever you have to do to keep your dignity once these men have you, but don't push that other impulse away. That darker, dirtier one that has you screaming my name as I spank your pussy and you come all over my fingers.

Give them that.

They *need* that.

And so do you.

THREE WEEKS later

"She wants to kill her father."

I stare out the window into the garden. I'm at home and I picked up Cassius' call right away. He didn't even bother to say hello. "She asked you to kill the mayor?"

"No," Cassius replies, sounding like he's about to lose his temper. "She was very clear about that. She wants to do it herself."

I remember what I told her the night she asked me to kill her father for her.

This is your life, Chiara. You want something changed, you fix it yourself. Grow the fuck up. Harden up. Do what needs to be done and don't fucking cry about it.

I guess she's done crying.

A smile spreads over my face. "That's my girl."

"Are you fucking kidding me? She only picked up a gun for the first time today. She's not ready to kill anyone."

My interest kindles at the thought of her holding a weapon. "She did? Is she a good shot?"

"She's not terrible," Cassius concedes. "But you and I know that target practice isn't the same as the real thing."

"If she does this, there really is no going back," I warn him. "This plan is shot to shit."

Literally. Chiara will put a bullet in our hopes.

"You've been ready to throw that plan away for the last ten months for Chiara so we assumed you were on the same page."

"It's not that I don't need—"

Cassius cuts across me. "You don't have to explain yourself. We get it. If it's a choice between that plan and Chiara, then we choose her."

A choice between our pasts and our futures.

"Even Lorenzo?"

"He won the fucking bet," Cassius growls.

I put back my head and shout with delighted laughter. "Lorenzo *fucking* Scava? That's the best thing I've heard in my life." I continue laughing until I realize there's silence on the other end of the line. It seems Cassius might be a tiny bit sore about losing that bet.

"All right. We're doing this, but first we're going to give Chiara what we never had."

"Revenge," Cassius replies. "You want to give her a gun and put her in front of her father? What if he kills her?"

I think for a moment, staring up at the clear blue sky. "I'll be right there with her. No one will harm a hair on her head. Here's what we're going to do."

3

Chiara

Salvatore gazes down at me, stroking the wet strands of hair back from my face as he finishes his story. He smells like blood and chlorine. Just thirty minutes ago, he was glaring at me with his green-blue eyes full of hatred and venom.

I touch my lips, recalling those hazy moments as someone gave me mouth-to-mouth and growled at me not to pass out.

Kiss me so I know you're still breathing.

I clasp his shoulders as I stare into his eyes, entranced by the expression of love in his handsome face. He was part of this all along. All the weeks that I missed him, he was biding his time until he could come back to me.

When he shot me in the stomach and dragged me out of

the swimming pool, he became mine again. He didn't know if I would be able to kill my father, but he understood it would be the hardest thing I'd ever do.

"I tried to do it. But..."

Salvatore holds me closer. "It's all right, baby. Take it easy on yourself."

Baby. How I've longed to hear him call me that. I rest my cheek against his shoulder and feel his strong arms come around me. I close my eyes, feeling them burn with tears. I tried to hate Salvatore after his harsh words on my eighteenth birthday, but my heart has been aching for him.

"You're really all friends again?" I whisper.

"We never stopped," Cassius rumbles beside me.

After my seventeenth birthday, there was only Salvatore by my side. Salvatore at the school gates. Salvatore who was my promised husband. The few times the five of us were all together, the other three snapped and snarled at Salvatore like starving wolves.

But they were all pretending. Because...?

I try to make sense of everything, but Dad's face keeps bursting into my mind every few seconds. I clench my fists on Salvatore's wet shirt. "I should have killed him."

I should have killed him so I'd never have to know that he would have happily let me bleed out in the swimming pool, just like my mother.

Lorenzo meets my eyes in the mirror and his gaze is pitiless. "It's not a total loss. The mayor would have tried to make you turn on us eventually. Now you know. He'd rather you were dead than be with us."

Cassius caresses my cheek with the back of his fingers. "You don't need him, *bambina*. You only need us."

Silence falls like a blanket as we drive. Vinicius drums on his thighs, and then switches the radio on. An old song plays. The late afternoon sun shines in through the window as we drive, dazzling me.

Vinicius hums the tune under his breath, and I see my mother, young and beautiful, holding her hands out to me as she smiles, dancing to the music, a record turning on the player.

The tears course down my face, silently at first, and then a shuddering intake of breath gives me away. Lorenzo's pale blue eyes meet mine in the mirror. Vinicius and Cassius turn in their seats to look at me.

Salvatore holds me closer while I sob. The mournful tune fills my heart with pain.

"Turn it off. Turn it off, please," I gasp. They either don't hear me, or don't know what I'm talking about.

"The radio," Salvatore snaps, finally understanding.

Someone hits a button and the music cuts off, but my tears won't stop. I wouldn't let myself cry for Mom because crying is weakness, and I told myself I wouldn't survive the year if I gave into my grief.

I give into it. The grief. The pain. With these four men surrounding me, protecting me, I have a few seconds to breathe. Salvatore holds me tight against his chest and I soak his shirt with my tears.

I'm sorry, Mom.

The car slows. I feel us descend and the world around me darkens. When we come to a halt, Salvatore scoops me up in his arms and gets out of the car with me. I don't look where we are. I can't summon the energy, though I can probably guess.

I feel myself taken upstairs and then placed onto a bed. I grasp a pillow with both arms. Why did I even think I could do it? These four men wouldn't have hesitated to kill the man who murdered their sisters, but given the same chance to avenge my mother, I crumpled up like paper.

Salvatore gets into bed with me and pulls my back against his broad chest. The searing heat of him surrounds me, but I can't stop shaking. His lips move against the nape of my neck. "I'm here. I've got you."

"Am I dead?" I ask.

"Officially, yes. How does that feel, baby?"

I turn in Salvatore's arms until I'm looking at him. His handsome face is close to mine, as breathtaking as the first time I laid eyes on him.

"But who are you? I don't understand why any of this happened."

"I'm the same man I always was," he says, pressing a kiss to my throat. "Yours."

All those times I saw the four of them together in the last year, they seemed to hate each other. Snarling at each other outside the Maxim Hotel when Salvatore took me to the fountain. Beating up the Geak who tried to have me raped and murdered. My heart turns over in my chest as I remember that night.

It was all four of them protecting me.

It's always been the four of them.

"The night of our engagement, I told you Dad had won by splitting you off from the others, but that's what the four of you wanted him to believe."

Salvatore strokes my hair back, drinking in my face like he's been starved of the sight of me. "That's right."

My fingers stroke his jaw, tracing over his full lower lip. "And you wanted him to believe that so you could...?"

He watches me with those deep blue-green eyes, saying nothing. There's something bigger and more important than me in play here. Something that they could get because of me but they...gave up for me?

Salvatore's lips stay closed.

These men are bank vaults when it comes to keeping secrets.

"When I was with the other three, I always felt there was something missing."

A smile spreads over Salvatore's lips and he dips his head closer to mine, but he doesn't kiss me. "Me? You missed me, baby?"

"They missed you. They did a good job of making me think you all hated each other's guts, but you were always on their minds. There was always someone missing."

Salvatore groans. "I can't tell you how much I wanted us all to be together. I've craved it so fucking much. But now we are. We're all together, baby."

He crushes me to his chest and slants his mouth over mine in a searing kiss. I whimper and thread my fingers through his hair and arch my breasts into his chest.

Touch me.

Make me know your body.

Give me what the others have already.

I pull away and press a finger to his lips. "I've had sex with all of them. You do realize that?"

A smile spreads over his face. "I thought that you might succumb to Cassius. Maybe Vinicius. But you had to have all of them, baby."

I feel my face flame. He's not disgusted, but is he calling me greedy? As the mayor's daughter I always had to be careful about my reputation. If it got back to my parents that I'd even kissed a boy, I'd have some explaining to do.

Now my promised husband knows I've had sex with all three of his friends, and he's grinning like the devil.

"I heard," he says slowly, fighting a smile, "that the day you lost your virginity was quite the event."

The day I lost my virginity, I was kidnapped and had sex at gunpoint, and then had sex with two men at the same time, while a third one watched.

"And weren't you engaged to another man at the time?"

I cover my face with my hands and moan. "Don't tease me."

"Oh, Chiara," he says, his voice filled with mock-reproach. "What a slutty time you've had while I was gone."

"Don't say that word. That's what my father called me."

Salvatore captures my hands and pulls them away from my face. "No, baby, no. I don't mean it like that. I'm sorry. I won't joke about it."

You little slut, trying to use your body to bargain for vengeance.

My mother would have never used such an ugly word, especially not about her own daughter. I like to imagine that if she saw me with these men and how they're trying their hardest to be tender despite their scarred souls, she'd understand why they want this. She might understand why I'm falling into this with all of them.

Well, most of them. I don't know what I'm going to do about Lorenzo.

"Is that how we make you feel? Cheap? You think I'm

angry that each and every one of my friends wants to rail you senseless, and *has* railed you senseless? They all made you come, baby, and I haven't been able to stop thinking about that."

Salvatore kisses me, a hard, demanding kiss. His hands slide up beneath Lorenzo's hoodie and squeeze my breasts, and he groans. He pants against my mouth, "The messages they were sending me about you were driving me crazy."

I give a shaky laugh. The *messages*. That goddamn group chat. It hasn't just been the three of them discussing my pussy. It's been the four of them.

"We're going push you hard. We're going to fuck you, one after the next, in front of each other, and you won't feel ashamed. You'll crave it. One of us won't be enough anymore, and you'll need this as much as we need you."

My mind is reeling. I can't keep up with everything that's happened today, and especially not while Salvatore is making me drunk from his kisses.

His knuckles brush my pussy over my underwear, and then slowly grind against my clit. "But first, I need you for myself."

My slipperiness is getting all over his fingers. He strips my underwear down and spreads my legs open.

The curtains are drawn but it's broad daylight and Salvatore's sitting up with a view of my everything from the waist down. His middle finger draws up my pussy and then sinks into me. He pumps it in and out while holding my other thigh against my shoulder.

"Tell me how they made you come," he snarls.

"You already know. They told you all about it," I whimper, my gaze locked on his finger. He's found a spot deep inside me behind my clit and he's rubbing it mercilessly. The pressure feels insane.

"*Tell me.*"

"Cassius...Cassius sat me in his lap and rubbed my clit," I moan, trying to form sentences from the images that are flying through my mind.

"He spanked those pretty tits of yours as well, didn't he?" Salvatore asks, his eyes narrowed with heat and desire.

I nod and sink my teeth into my lower lip trying to remember what came next. "Vinicius licked me. I couldn't bear not coming as he teased me. He made me beg for it. Lorenzo licked me as well. He tied me up. I thought he was going to beat me senseless and I was so scared and turned on at the same time. Oh, God, Salvatore," I cry, reaching up to brace my hands against the headboard. I'm not coming yet, but what he's doing is so overwhelming I can barely breathe.

"And then he fucked you?"

I nod, swallowing and gasping for breath. "With a gun to my head. He told me not to move my hands but I...I..."

"You couldn't help yourself. You were squeezing his dick with this pretty pussy of yours as you came and you held onto him for dear life."

I force my eyes open and look at Salvatore. He's looking at me just like Lorenzo did as we had sex. And Cassius. And Vinicius, while he was teasing me with the tip of his cock. Utter focus. Complete control.

"And then what, baby? I want to hear everything." He draws his finger out of me, sucks on it, and then goes deep with two at once.

I can't think. What happened next? That day is all jumbled together in a hot mess. "Then...then I sucked

Lorenzo's cock while Vinicius pounded me from behind, and Cassius watched."

Salvatore groans and thrusts deeper with his fingers. "Fuck, baby, that must have been a sight. I wish I'd been there. And then?"

His fingers slam into me and my body arches up off the bed.

Salvatore laughs. "Can't speak, baby? That's okay, I'll fill in the rest. Cassius took you to bed and sat you on his cock, and watched you slide up and down on his length until you burst all over him."

He really does know everything. They shared *everything*.

Salvatore leans down and swipes his tongue against my clit, once, twice, three times. It's barely anything, but it sends me over the edge so fast that I yell in surprise. The yell goes on and on, getting louder as I come and he goes on licking me.

Finally, I fall back limply on the bed.

Salvatore strips his clothes off, and his cock is jutting out, thick and veiny. "I think they all heard you just now, baby. Let's give them a bit more of a performance, shall we?"

Before I can catch my breath, Salvatore has grasped me around the hips, yanked me down the bed toward him, and sank his entire length into me. Cursing and growling, he fucks me hard. Deep, selfish thrusts to slake a need that's been burning within him for a year.

"Fuck, yes," he says through clenched teeth, watching his cock disappear inside me, over and over. "That's my good girl. That's my good fucking girl."

Salvatore grabs me around my waist. Pain erupts in my belly and I gasp in shock.

His eyes widen and he stops thrusting. "Chiara?"

Slowly, I draw Lorenzo's hoodie up until my midriff is bare. There's an angry red and purple bruise on my belly, right where Salvatore shot me.

He pulls out and slides down my body to plant a gentle kiss on the angry red mark. "Ah, fuck. I'm sorry. You're going to be sore for a while. I should get Lorenzo to take a look at you."

Salvatore sits up as if to go and get his friend. Panic shoots through me at the thought of being naked and close to Lorenzo while I'm turned on. He'll smell it on me. The word *no* doesn't hold much meaning for Lorenzo, and he still hasn't apologized for scaring me out of my goddamn mind the day he took my virginity. He'll probably want to check my stomach by sticking his fingers in my pussy. The image of me sucking Salvatore's cock while Lorenzo slams two fingers into me sashays across my mind. While Lorenzo's wearing those black latex gloves.

That weirdly makes me hornier.

Yeah, he *cannot* come in here right now.

"I'm fine. Just don't grab my stomach." I pull the hoodie up over my head, and the distraction works. I'm naked and Salvatore's gaze is drawn to my breasts. I cup the nape of his neck and bring him down to me, and he sucks my nipples, one after the other. I wriggle beneath him until I have my legs wrapped around his hips and his cock is nudging at my entrance.

It doesn't take much encouragement to have him thrusting back into me. He goes slowly at first, searching my face for any flickers of pain, but I feel nothing but the sweet oblivion of his cock filling me until I'm bursting.

"What will you put in the group chat about this?" I ask him, watching the way the muscles of Salvatore's stomach and torso bunch and flex as he moves. I glance at the doorway, because it almost feels strange that Cassius isn't watching me have sex.

His smile is savage. "Thinking about my friends while I'm balls deep in you, baby?"

I lick my lips and stroke my fingers down his chest. I've never seen Salvatore naked before and he's so sexy it's ridiculous. I can see now why he swaggers around like God's gift to women. "I like to know how I'm being talked about."

"I'll tell them that your pussy tastes like watermelon sugar and you look like you're drowning in pleasure the closer and closer you get to coming. I'll tell them you said all their names while my fingers were slamming into you. Their balls will tighten, their dicks will get hard, and they'll calculate how soon it will be until they can tear your clothes off and sink into your mouth or your pussy or your ass."

Salvatore pushes my knees up to my shoulders and leans his full weight on me as he pounds me deep.

"That's it, baby, give me what I've waited a fucking year for."

He slams into me over and over as I twine my hands up his arms and hold on for dear life. His hungry eyes drink me in with every thrust.

Without warning, Salvatore groans and pulls out of me. "Off the bed. Get on your knees, open that mouth." He speaks urgently, pumping his cock in his fist.

I slip from the bed onto my knees as he stands over me, one hand braced against the wall and breathing hard. I suck the tip of him for a moment, and then lick him, keeping a close eye on his face. I want to see it, the moment he comes. Salvatore is beautiful when he comes.

His head tips back with a groan, and his cum shoots over my tongue. His fist still moving up and down his length, he gasps, "Open your mouth. Let me see."

I do as I'm told, his cum rolling over my tongue.

"That's my good girl," Salvatore growls. "Now swallow me down."

I swallow, and he cups my chin and smiles breathlessly. "Aren't you fucking perfect?"

He lifts me in his arms and we lay down on the bed with his strong body wrapped around me.

"No more tears, baby," he murmurs, lips against my brow. "You faced him like a queen. Do you know how fucking proud I was of you in that moment?"

I don't feel like I've done anything to be proud of seeing as I blew it, but I have Salvatore back. I burrow into his chest, breathing him in, my heart pounding hard to the same rhythm as his. Just a few days ago, I was holding Cassius like this and asking myself if he might be the man for me. How will they feel if I develop feelings for one of them? Or more than one of them?

"Salvatore," I whisper, not opening my eyes.

"Yes, baby?" he murmurs sleepily.

"You're the first man I ever felt things for. While you were gone those ten months before our wedding, I missed you so much."

"I missed you, too."

"But then I developed feelings for someone else. For...Cassius."

Salvatore draws back. My heart races in panic. Will I see hatred and jealousy burning in his face?

Salvatore tips my chin up to his. "Say it again."

I open my eyes. "I have feelings for Cassius."

Salvatore groans and presses a lingering kiss to my lips. "That's beautiful, baby. That's just perfect. And the other two?"

"I don't know. I make a difference to Cassius. I felt the warmth in his heart for me." I reach up and touch Salvatore's cheek. "I feel it from you, too. While you were shouting at me to be smarter and toughen up, you were scared that I wouldn't be strong enough to survive, weren't you?"

He laughs softly and presses his mouth over mine. "Fuck, I'm an asshole."

Yeah, he is. Being an asshole is apparently his love language.

"Vinicius is aloof. Lorenzo is cold. They don't seem interested in getting to know me. They don't need me."

"They need you, baby. They haven't shown you how they need you, but they do."

Salvatore pulls me into his arms and cradles me close. I try to imagine feeling this same warmth and tenderness from Vinicius and Lorenzo, but I can't. I remember what Vinicius said about each of them having one piece of what a woman might grow to love. Maybe those two are just too broken to offer anything but their intelligence, or their muscle, or their bodies.

Maybe I am, too.

I must fall asleep for a moment because the next thing I know, Salvatore's arms are gone and someone's drawing the sheets down my body.

When I open my eyes, there are two pale blue savage ones peering at my naked body. I grab for the sheets. "Get out!"

Lorenzo glares at me and doesn't let go of the sheet. "Salvatore said your stomach is bruised. He's worried about you. Though not so worried he didn't fuck you first," he mutters, glancing at the disheveled sheets and my bed hair.

Lorenzo's wearing a loose tank that shows off his biceps and a lot of his muscled, tattooed chest. I try not to stare at him in case he thinks I'm panting for more dick right now. "My stomach's fine."

"I'm not leaving until I've seen for myself."

I wrestle with the sheets for a moment and then give up. "Fine. Turn around and let me put some clothes on."

"Are you fucking kidding me? I've seen you naked before."

Yeah, because he sliced my clothes to ribbons with his knife. We glare at each other until he growls, "Fine," and turns around.

I pull on my underwear and his hoodie because it's the only thing I have to wear, and stand in the center of the room. "Okay. I'm ready."

When he turns around he gazes at me in his clothes and rubs the back of his neck, a faint smile tugging at the corner of his mouth. Almost like he thinks I'm cute.

He points at the bed. "Lie down on your back."

"Piss off."

"Do as you're fucking told. I can't check you properly if you're not lying down."

I point a warning finger at him. "No funny business. I'm not in the mood."

"Who, me?" he asks innocently, following me to the bed. He sits down on the edge of the mattress and pulls the hoodie up to my ribs. I study his face as he pokes and prods my belly. Lorenzo is almost as good at trickery as Vinicius. Every time he's gotten close to me, I've ended up completely at his mercy.

"Relax would you, I'm not going to bite."

I hold up my arm, which still bears his faint teeth marks just above my wrist. "Oh, really?"

He smiles as if it's a fond memory. "Oh, yeah. That was great. We should do that again sometime."

"It wasn't a date. I tried to kill you." I wince as Lorenzo's fingers prod at my bruise. "What are you doing?"

"Checking to see if your liver is healthy and how many lobes I can harvest."

"I wish you'd stop joking about that."

He grins nastily and then pulls the hoodie back down. Bracing one hand by my head, he leans closer. He's freshly shaven and he smells like sharp, cold cologne, and his pale eyes glitter.

I stare up at him, wide eyed, my breath coming faster.

"You're bruised, but it's superficial," he speaks softly, his eyes glowing with thoughts that have nothing to do with my injured stomach. "The pain will go away in a couple of days and the bruise will fade in a week or two."

"Um, okay."

"You smell like sex, princess."

I put my hands against his chest and push, but he's a wall of solid, malevolent muscle, and he doesn't budge.

"We've all fucked you now. I'm actually surprised. Who

knew a stuck up princess like you would enjoy so much cock?"

My face burns with anger, and his smile widens, as if this is exactly what he was hoping to see.

"We're not nice or gentle men, but you haven't run screaming from us yet."

His gaze slips down my body. "Makes me wonder what else we could do with you."

I haven't got the stomach for being tormented by him right now. I turn my face away from Lorenzo and curl into a ball. "Please leave me alone."

His sharp eyes are on my neck. I wonder if he's going to seethe at me for turning my back on him, but Lorenzo growls, "Say the word and I'll do it. However much torture you want, princess. He can die quick or slow."

Despair washes over me. If only Dad being dead would take away all my pain and bring Mom back. When I don't reply, Lorenzo tucks the blanket around me with surprisingly gentle hands, and then leaves, closing the door behind him.

WHEN I WAKE UP, the light outside has shifted and mellowed, and I think it must be late afternoon. I feel someone standing over me but, I'm not feeling strong enough to talk yet. Whoever it is, he'll tell me it's fine, it doesn't matter that I couldn't kill my father, but I won't believe him.

"*Bambina?*" a voice calls softly.

Cassius.

He never wanted me to go through with my revenge plot in the first place. Murder would be a stain on my innocence, or I was too naïve to go through with it. He might even say *I told you so.*

A moment later, the footsteps recede and the door closes quietly.

A savory aroma fills the air. I sit up and see that something has been left on my bedside table. A bowl of soup. Creamy chicken with macaroni and pieces of carrot and celery. Cassius cooked this for me? I take a spoonful and it tastes rustic, like an old family recipe. He didn't know how to comfort me while I was upset, and so he set to work with his hands, slicing onions and shredding chicken.

I manage to eat half the bowl before exhaustion overwhelms me and I lay down again. Sleep. Sleep is a release. Just one long sleep and I'll be ready to face the world again.

The night passes fitfully. Occasionally I think I hear deep male voices speaking in hushed tones, but mostly the house is silent.

In the morning, I awake feeling groggy and more tired than when I went to sleep. I need water. I need a shower and some fresh clothes. I need to figure out what the rest of my life is going to be like from now on.

But first I have to deal with the man in my room.

Lorenzo's sitting by the open window, rocking back on two legs of a chair. The sunlight catches on his blond hair and outlines his severe expression.

"Morning, princess," he says, not looking away from the window.

He doesn't do anything but sit there. Doesn't he have anything better to do?

Don't I, other than lay around in bed?

As I sit up, heaviness settles over me and I want to lay back down again. I make myself stand up and head over to the bathroom. Someone's stacked some of "my" clothes on a set of drawers—the clothes I was wearing at Cassius' apartment. I suppose Cassius brought them for me.

I take a shower and dress myself, and when I'm done my legs and arms feel like solid lead bars. I can't face the stairs, let alone talking to anyone, so I crawl back into bed.

As I drift off to sleep, I hear Lorenzo talking quietly on the phone. From his tone, I think they must be work calls, or in his case, crime calls, but whatever he's saying, his deep voice is soothing.

Sometimes when I wake up, Lorenzo's there, but other times he's gone, and there's food on my bedside table instead. When he's there he doesn't yell at me to get the fuck out of bed, though I sense that he wants to.

For hours at a time, he sits next to the open window and stares outside. A silent sentinel keeping watch over me. Sometimes I catch him staring at me. Sometimes he's writing in a battered blue notebook. He writes pages and pages. A diary? Or is he planning something? I can't read his scrawl from here but he fills entire pages in his slanted handwriting. Long sentences that go on and on, as if there are too many thoughts in his head and he's trying to pour them onto the page.

Four, maybe five days go by. I don't see the others, but Lorenzo seems to be in that chair every night, and sometimes during the day as well, usually with a pen in his hand. He hasn't said a word to me in days.

"That song on the radio. Mom used to play it on our old

record player." My voice is crackly with disuse. I haven't been able to get that song out of my head. The one that was playing in the car.

Lorenzo stops writing, but he doesn't look up.

"She'd take off her high heels and dance in her stockings. Like her mother did with her, she'd say, holding out her hands to me."

I can picture her as a little girl, dancing with grandma. Smiling and smiling, like I did as a child, back when we didn't know any better. As I grew older, she stopped dancing.

"Cool story," he deadpans, still staring at the page.

I roll over and turn my back on him. I don't know why I bother trying to talk to Lorenzo.

Hours later, I awaken, and hear rain lashing my window. The room is almost pitch dark and I don't know what brought me into consciousness. Perhaps it's the storm. I lay there with my eyes closed, listening for thunder, when I feel the mattress move.

Someone's in bed with me.

I presume it's Vinicius, as he's snuck into my bed before "just to cuddle." That cuddling turned into making out, which turned into him going down on me with that wicked tongue of his, which turned into us almost having full-blown sex.

A hand reaches out and grasps my shoulder and rolls me onto my back. I keep my eyes closed. If Vinicius wants some secret, late night making out, then fine. I'll welcome the comfort of his kisses, as long as he doesn't want to talk.

A thumb swipes slowly across my lower lip.

My heart jolts. This isn't Vinicius. Only one man touches

me like this and having him in my bed isn't going to be the least bit comforting.

Wild, probably.

Crazy, definitely.

There's pressure on either side of my head as if he's braced his hands by my pillow. His face dips closer to mine. He's so close I can feel him breathing.

Lorenzo is going to kiss me?

Lorenzo never kisses me.

I lay perfectly still, my eyes closed. Alone in the dark with Lorenzo in the middle of the night. What's he going to do to me while he thinks I'm asleep?

"What's your blood type, princess?"

My eyes pop open.

I can just make out Lorenzo looming over me in the dark. The light from the window hits the sharp line of his jaw and cheekbone and glints in his wintry eyes.

His eyes widen in a *you heard me* way. When I don't answer he slips both arms beneath my body and hoists me out of bed.

"What are you—"

"Shh," he hushes, carrying me downstairs.

Lorenzo's grim expression tells me that kissing is the last thing on his mind right now. He's wearing a tight black T-shirt that shows the tattoos that are inked up the side of his neck. Beautiful, ornate tattoos. I've never looked at them closely before. I've had other things on my mind when I've been this close to Lorenzo in the past.

Like, is he going to fuck me or kill me, or both?

The stairs are steep and I wrap my arms around his neck and hold on. We reach the ground floor, but we keep going.

"I can walk, you know," I remind him.

"I thought you might run away."

My arms tighten in surprise. "Why? Where are you taking me? You better not be kidnapping me again."

I'm in his *house*. How much more control over me does he need?

Lorenzo steps through a door into his ghastly operating-style room that's full of medical equipment.

Oh, shit. Is this when he harvests my kidneys?

Lorenzo puts me down, my bare feet on the cold concrete, turns his back on me and crosses the room. A man with as many muscles and tattoos as Lorenzo is laying on one of the metal tables.

Unlike Lorenzo, this man is unconscious and riddled with circular wounds. Blood drips from the metal table onto the slanted ground, flowing toward the drain like a crimson river.

So much blood. How is he still alive?

I'm so busy staring at his lifeless body that I barely notice Lorenzo advancing on me with something pointy glinting in his gloved fingers.

I back away from him. "What are you doing?"

"I need blood. There are seven people under this roof tonight and everyone's the wrong type. I need to know yours."

I stare at the needle in his hand and then over at the man on the table. A hundred questions are swarming in my mind, but if I don't answer quickly then Lorenzo will hold me down and stab me with that needle. "I'm A-negative."

"Perfect." He throws the needle aside, grabs a rubber ligature, picks me up by the waist, and sits me on a table.

I study Lorenzo's face. He *looks* like he's focused on getting blood for a dying man, but who knows what hidden agendas he might have. The concrete room is as cold as the metal table beneath me, sending a shiver up my spine. "This feels suspiciously like the first time you stuck me with a needle. Are you going to trick me again?"

"You don't trust me, princess?" he asks, fitting the rubber band around my arm.

"No."

"You're in luck. I don't have time to screw with you right now." He pulls the ligature tight. "You know what to do. Let's see those pretty veins."

I hesitate for a moment. "What happened to that man? Can't he go to the hospital? Who is he?"

"Acid," he says, ignoring the rest of my questions.

Acid. His name is Acid? He hasn't moved since I came in here, his skin is alarmingly pallid and his chest is barely lifting up and down. Acid looks like he's at death's door.

"Lorenzo—"

Lorenzo's jaw flexes as he glares at me, and he holds up a needle. "Either you let me stick this in your arm or we go over there and watch a man die. Shouldn't take more than ten, fifteen minutes. I'll make you watch, princess. You know I will."

I swallow down the rest of my questions and hold out my arm.

Lorenzo swabs the inside of my elbow and slips a needle into a bulging vein. Dark red blood flows along a clear plastic tube and collects in a bag.

Lorenzo's fingers trail down my arm. For a moment, his focus slips and a heated expression slides over his face. He makes an appreciative noise in the back of his throat as he cups my elbow with his large hand.

"Perfect, princess," he murmurs, his voice husky.

God, he's weird.

He turns away and goes back to the injured man, changes his gloves, and picks up a silver instrument that looks like a pair of pliers.

"You sure you want to watch this part?" Lorenzo asks without turning around.

"How do you know I'm watching you?"

"I can feel you." Without waiting for a reply, he digs with the instrument inside one of the wounds. Thank God Acid is out cold because it looks painful, and Lorenzo isn't gentle. A moment later, he draws out something small and shiny and throws it into a metal dish with a heavy *plunk*.

"What was that?"

"A bullet. One down. Four to go."

One by one the rest of the bullets are extricated from the man's body and thrown into the dish.

The bag of blood next to me is growing bloated and I'm starting to feel light-headed. I want to ask Lorenzo if he can please take this needle out before he drains all my blood, but he seems to be struggling with one of Acid's wounds.

"Damn it all to fucking hell," he growls under his breath, beads of sweat on his brow.

He strides back over to me, pulls the needle out of my arm and slaps some plaster over the wound. "I've got about two minutes to sew this blood vessel up before he's fucked. Can you stand?"

It's not really a question when he's already helping me to my feet and walking me over to the table. He gives me a pair of black latex gloves to put on and puts a stool under me I can perch on. Black spots are swarming in front of my eyes as I wriggle into the gloves.

With a scissor-like instrument that has curved, blunt ends, Lorenzo digs inside a wound in Acid's shoulder, and then angles the handles toward me. "Here. Take these. Don't let up the pressure and *don't* fucking faint. I need to get that blood into him now."

I grasp the clamp and hold it as steady as I can. Acid's face is slack and pale. He looks like he's already dead. The scent of blood and gunpowder is sickeningly overpowering.

Don't faint.

Don't faint.

Blood doesn't make me squeamish but I'm struggling to keep my eyes open. My head starts to droop as Lorenzo sticks a needle in Acid's arm.

There's a sharp tug on my scalp and my head is yanked up.

"Don't you fucking faint!" Lorenzo shouts in my face.

"I'm trying," I mutter, blinking hard as Lorenzo lets go of my hair. I've donated blood before and I've never felt this awful. How much did he take?

"What am I holding closed?" I ask, checking that my grip is secure, hoping that talking will help me stay conscious.

"His blood vessel."

I'm keeping Acid alive? Great. No pressure. I dig the nails of my other hand into my palm, hoping that the pain will help me focus. My blood is flowing into Acid's vein through his other arm. I glance again at the man's face. He has beautiful brows, sculpted cheekbones and close-cropped hair. A tattoo of a black skull with flaming green eyes stands out on his throat against his deathly pale skin. He's someone's son. Someone's friend. He's moments away from death. I can feel it in the way Lorenzo's eyes keep darting from the suture he's putting in the blood vessel I have clamped, to the blood drip, to Acid's face.

Please let him live.

This man is probably a criminal and maybe he's done terrible things, but it's his heart that's desperately pumping a trickle of blood around his veins. His body that will turn cold and lifeless in front of us.

Lorenzo's hand covers mine, and I realize he's loosening my grip on the clamp and putting it aside. He sews up Acid's flesh and then rests both his hands on the table, glaring at the man's face. "You'd better not die after all that, you motherfucker."

"Who is he?"

"I told you already."

"Acid. Yes. But why is he here?"

"Hospitals mean questions. Questions mean cops. Cops mean prison because Acid has about a dozen warrants out for his arrest."

I glance around the room and back to Lorenzo. "You weren't kidding when you said you're a doctor."

He shakes his head. "I'm not a doctor. I didn't finish my medical degree and I never did a surgical residency. One of my mom's uncles was a surgeon. He helped me set this place up and taught me the basics. I can dig out bullets and stitch up stab wounds. It keeps my men out of the hospitals and I can give them somewhere safe to recover if there's a hit out on their asses. Most of my men are wanted by someone. Satisfied?"

Not even close.

"Is that what you wanted to be? A surgeon?"

I've heard that surgeons are clever but sometimes callous people. What makes them good at cutting people open and taking risks in the operating room means they're arrogant and cold-hearted outside it. Lorenzo probably would have made a great surgeon.

He sighs and scrubs the back of his forearm over his face. "It's late, princess. Come on. I'll take you back to bed."

Lorenzo takes off his gloves and tries to pick me up in his arms, but I put my hand on his chest. "Let me sit with him while you clean up." The medical equipment in this room is pretty basic. He hasn't even got a heart rate monitor. Acid could die while Lorenzo's back is turned.

Lorenzo stays where he is, gazing at me with his brows drawn together. "You watch as I stick needles in you. The night Vinicius blew that Geak's brains out, you didn't even look away. All this blood and gore doesn't turn your stomach?"

It should, shouldn't it?

To be fair, I nearly threw up at the sight of Griffin's brains splattered all over the broken concrete. But I didn't look away.

"I'd just rather know." That's the only thing I can say. I don't really understand it myself. If horrible things are happening all around me, then what use is it to turn my face away and pretend they're not?

Lorenzo straightens up and lets go of me. "All right. Keep an eye on him while I clean this mess up. Check his pulse occasionally and tell me if he stops breathing."

I press my fingers against the side of Acid's neck until I

feel a faint pulse. His heart's beating, but I don't know if it's at a good rate or a dangerous one. Above my head on a metal stand, my blood drains down a thin tube and into Acid's arm.

Lorenzo puts on fresh gloves, picks up all the medical instruments and bloodstained bits of gauze and takes them over to a bench.

I rest my chin on my hand, doing my best to keep my eyes open. "Those black latex gloves are kind of sexy."

Lorenzo keeps his back to me but I hear the smile in his voice. "You little weirdo."

"You think so too, otherwise you'd wear normal ones."

Lorenzo laughs under his breath, but he doesn't argue with me. A moment later, he rubs his face with his forearm again.

"Are you tired? Have you not been sleeping?" I ask.

"I'm fucking exhausted. I've barely slept this week."

"Why?"

"I've been watching over you, princess. The others have been busy during the day."

Oh. No wonder he's exhausted. He's been worried about me. Scared I might do something stupid if I'm left alone?

"Thank you," I whisper. "I'm...I'm sorry I've been such a mess."

"It's why we're four, princess."

He says this matter-of-factly. No complaints, like he's used to them picking up the slack for each other. This is how they function as friends, and now they're bringing me into it.

Lorenzo comes over and presses his fingers to Acid's throat.

"Good pulse," he murmurs, and his shoulders relax a

little. All my blood from the bag has drained into Acid's veins, and Lorenzo replaces it with a saline drip. "Thanks for the blood."

"Um, anytime."

"Do you want to go back to bed yet?"

I shake my head. I've spent enough time in bed. There's so much blood all over the cabinets and trailing over to the door. I guess Acid was dragged in here bleeding profusely. Lorenzo gets buckets and cloths and starts cleaning it up.

I try to stand up and help him, but Lorenzo clamps a hand to my shoulder. "I took two pints out of you. Sit the fuck down and watch Acid. I'll do this."

Color has returned to Acid's cheeks and he looks like a human being again rather than a corpse. Lorenzo works in silence around me. He glances at Acid occasionally, but doesn't seem as worried about him as he was an hour ago.

My eyes burn with fatigue and my head spins. There's a tiny bit of space on the table next to Acid's unconscious body. I take off my gloves, pillow my head in my arms and close my eyes, intending to rest them just for a second.

Instead, I pitch head-first into inky blackness.

Sometime later, my arms feel numb and tingly, and I raise my head. I must have fallen asleep.

"Well, hello," a deep voice rumbles.

I sit up and find the tattooed man gazing at me. His eyes are the most vivid shade of green I've ever seen.

"Acid?" I ask him, staring into those eyes. If Acid is his nickname, I think I've just discovered the reason why.

"Are you my guardian angel?" he asks, his voice husky. "Sorry, baby. I've been a bad boy."

Acid is looking at me with the same hungry expression

that my men give me, except it's discomforting from a stranger. How is he finding the energy to flirt when he's riddled with bullet holes?

"No, I'm Chiara."

He reaches out a large forefinger and strokes my cheek. "Aren't you pretty, Chiara."

As Acid's gaze slips down my body, suddenly I'm hyper-aware that I'm only wearing a white tank and tiny shorts, and the material of both are thin.

"Touch her again and I'll put every one of those bullets back, and a couple more," growls a voice from the other side of the room.

A smile quirks Acid's mouth, but he doesn't look away from me. "Your nurses are prettier these days, boss. This is better than waking up to your surly face."

"She's not your fucking nurse." I feel Lorenzo come up behind me and drop a hoodie around my shoulders. I push my arms into the sleeves and zip it up.

"Chiara, this is Acid, a lowlife piece of shit who works for me down at Strife. Acid, this is Chiara Romano."

Strife. What's Strife?

Acid's eyes widen as he studies me. "Romano? The mayor's daughter? Fuck, what are you doing with this asshole?"

Lorenzo wraps his arms around me and strokes my hair back from my face as he glares at Acid. "Say thank you for the two pints of blood Chiara gave you."

A smile spreads over Acid's face. "Two pints of blood from the Princess of Coldlake. I'm honored."

"You're welcome. Did you deserve to be saved?"

His smile widens. "Not a chance in hell."

"I'm not bleeding her again for you, so be more fucking careful next time," Lorenzo tells him. "So, what happened?"

But Acid doesn't seem interested in talking about last night's events. His expression is full of incredulity. Big, bad, dangerous Lorenzo has his arms around the mayor's good little daughter. "She's your woman? The mayor's daughter?"

Lorenzo's fingers briefly caress my cheek. "Answer the question and you can have some morphine."

Acid sighs. "Fine. It was that fucking Geak leader."

I can't help my exclamation of surprise. "Jax?"

Nearly a year has gone by, but I still remember his name. It's thanks to Cassius, Vinicius, and Lorenzo that I didn't end up raped and left for dead by Jax and the rest of the Geaks, as punishment for my father who'd put some of their members in prison.

Acid laughs, and then winces in pain. "You know Jax?"

"Not personally. I nearly had a run-in with him last year. I met a Geak called Griffin and I nearly didn't make it out alive."

Lorenzo's arms tighten around me at the memory. "So we beat him to a pulp and blew his brains out."

Acid glances between the two of us. "You aren't what I was expecting, Miss Romano. Yeah. Jax. The pain in all our asses for ten years now."

Acid explains how he was doing a dead drop with some of Vinicius' merchandise—he doesn't say what sort but I'm guessing it's nothing legal—when several Geaks ambushed him, along with some members of another gang called the Blood Pack.

I find myself settling back against Lorenzo's broad chest and let myself be supported by his strong arms as I listen to

Acid. My head's still spinning slightly and I'm sleepy, but I want to hear this.

"We managed to get the goods back but Jax pumped half a clip into me, and here we are." Acid glances at me. "I'll forgo the morphine if she tells me her story."

Lorenzo scoops me up in his arms. "She's going back to bed. Stay where you are. If you rip your stitches out I'm not putting them back in."

He carries me out of the room, and I put my head down on his shoulder as he walks upstairs with me. Lorenzo might not have a medical degree, but he worked skillfully to save Acid's life. "It was good of you to save him."

"He makes me money."

"Is that the only reason? You seem like you're friends."

A moment later we're upstairs in my dimly lit room and Lorenzo's got a knee up on the bed as he lays me on the mattress.

Before he can stand up, I wriggle closer, wrap my arms around his neck and draw him down to me. If Lorenzo can hold me to show that I'm off-limits to other men, then he can hold me when we're alone, too.

"Chiara, I have to get back downstairs," he whispers, but he doesn't move away. His hands hover over me, as if he doesn't know what to do with them.

"What time is it?" I whisper, eyes closed, listening to his heart thumping. Salvatore, Vinicius, Cassius, and Lorenzo all do dangerous things all the time. It could have been one of them laying on a metal table and bleeding out tonight.

Slowly, Lorenzo rests his hands against my back. "Nearly five in the morning."

I reach up and cup his cheek in the darkness. Lorenzo

has never kissed me. This is when he should kiss me, even if it's a brief press of his mouth. We worked together to save his friend and now he's holding me close in my bed. His blond head is on the pillow and he's staring at me with wide, pale eyes.

Lorenzo doesn't move. His whole body is rigid muscle, braced for a brutal assault.

But it's just me.

And I'm supposed to be the one afraid of him.

"You're strange," I whisper. His cheek is cold and his stubble rasps against my fingers. "You fight so hard to keep me, but none of you seem to want me to get close."

Lorenzo reaches up and takes hold of my throat. He doesn't grab. He doesn't squeeze. His fingers slide around me and hold, pressing against my arteries.

"What are you doing?"

"Do you know what a miracle it is that you're still alive?"

My heart starts to throb in my chest. Is he threatening me? Lorenzo seems to feel my pulse quicken and he glances at his fingers.

In that same quiet, icy tone, he continues, "We don't shower you with rose petals and love poems, but every one of us burns with gratitude when you walk in the room, still breathing."

I suck in a breath.

"I drained two pints of blood from you and pumped them into a dying man, right in front of you, and you still think breathing isn't a privilege in this world? You know what would have happened to Acid if he'd died in my base-ment? His body would have been wrapped in plastic bags and buried in a shallow grave in the woods. No pretty coffin heaped with white roses and people singing hymns in Cold-lake Cathedral. That could be any one of us. That could be you. So be fucking grateful for what you've got."

Lorenzo rips his hand from my throat, stalks to the door, and slams it behind him.

I roll onto my back and stare at the ceiling. The ghost of his cold fingers are on my neck. Those are my choices, to exist, or to be consigned forever to an unmarked grave?

No.

I won't settle for that.

Either I'll find a way to be happy, or I'll upend anything and anyone in my path to make it happen, including these four men.

I press my fingers over my mouth, remembering the swipe of Lorenzo's thumb there. Even when we've been naked and he's been buried deep inside me, Lorenzo's lips have never touched mine. He thinks he has to stay hard all the time. Vigilant, or he and the people around him will end up dead.

I rub my hand over my face, feeling like shit in my body and my heart. I don't want the pieces of four broken men. If they're going to demand every piece of me, shouldn't I have all of them?

4

Vinicius

I wake up to the sun blushing the high ceilings of my airy loft and the sound of my phone buzzing insistently on the nightstand.

Morning. It's been a week since Chiara tried to kill her father, and I wonder what she's doing right now. My cock is standing to attention and I reach down and wrap my hand around it and close my eyes, picturing her in bed in tiny panties and a little T-shirt, all warm skin and sleepy innocence. She tasted like honey against my tongue. The memory of her cries and her fingers threading through my hair as I sucked her clit has me groaning. Lorenzo says she won't get out of bed. If I hadn't been so busy this week, I could have enticed her out by now. An orgasm or two in my mouth, a pounding into the mattress to remind her she's alive, and a few rounds of target practice with a big gun to refocus her attitude. That's what she needs.

I'm not busy today. I think I'll pay a visit to my sweet kitten.

My hand is working faster up and down my cock as I picture her bent over in one of the shooting range cubicles, her pussy on display for me and shimmering with wetness.

Buzz.

Buzz.

Buzz.

For *fuck's* sake.

I grab for my phone and squint at the screen. The boys are in the group chat.

Lorenzo: *Go easy on our princess the next couple of days.*

Salvatore: *Why? What did you do to her?*

Lorenzo: *Bled her.*

Cassius: *WHAT?*

Lorenzo: *One of my men got shot. She was the only A-neg at the compound last night.*

Salvatore: *Is she all right?*

Lorenzo: *She's fine. I'm watching her sleep right now. Could use some fucking sleep myself.*

It sounds like he's been up all night, and after the week he's had he must be exhausted. I tap the screen and start typing. *The factory can run itself today. I'll come.*

Lorenzo: *Make it quick. My eyes are falling out of my head.*

Smirking, I add, *Did you...?*

Lorenzo: *I would have said if I had.*

True, but he could have been drawing it out for dramatic effect. Making us wonder enviously about the moments he spent in Chiara's arms—though that's something I would do, come to think of it, not something Lorenzo would do.

I send, *On my way*, swing out of bed and head to the shower. If I'm going to spend the day with Chiara, I need to be looking my best. After washing and drying my hair and shaving, I do a little manscaping, buzzing off all the hair around my cock. First of all, it's only courteous to keep things neat down there for a lady.

Second of all, it makes my cock look huge.

I push my fingers through my blond hair and angle my body from side to side, wondering if I should add some extra sit-ups to my workout from now on as my abdominal muscles aren't popping as much as they could. I should train with Cassius more often. That man is a beast.

From my wardrobe, I select an Italian suit, a charcoal shirt without a tie, and some Prada loafers. I'm fastening a gold watch around my wrist when I hear my phone buzzing repeatedly again on the nightstand, and I glance at the screen.

Lorenzo: *I*

Lorenzo: *will*

Lorenzo: *kill*

Lorenzo: *you*

I grin and shove my phone into my pocket and head downstairs. There's no point telling him I'm just leaving now. The man will pop a blood vessel in his brain.

Twenty minutes later, I pull up at Lorenzo's compound. One of the guards lets me in at the gates. I drive down into the garage, and then walk up to the room Chiara's been using. She's asleep on the bed in one of Lorenzo's hoodies, her back to me and her hair laying shiny gold across the pillow.

Wearing Lorenzo's clothes but they haven't had sex. Has he been nice to Chiara without getting anything in return?

Then I remember what he said about bleeding her. He couldn't manage a hug or a kiss after, probably, so he gave her his hoodie as a consolation prize.

Poor baby. I'll make it up to her.

Lorenzo's slumped in a chair and rubs his bleary eyes as he sees me walk in.

"You look like a wreck," I whisper, so I don't wake Chiara.

"Fuck you, too. Goodnight." He pats my shoulder heavily as he heads for the door.

Chiara's breathing is irregular, as if she's on the verge of waking up, and so I sit down on the edge of the bed and stroke my hand up her back, cupping the nape of her neck. She breathes in and opens her eyes.

"Kitten."

She blinks sleepily and rubs the back of her hand over her eyes. "Vinicius, when did you get here? What a night it's been."

I can imagine. "I got here just now. How are you feeling?"

Chiara puts her hand in mine and I help her sit up. She unzips the hoodie and pushes it off, and I see that there's a plaster at the bend of her elbow and blood spatters down the front of her tank top. Quality time spent with Lorenzo.

After checking herself over and pushing her hair off her face she says, "Um...not too bad, actually."

She's pale, but her eyes are bright. Maybe witching hour surgery and blood-letting was what she needed to shock her out of her funk. "Wonderful. I want to take you out today. You up for it?"

"I think so. As long as you don't ask me to hike up any hills."

"No hills. All you have to do is sit in my car."

"I can do sitting. Where are we going?"

I smile at her. "Here and there. Go shower. I'll wait here."

"You can wait downstairs."

"I'll wait here," I repeat, making myself more comfortable on her bed and taking out my phone. She's tiny, and Lorenzo took enough blood from her to save one of his men. "Call out to me if you feel faint."

"I feel like I'm never alone," she mutters as she heads through to the bathroom.

That's the idea, kitten. If you're never alone, nothing bad can happen to you.

Ten minutes later she emerges in a towel from a cloud of steam, grabs some clothes, and disappears. Finally, she comes out dressed casually in jeans and a T-shirt.

I smile at her and stand up. "You look beautiful. Let's go."

She plucks at her T-shirt and raises her eyebrows as we walk downstairs. "Me? You look like you just stepped out of a magazine ad. I look like a frump."

I press a kiss to her lips as I open the passenger door to my car, and reaffirm, "You look beautiful." But if she wants new clothes, that can be arranged.

I hand her a pair of my sunglasses. "Keep these on and your hair around your face."

She does as she's asked, finger-combing her long blonde tresses to frame her face, and I drive us out of the underground garage.

I head up the road for half a mile and then turn into the drive-thru lane of a chain restaurant. "Breakfast will have to be cheap and cheerful. Uber Eats doesn't deliver to Lorenzo's impregnable fortress and I can't take you into a restaurant."

"Why?"

"Because you're dead, kitten."

"Oh. Yeah, I forgot."

"What do you want? Hungry?"

Chiara leans over me and studies the menu. "I am actually. Umm...the breakfast biscuit with an extra hash brown and a latte, please."

I speak our order into the mic and add a black coffee for myself, and then drive up to the window to pay. The teenage boy at the till stares at my car. I don't suppose he sees many Lamborghini Aventadors in the drive-thru.

"Sick car, bro."

I smile as I pass him a hundred dollar bill. "Keep the change."

"You're such a show-off," Chiara mutters, shaking her head as we pull up to the next window to wait for our order.

I roll my head to the side to smile at her. "I just like spreading goodwill and cheer wherever I go."

Another boy passes us our order and I set it on Chiara's lap before driving back out onto the street. She gazes around at the cream leather interior of the Lamborghini.

"I can't eat in here. What if I spill something? There aren't even cup holders."

This is a supercar. Of course there aren't cup holders. "Eat your breakfast, kitten. Don't worry about my car. Keep my coffee in the bag, okay?"

"Well, if you're sure..." Chiara delves into the bag and

pulls out her biscuit, tucking our coffees between her feet. She bites into her bacon and egg biscuit with an appreciative sound.

"How's that?" I ask.

"Mm. So good. I'm starving. Laying around for a week can really take it out of you, I guess." She takes a small bite, chews for a moment, and adds, "Sorry I've been such a mess."

Chiara's been through a lot in the last month. Salvatore was a nightmare to her on her birthday and then the three of us put her through hell. Being shot in the stomach by Salvatore and thinking she was going to die like her mother was probably the cherry on a shit sundae.

"Today we're going to put that behind you. I'm taking you on a tour of Coldlake."

"I've lived here all my life. I know Coldlake as well as you do."

"You know the lake and the bridges and the tourist spots. But do you know the streets?"

"Of course. I used to walk—"

"Not the streets. The *streets*. The invisible boundaries of this city. Who owns this borough? Who runs that gang? The man you gave blood for last night, where did he come from? What does he do?"

"Lorenzo wouldn't tell me much. Something about a place called Strife."

Of course he didn't. Lorenzo wants to protect his princess from all the dangers in this city. If it were up to him he'd lock her up in his fortress where no one could see her, let alone touch her, while he prowled the streets with his guns and his muscle and came home to her covered in blood.

But it's not up to Lorenzo. It's up to all of us.

"The city is divided into four pieces that each of us control. This part," I say gesturing out the window. "Which of us runs this part?"

Chiara gazes out the window at the passing houses and buildings. It's an older part of the city with brick houses and wide streets. Clean but unlovely and rough around the edges. Like the man who runs it.

"Seeing as he lives here, I'm guessing Lorenzo."

"That's right. Everything northwest of Coldlake Bridge is Lorenzo's. He's in charge of the gangs that operate here, too."

"These are some rough areas."

"Lorenzo is a rough man. He and I do a lot of business together."

"His gangs shift your merchandise?" she asks, nibbling her biscuit.

I turn my head away from the road and stare at her. "How the hell did you know that?"

"I listen. What's your merchandise?"

"Oh, this and that. The north is mine. The inner north and the east belongs to Cassius. The inner south and the southeast is Salvatore's."

Chiara gazes in the direction of her old home, though she can't see it from here. The southeast is the wealthiest part of Coldlake. All the richest people built their enormous houses there. The streets are wide and lined with trees and children ride yellow buses to huge, handsome schools with fancy crests on the gates. Chiara must have had an idyllic childhood.

Nothing like my own.

"So, I lived in Salvatore's part of Coldlake all my life. Or I did once he took control from...who? His father?"

"Yes, Francesco Fiore. The old man was the boss of the whole city. We're the ones who split it up into four pieces nine years ago when Francesco got sick. He hated that we formed the Coldlake Syndicate. Many people did, actually."

"Why did you do it? And why did people hate it?"

My hands grow sweaty on the steering wheel and my heart pounds, sick and fast. This is skating too close to a topic I don't want to talk about today, and probably not ever. How do the others shut down conversations like this with Chiara? Cassius probably forbids her from asking questions and threatens to spank her, and I suppose Salvatore loses his temper and shoves his cock in her mouth. Lorenzo solved the problem by being too fucking scary to be asked questions in the first place.

None of that's my style, though. I glance at Chiara and smile. "Because we wanted to share."

She raises one eyebrow. "Why do you sound so flirty when you say that?"

"Say what?"

"*Share.*"

I laugh, mostly in relief that my deflection has worked and I can move the conversation elsewhere. "You haven't asked about the southwest part of the city. The only part that isn't run by the Coldlake Syndicate."

"Who runs the southwest part of the city?"

"You tell me."

Chiara had her own tour of the southwest last year when she got into a car with a boy she was hoping would take her virginity. It was a pleasure to blow that fucker's brains out.

"The Geaks," she guesses, a shadow passing over her face.

"The Geaks, the Blood Pack and a few other gangs."

"I met a man called Acid last night. He was shot by Jax, the leader of the Geaks." She hesitates and adds, "The one who planned on raping me with broken bottles."

Being the daughter of a tough-on-gangs mayor put a target on her back. Being with the four of us puts an even bigger target on her back. The gangs in the southwest hate us with the power of ten thousand suns. If they got their hands on Chiara now, the death she would have suffered last year would be merciful in comparison.

"You don't have to worry about Jax and the gangs, kitten. We're never letting you out of our sight."

I change lanes and we head toward Coldlake Bridge, a massive suspension bridge that spans the northwest side of the lake that gives the city its name. The sun is glittering on the surface of the water and the skyscrapers are outlined proudly against the blue sky. It's a perfect morning for a drive.

Chiara gazes out the window as we fly up the long incline onto the bridge, sipping her coffee as she takes in the sights.

"You see it differently now, don't you?" I ask when we reach the top of the bridge. "The city, I mean."

"Each quadrant belonging to a different man. I guess it's more manageable this way than trying to control the whole city by yourself."

"That's the idea, kitten."

When we reach the other side of the bridge, I drive north, into my own territory. Once we're out of the city I head for a park that has a view of Coldlake. I park by the observatory and we gaze out across the city. It would be a beautiful day for a walk, but Chiara's looking pale. Also, she's officially dead so she probably shouldn't be seen.

Chiara passes me my coffee. She must have been thinking the same thing, as she asks, "How long will I stay dead?"

"I'm not sure. However long we can keep it secret. Or maybe we won't bother. Plans change, and we adapt to them."

"Maybe I won't be with you very long."

"*That* part of the plan isn't going to change." I reach out and thread my fingers through hers, holding her hand tight. Chiara staying with us is the only thing that's set in stone.

"That depends," she says, taking a sip of her coffee.

My eyes narrow. "On what?"

"On whether I want to stay with you all. What did Cassius call me a few weeks ago? A little stray cat. I don't intend on being anyone's stray for the rest of my life. Maybe I'll leave and go somewhere else entirely."

Behind her dark glasses, Chiara surveys the city, her interested eyes flickering over the streets and houses of Coldlake. She can't fool me. This city is a part of her as much as it is anyone of us.

Finally, Chiara turns to me. "Can you tell me about your sister?"

The sudden change in topic makes me wince. The short answer is, *No.*

The long answer is, *Fuck, no.*

The even longer answer is, *Fuck no, and don't ever ask me that question again.*

I presume it's not a coincidence that the subject has changed from whether she's staying with us to personal questions about myself. Chiara's way of saying, *You want me? You have to open up to me.*

"My sister. Amalia." I take a deep breath and let it out slowly. "I don't really talk about her, kitten."

Her expression softens. "I know, and I understand. Salvatore didn't want to talk about Ophelia, and Cassius could only manage a few words about Evelina. What a terrible thing to have happened to them."

Terrible. What an inadequate word to describe what happened to Amalia. *Unthinkable* comes closer. Her bleeding, brutalized corpse was something out of a nightmare. It made what the Geaks threatened to do to Chiara look like a fun night out.

"We were twins, and we were really close as we were growing up," I say, watching the cars driving over Coldlake Bridge, their windshields glinting in the sunshine. "We did everything together. A couple of troublemakers. I miss her every day."

"What kind of trouble would the two of you get into?"

I rest my hand on the steering wheel of my Lamborghini. "Rich kid bullshit. Rich kid *crime* bullshit. Mom spoiled us, and with a father like ours, no one dared to touch us. We were expelled so many times but the school always had to let us back in again. I saw the inside of a jail cell half a dozen times before I was sixteen."

"You were arrested that many times? And you were never charged?"

I smile wider. "No charges. Nothing stuck. Nothing ever does."

"One of the first things I learned about you was that you were arrested and then they just let you go. How do you manage that?"

I merely smile and take a sip of my coffee.

She gives an exasperated shake of her head. "Vinicius, have you ever suffered a single consequence of your actions in your entire life?"

"Consequence?" I say the word slowly as if it's in a foreign language. "Never heard of it."

"What about Amalia? Did she get into trouble to?"

I shake my head. "No fucking way. Even though we were from a notorious crime family, her nickname was Angel because everyone thought she was one. One time when I was fifteen I was teaching myself to paint by copying out of an art book. I complained that I couldn't see the brush-strokes clearly enough, and so she broke into the city's art gallery and stole a Monet for me."

Chiara's mouth falls open. "You're kidding. Did she get caught?"

"I spent the summer copying it, and when I had made the perfect forgery, Amalia dropped the copy on the front steps. It's still hanging in the gallery today. Nobody ever suspected."

"Most people would have told you to take an art class."

"Amalia isn't most people." My smile slips from my face and I take Chiara's empty coffee cup and mine and crush them in the paper bag. "Wasn't most people."

She puts her hand on my sleeve, and her eyes behind her glasses are big and filled with sympathy. "Thank you for telling me about her. I know how painful it must be for you."

I put an arm around her shoulders, pull her close, and

press a kiss to her forehead. "You know what, kitten? It actually feels good to talk about her for a change. Thank you for that."

I start the engine and we head out of the park and back toward the city.

"Where are we going now? Back to Lorenzo's, or to see more of the city?"

"Something more fun. You've been wearing the same clothes that Cassius bought you for weeks. I'm taking you shopping."

Chiara looks down at herself. "Cassius bought these? They're fine. They're comfy."

Comfy is for eating Chinese food on the sofa, but no girl of mine is going to put up with department store joggers when she could be wearing designer.

"Where can we even go shopping? You said yourself I'm supposed to be dead."

I voice activate my phone and ask it to call Daphne's Boutique. A woman with a gracious customer service voice picks up on the other end.

"Hello, Daphne's Boutique. How may I help you?"

"Hello. I'd like to do some shopping. My friend is sensitive about her appearance and doesn't want to be seen, by anyone. The CCTV needs to be turned off and there are to be no shop assistants. If there's a fee for this, I'll pay it."

"Well..."

"I forgot to introduce myself. My name is Vinicius Angeli."

There's a short silence on the line, and then the woman replies in an entirely different tone, "Of course, Mr. Angeli. When would you like to bring your friend to Daphne's?"

I glance at my watch. "In about ten minutes."

"We can manage that."

"Thank you. We'll arrive via the back entrance. No one, and I mean *no one*, is to look at my friend or I'll be very upset." I'm speaking lightly but if she has half a brain she'll realize what *very upset* means from a man like me.

"Of course, Mr. Angeli," she says, her tone slightly strangled now. "The shop assistants and I will be upstairs."

I hang up, and notice that Chiara is gazing at me, amused.

"You do like getting what you want with just your tongue," she says, referring to something I told her while I was licking her clit for the first time.

I laugh softly. "Always, baby."

A few minutes later, I pull into a narrow street behind Belrose Avenue, give Chiara my suit jacket to put over her head and walk her inside. The manager has done as I've asked; the store is deserted, and the front door is locked.

Chiara gazes around at the array of dresses, tops, blouses, skirts, and shoes, all designer, and all expensive. The perfect selection for a girl who's found herself without her wardrobe.

I press a kiss to her lips and go and find the manager, calling over my shoulder, "Get whatever you want. I don't know when I'll be able to take you shopping again so don't hold back."

I find the manager upstairs in the break room with four shop assistants. They all stare at me with a mixture of admiration and trepidation as I hand over my platinum credit card with a smile. The assistants surreptitiously lean forward to check the name on the card, and their eyes widen.

Yes, it really is me.

"My friend will need around an hour. I'll bring her purchases up to you, and then we'll be on our way. Thank you *ever* so much for accommodating us."

I give them all my most charming smile. I can only imagine what they'll tell their friends over cocktails tonight.

That slippery devil who's always in the news and in the casinos came to the store today. He spent thousands. *Dirty money, obviously, but his credit card went through so we weren't going to turn him away.*

As I walk back downstairs I send a message to the group chat. *I closed down a boutique on Belrose Avenue and I'm shopping with Chiara. Anything special I should get her?*

Salvatore: *A couple of cocktail dresses. I've got a surprise planned for Chiara.*

Lorenzo: *Lingerie. White. Pink. Cute shit.*

Cassius adds an emoji of a finger pointing up at Lorenzo's statement.

I smile as I type my reply. *You're a couple of pervs. Done.*

Chiara has taken some clothes into the changing room. I saunter over to the lingerie section and browse the lacy bras in white, cream, and pastel colors. Chiara wearing these would be enough to bring a hard, dangerous man to his knees.

Or four hard, dangerous men all at once.

"Kitten, what's your bra size?" I call, flicking through them.

"28C. But I already grabbed some bras."

The bras she's chosen are probably ones that are meant

to be worn. The ones I'm looking at are meant to be taken off. I grab a few and stick my hand through the curtain.

"By request of Cassius and Lorenzo."

She mutters something that sounds like *dirty bastards*, but accepts them from me. "Are you sure they're not by your request?"

I draw the curtain aside and peer in at her. She's wearing only panties and a lilac sweater. "I prefer you naked."

She grabs the curtain from me and pulls it closed again. "Vinicius! Get out."

"Let me come in there and help you try things on. We've got the whole store to ourselves."

"Go and find me some shirts, would you? Silk and cotton. White, black, and patterned, please."

We spend the next hour that way, wandering around the store selecting clothes for her to try on and me putting everything that looks good into a pile. The heap is getting bigger and bigger.

Chiara stares at it and shakes her head. "That's more than enough. Let's get going."

"One more thing. Salvatore has a surprise for you and he wants you to wear a cocktail dress. He'd want you in something Italian. We all would, actually." I pick out a selection from Gucci, Dolce & Gabbana, and Moschino, and she goes to try them on. I sit down on a sofa and call after her, "Come out and show me."

A few minutes later, Chiara steps out of the fitting room in a red, off-the-shoulder dress with long sleeves and a short skirt.

"You look fucking incredible. Come here." Chiara comes to stand between my knees and I grasp her waist.

"You have good taste in dresses."

"I have good taste, period," I purr, slipping my hands down to cup her ass. I'm about to pull her down onto my lap when she slips out of my grasp.

The other two dresses are perfect as well, and I'm hard as hell watching her parade about in them, showing off her slender legs and perky tits.

"Which one?" she asks, gazing at herself in a tight, rose-printed dress.

"All of them."

"I only need one, and they're ridiculously expensive. I'm only going to... What, why are you laughing?"

"You have four boyfriends who are going to spoil you rotten. *Only one* isn't part of your vocabulary anymore."

Chiara's cheeks flush with annoyance. "Remember my seventeenth birthday when you all tormented me for being spoiled? I thought you wanted me to toughen up."

I stand up and take her face in my hands. "You are tough. We've put you through hell and you're still standing. We're getting the dresses."

"Why do I feel like this is bribery for putting up with all the hell you're going to continue to put me through?" she grumbles as she goes back into the changing room to put on her own clothes.

Because she's too smart for her own good, that's why.

As Chiara gets changed back into her own clothes, I go and have a word to the manager about having everything delivered to Cassius' penthouse, which is only a block down the street. There's not much trunk space in a Lamborghini.

"What do we do about all this?" Chiara asks as she

emerges from the changing rooms a few minutes later and stares at the pile of clothes.

I cover her head with my suit jacket again and walk her out. "All taken care of. They'll go to Cassius' place and he'll bring them around to you."

Once we get into my car, Chiara leans back in her seat with a smile. "Thank you for this. I feel relaxed when I'm with you. You're so lovely to spend time with."

I smile and press my mouth against hers. "I'm just happy to see you up and about again. You had us all worried."

She starts to say sorry, but I press a finger against her lips. "No sorries. Just keep that beautiful head up, kitten."

I kiss her again, parting her lips with my tongue and tasting her sweetness. If Chiara's smiling, then we know we're doing something right.

As I start the Lamborghini, Chiara straightens her sunglasses and says, "I thought you couldn't help but tells lies, but you didn't tell one lie all day, did you?"

"No, not one," I say, driving out onto Belrose Avenue and telling my second lie that day.

5

Chiara

I'm so worn out after our drive and shopping that Vinicius has to carry me upstairs at Lorenzo's compound and tuck me into bed. He tucks himself in with me, and at first, he kisses my neck and slides his hands beneath my clothes. There's nothing I want more than to lose myself in whatever he's hungry to do to my body, but every time I reach for him, my arm falls boneless onto the mattress and my eyes drift closed.

"You sleep, kitten," Vinicius murmurs, pulling the bedclothes around me.

"No, don't go..." I reach for him and he kisses the palms of each of my hands and tucks them beneath the comforter. As he stands up, I fall into an exhausted, dreamless doze.

A few hours later, I wake to find that it's dark outside. I slept the day away.

I sit up and glance at the alarm clock on the side table and see that it's seven in the evening. There are dozens of shopping bags from the boutique lined up along one wall. Cassius must be here, or has been here. My heart melts at the thought of the big, grumpy Italian. I haven't been alone with him since I "died," and I wonder if he's still at the compound.

I get out of bed and head for the door in my oversized T-shirt and panties, feeling much more myself after sleep. The effects of having been bled are finally wearing off.

There are voices from downstairs and I make my way toward them. Lorenzo and Salvatore are sitting on the sofas and Cassius is in the kitchen, making drinks. Tall, cold ones full of ice and mint.

Lorenzo studies me as I cross the room, his brows drawn together. "Dizzy, princess? Do you need to eat?"

"I'm fine, thanks." I go straight to Cassius and put my arms around his neck. I have to reach high and stand on tiptoe because he's so tall. He smells like the mint he's tearing up and his rich, masculine cologne. His white shirt is crisp and pristine, as always, and his beard is mathematically neat.

"*Bambina*," he murmurs, turning toward me and capturing my waist with his big hands. The heat from his body envelops me like a hug.

I rub my thumb over the dark hairs at the V of his shirt. "I've missed you."

A smile quirks the corner of his mouth. "You could have

asked for me anytime and I would have been right by your side."

I know, but I wasn't ready for him to be disappointed in me. I'm barely ready for it now. "You can say it if you want. *I told you so.*"

"Why would I say *I told you so*?" His deep voice rumbles against me.

"Because you knew I wouldn't be able to kill my father."

He strokes my cheek with the backs of his fingers, his eyes running over my face. "I didn't know that. I was worried about you. I didn't want you facing that *cazzo di merda* without me, but Salvatore was there to protect you. Nothing was going to happen to you."

I should have realized my three unhinged and obsessive men wouldn't have let me walk into the lion's den unprotected. Especially Cassius.

"If you and Salvatore were really enemies, would you have let me go through with my idea to try and kill Dad myself?"

His face transforms in shock at the mere idea, and anger races through his muscles. "*Bambina.* Let my woman face two enemies armed with nothing but a handgun and a bouquet of flowers? Every Ferragamo would turn in his fucking grave."

His woman.

Their woman.

Am I theirs?

I'm still wearing Salvatore's engagement ring that Cassius put on my finger just after the three of them kidnapped me. At the time I thought they were taunting me by telling me I was engaged to all of them. I think they're actually serious.

I glance at the ring on my left hand, which is resting on Cassius' muscular chest. He sees what I'm looking at and reaches up and takes it, holding my hand between us so we can both see the enormous diamond sparkling.

"You never looked at this ring closely after I put it back on your finger, did you?"

It looks the same, though I only had it a few minutes before giving it to Stephan to take to Cassius. "Why? Is it a fake?"

"No, *bambina*. While we were waiting to kidnap you, I had it engraved."

I slip the ring from my finger and peer inside the band. There are four prongs that hold the diamond in place and each one is engraved with a set of initials. *SF. VA. CF. LS.*

Salvatore Fiore. Vinicius Angeli. Cassius Ferragamo. Lorenzo Scava.

And then on the band, at the center of the other initials, *CR*.

Chiara Romano.

I carried the truth on my hand all this time.

The four of them and me.

"I had days and days alone in your penthouse with nothing to do. What if I'd taken off this ring and looked closely at it?"

Cassius slips the ring back onto my finger and pulls me into his arms. "We agreed that we would get to know you and then decide whether to give you back to Salvatore to marry. I'd already made up my mind. I wasn't going to give you back. So what if you saw the engravings?"

He dips his head and slants his mouth over mine. His sudden, ferocious kiss steals the breath from my lungs. When he pulls back, his eyes are glittering. "Remember what I told you the night of your seventeenth birthday?"

He promised he'd be back for me. I see another promise burning in his gaze. That he'll never let me go again. I reach up to touch the dark bristles of his beard. I'm in the arms of one of the most powerful and demanding men in Coldlake, and his dark brown eyes gleam with hunger.

Desire races through my body. I've only had sex with Cassius once, and it's not enough. Suddenly, all I can think about is tearing off his clothes and feeling his cock—too big, too thick, absolutely perfect—hammering into me while I cry out his name.

Cassius' expression tells me he's had exactly the same idea when someone clears their throat from the doorway. I nestle closer to Cassius, my breasts tight against his chest. His arms crush me possessively against his body. Normal people would take the hint that we're in the middle of something and leave us alone.

"Come here, you two. You're going to want to see this."

"Later. We're busy," Cassius mutters, not looking away from me.

"I'm serious. Get in here." Salvatore jerks his head toward a laptop that's open on the coffee table. A news program is showing. I can't make out any of the words as Cassius lowers his mouth to mine again.

Then I hear her say my name.

Cassius looks up in surprise. "*Che cazzo?*" *What the fuck?*

I hurry over to the laptop and see a blonde newscaster in

a blue blazer is speaking earnestly into the camera. "...cross now to Mayor Romano's press conference."

The picture changes to the front steps of City Hall where a podium and a dozen microphones have been set up. There's a red box in the corner of the screen that says LIVE, and rolling text at the bottom reading, *Mayor Romano speaks: "My daughter is missing."*

"Missing!" I exclaim, sinking onto the sofa in front of the laptop.

The men cluster around me and we watch as the front doors of the imposing building open. There's an eruption of camera flashes as Dad approaches the podium dressed in a somber black suit and wearing a grave but determined expression that I know well. It's his "natural disaster" face. His "senseless murder" face. "We have all been shaken, but we'll carry on," that expression says.

He braces his hands on either side of the podium and gazes out across the crowd. "One month ago was meant to be the happiest day of my daughter's life. It was meant to be the proudest day of mine. The day I gave her away in marriage to the man she loved, Salvatore Fiore."

Dad pauses for emotional effect, and I exchange glances with Salvatore. Are we going to be the heroes of this story, or the villains?

"Instead, she was ripped from my arms and his by notorious criminals."

Gasps from the gathered crowd.

"You'll all be wondering why news of this despicable crime is only being revealed to you now, after a whole month has passed. That was my decision, and my decision alone. I have been hoping to negotiate with her kidnappers. I would pay any ransom to have my daughter returned to me, but they have remained silent. The time has come to unmask the men behind this crime."

Dad takes a deep breath, as if composing himself, and looks into the camera.

"She is the prisoner of three men. Vinicius Angeli. Cassius Ferragamo. Lorenzo Scava. These names are recognizable by all who live in Coldlake. Each are known members of the mafia, criminals, extortionists, and cold-blooded killers. These are the hands my innocent daughter has fallen into."

"And what a delicious innocent morsel she is," Vinicius says, over my head.

"Not so innocent now," Lorenzo say with relish.

Another pause from Dad. "Or so I thought."

I sit up straight. What's this? Is he going to tell everyone in Coldlake I tried to kill him?

"I have just learned that there's a fourth kidnapper. A man I thought I could trust. My daughter's fiancé, Salvatore Fiore. I invited him into my home. I broke bread with this man, and all along he planned to betray me. Salvatore Fiore, I'm shocked to learn, is as despicable and corrupt as his late father."

I glance at Salvatore, who's glaring at the laptop screen. Dad's not only dragging his name, but his father's, as well.

"The time has come to ask you all for help," Dad says. "The people of Coldlake have always been there for me, and I need you now more than ever. I'm announcing a reward of one million dollars for information leading to the capture and arrest of these men, and the whereabouts of my daughter. One million dollars each."

I gnaw on my lower lip. Five million dollars. That's a worrisome amount. How many of these men's friends would sell them out for cash like that?

Dad's voice becomes more strident. "I am authorizing everyone in this city to make a citizen's arrest of these men, if safe to do so. Immunity from prosecution will be granted to anyone who can deliver Salvatore Ferragamo, Vinicius Angeli, Cassius Ferragamo, Lorenzo Scava or my daughter to the nearest police station."

"Holy fuck," Lorenzo mutters.

"These four men will not be allowed to continue their reign of terror in Coldlake. This is war."

A journalist calls to Dad, "Mayor Romano, do you have any words of comfort for your daughter? She could be watching this broadcast."

Dad looks straight into the TV camera, and all the hairs stand up on the back of my neck as his eyes bore into mine.

"I'll find you."

I laugh weakly. "Is it just me, or did that sound like a threat?"

Cassius isn't laughing. He reaches out and mutes the laptop. "Every lowlife piece of shit, every cop, and every investigator in this city is going to be hunting down us and Chiara from this moment on."

Vinicius sighs and scrubs a hand over his face. "This is my fault for taking Chiara all over town today. Someone saw her and it got back to the mayor."

"If I find out that Acid opened his fat fucking mouth—" Lorenzo begins.

Salvatore speaks over him. "It wasn't your fault, Vinicius, and it wasn't Acid, either. It was me."

I turn around in surprise. "You?"

"The mayor has been calling me day and night. I think he's realized that he's been played."

"What have you been saying to that *bastardo*?" Cassius spits the word like it's rotting flesh in his mouth.

A smile spreads over Salvatore's face. "Me? I haven't said anything to the mayor. I haven't been taking his calls. I had a year of pretending to like that asshole, and once we got Chiara back, I couldn't be bothered anymore."

Vinicius glances at the laptop. "He didn't say her name once, did you notice? It was always *my daughter*."

"I'm more valuable to him as a prop than as someone he loves." I glance around at the four men. They kidnapped me and manipulated me into being theirs, but now that I am, they have no plans to use me for any purpose other than their lover. That I know about, anyway.

Lorenzo isn't saying anything, so I ask him, "Are you all right?"

"No. None of us are. Did you hear what your father said?"

"Yes, that there's a reward on all your heads and he wants me back."

He folds his arms and looks at the others one by one. "Not that part. The immunity from prosecution part. The mayor just gave anyone who drags one of our bleeding corpses to the nearest police station the keys to the fucking city."

"But that's not what he said. Is it?"

Lorenzo raises his eyebrows at me, and I recall Dad's exact words. *Immunity from prosecution will be granted.* And he never mentioned whether we should be alive or not.

Oh, shit.

"Every gang member in the city is going to be hunting us down. Hunting *you* down, princess. The Geaks, the Blood Pack and more. A free pass to do whatever they want? It's like Christmas to them."

"This is just the enticement they need to come out of the southwest and rain down chaos on the city," Vinicius says. "It could be worse than when we took over from Francesco Fiore."

Worse than when all their sisters were killed?

It really is war.

Cassius stands up, goes into the kitchen, and comes back with the cocktails he was making when I came downstairs. As he passes them out, he says, "We knew this might happen. We prepared for this, and in the end, we'll win."

"Nothing changes," Salvatore affirms. "We were never planning on letting Chiara out of our sight even before the mayor announced open season on us."

"It's not just me, though," I say, casting worried looks at them all. "You have to be careful of yourselves as well."

Vinicius smiles. "Ah, kitten. You're worried about us."

I don't want their dead bodies splashed all over the news while my father gloats over their demise.

I don't want them dead at all.

Lorenzo holds up his glass. "If the mayor wants war, then we'll bring it. Won't we, princess?"

Cassius hands me a glass, and I stare at the mint and ice cubes. Every lie Dad told on that broadcast burns through me. If only the people of Coldlake could see him murdering Mom the night of my birthday then they wouldn't be gasping in sympathy for him. He's the one who deserves to be hunted down like an animal.

I hold up my glass. "It's war."

Dad keeps betting on being able to manipulate these men, but now the odds are stacked against him more than ever. He hasn't got Mom at his side, and he hasn't got me.

As I drink the cocktail, a familiar face appears on the news. They're back in the studio, focusing on a pale man with an unhealthy complexion, sunken eyes, and a sticklike neck.

"That's Christian Galloway, Dad's political opponent."

Salvatore leans forward and unmutes the laptop. Galloway speaks in a rapid, breathless voice.

"...and we have to remember that it's during Mayor Romano's so-called tough-on-crime terms in office that we've seen organized crime flourish in Coldlake. He was planning on wedding his own daughter to one of the most suspect men in the city. I don't believe that the mayor thought Salvatore Fiore was a law-abiding citizen for a second, let alone for an entire year. As mayor of Coldlake, I'll stamp out..."

Salvatore mutes it again, and he's grinning. "My good name is taking quite the beating today."

"He's a creepy motherfucker," Vinicius observes, looking at Galloway. "He looks more like an undertaker than a politician."

"Close. He was a coroner," I tell him.

"He's got as much charisma as a shriveled vegetable," Cassius says.

Dad's going to get so much attention and sympathy in the lead up to the election. Galloway is toast, even if he does speak the truth.

"Go and put on one of your new dresses, Chiara. We're going out."

I look up in surprise at Salvatore. "Out? When there's a price on all our heads?"

"We're going to my house."

Salvatore's house. I'm interested to see where Salvatore lives. Cassius helps me to my feet and starts moving us toward the door. His eyes have sharpened with desire once more.

"I'll help her get dressed."

"We haven't got time for that sort of help, Cassius. They're waiting."

Cassius shoots Salvatore a dark look. "Easy for you to say. You've already taken Chiara to bed."

"I had to wait a fucking year and then listen to you all tell me how good her pussy is. You can wait a few more hours."

Cassius' temper is simmering just beneath the surface as he glares at Salvatore. Finally, he grasps my jaw and tilts my face up to his with a fist in my hair. "We'll finish this later," he growls, and then gives me a savage kiss.

I practically melt through the floor and there's a rush of heat between my thighs. I consider slinking closer to him and whimpering, *But my pussy's wet*, just to get my own way, but something Salvatore said makes me turn to him.

"Who's waiting? Is it Ginevra and Antonio?"

Salvatore is staring at my hard nipples like he's regretting making plans tonight. "Go and get ready. You'll find out."

Lips tingling and slightly breathless, I make my way back up to my room, carrying my cocktail. I can manage the steps without getting dizzy so I guess my blood pressure is finally getting back to normal.

After I take a shower, I let my hair dry naturally while I sort through the clothes. I'm about to regret not telling Vinicius I need makeup when I see a bag from a department store which is filled with boxes of blusher, eyeshadow, lipstick, and mascara, as well as various shades of foundation and concealer. It's the sort of selection a shop assistant might put together if a man walked up with a credit card and said, *I don't know, she needs everything.*

Forty minutes later I come downstairs wearing the Dolce & Gabbana rose print mini-dress with spaghetti straps and a pair of black stilettos. My cheeks and lips are rosy and I'm wearing mascara and eyeliner. I haven't dressed up since Salvatore took me to one of his casinos a year ago.

I'm clicking down the hall in my high heels when someone appears at the other end. Lorenzo has put on a suit, and I realize it's been a while since I've seen him dressed up, too. My mouth waters at the sight of his tattooed hands and throat against his white shirt and suit jacket.

He prowls toward me, his gaze slipping hungrily down my body. "Fuck, princess, you look good enough to eat. You wearing pretty panties like I requested?"

Lorenzo snags me around the waist and pulls me against him. I nearly moan from the feel of his arms around me. Being near the four of them puts me into heat.

"I don't know. Am I?"

A heated smile slinks over his face. I've never been so blatant about my attraction to Lorenzo. Reaching behind me, he works his finger between my legs and strokes the lace of my G-string, right over my pussy.

My hands clench on the lapels of his jacket and my ankles tremble in these sky-high heels.

"Fuck, they sure do feel pretty."

At the end of the hallway, Salvatore appears around the corner and his expression flattens into annoyance as he sees his friend with his hand up my dress. I've been horny as hell since Vinicius tucked me into bed, but first exhaustion got in my way, and now Salvatore.

I pant against Lorenzo's mouth, "Why do you all have to turn me on so much when Salvatore's hurrying us out of here?"

He groans and buries his face in my hair. "Don't fucking tell me that, princess. I already want to lock you up in a cage way too much. The last thing you need is to give me another reason."

There are rapid footsteps toward us, and I feel an arm loop around my waist and drag me out of Lorenzo's grasp. I run my tongue over my upper lip and smile at Salvatore. "I got ready as fast as I could."

"You look beautiful, baby," he murmurs, but I don't get the kiss I was hoping for. Now I'm feeling better all I want is sex and Chinese food on the sofa with all of them. Like how it was at Cassius' place.

It was way better being kidnapped.

Cassius is walking toward us, adjusting the heavy watch on his wrist, and my gaze is drawn to his fingers. Long, thick fingers and tanned hands with veins that stand out on the backs. His dark gaze catches mine and I think he knows I'm thinking about his hands.

"Are you going to behave, *bambina*? I'd hate to have to spank you again."

God.

Why does that turn me on as well?

I turn to Salvatore. "Do we have to go out? Can't we stay here and get take-out? It's so much nicer when it's just us."

Salvatore gazes at me, amused. "You *are* feeling better. Sorry, baby. You'll disappoint your guests if we don't go, and I promise you won't want that."

"Chinese food and sofas tomorrow?" I ask hopefully as he takes my hand and leads me toward the cars in Lorenzo's underground garage.

"Anything you want, baby," he murmurs and kisses me behind the ear. "Vinicius is joining us there."

I can feel Lorenzo close behind me like a wolf alpha pursuing his mate. *I already want to lock you up in a cage way too much.*

I'm not turned on by that.

I'm *not.*

Crap.

Lorenzo steps past me and opens the passenger door of Salvatore's gray Maserati and flips the front seat forward. "After you, princess."

Salvatore glares at Lorenzo, who's getting into the back seat beside me. "Drive yourself. You've got five cars of your own."

The blond, cold-eyed man settles back on the leather seat next to me. "You drive. You can bring me home when you bring Chiara back. Hurry up, I thought you said we were late."

Salvatore slams the passenger door closed in his smirking face.

Lorenzo doesn't even look at me as we drive out of the compound and through the streets. Cassius, in his white SUV Porsche, is just behind us. As soon as we're on the freeway, Lorenzo slides closer to me, a wicked glint in his eyes that makes my heart pound faster.

"Are you sure you haven't felt faint today? I'd better check your pulse." Lorenzo slips his hand between my knees and pulls them open. I don't know what vein he thinks he's going for but nobody's ever taken my pulse down there before. There isn't a lot of space in the back of the car and he's crowding me against the door.

Crowd me harder, please.

"How is Acid, anyway?" I ask, trying to pretend everything's innocent in the back seat as I stare down at tattooed hands between my legs.

"He'll live," Lorenzo says as he slips two fingers inside my panties and feels how wet I am. His eyes dilate and he mouths three words, his lips just inches from mine.

Jesus fucking Christ.

Then he slides two fingers straight into my pussy.

A loud cry rushes up my throat but I manage to swallow it down. I angle my hips forward, and Lorenzo curls his fingers wickedly around my G-spot. He puts his lips against my ear and speaks softly so only I can hear him.

"I kept the sheets I fucked you on. They're smeared with your blood. When will you be on your period? I want to recreate that moment as soon as possible."

My face flames and my pussy spasms around him as he works his fingers in and out of me. Hard. Deep. Merciless. I moan and edge my knees wider. "That's gross. You're gross."

He laughs as my breathing gets faster and faster. "Sure, princess. Lie to me while your pussy is getting wetter by the second."

I can hear that my pussy is wet. Every thrust of his fingers is making an obscene squelching sound. Apparently, Salvatore can hear it, too.

"What's going on back there?"

"Nothing," Lorenzo says innocently, pressing two fingers to my throat. "Her heartbeat's strong. Maybe a little too fast, but I do that to women."

I don't know about other women, but he's doing it to me.

"Chiara?" Salvatore asks.

"Um, hi—oh, *God*," I gasp, my head tipping back, pleasure cascading through me. Lorenzo's fingers pressing on my throat becomes a grab. He pulls his fingers out of my pussy and goes back to my clit.

Salvatore adjusts the rearview mirror, and snarls, "Oh, for fuck's sake, Lorenzo."

"Eyes on the road," Lorenzo tells him, and then nips at my neck with his teeth. "Moan louder for me, princess, it feels like a fucking lifetime since I've touched you."

It does feel like a lifetime since he had a gun to my head as he obliterated my virginity in his bed. Being alone with him was intense. Blowing him while Vinicius pounded me from behind and Cassius gazed on was inconceivable for the Mayor of Coldlake's good little daughter. Letting him finger-fuck me in a car on the freeway while there's a price on my head is mind-blowing.

"Call Cassius," Salvatore says, and then there's a dial tone.

I choke off my moan, but Lorenzo laughs. "You trying to get me punched in the face?"

"Always," says Salvatore, a grin in his voice.

A moment later an accented voice snaps through the car. "Yes?"

"Lorenzo's jumping the queue."

"*Che cosa*?" *What?*

A white SUV roars up beside us and I can just make out Cassius in the car. I doubt he can see much because of the tinted windows, but he can hear.

"Scava, what the fuck are you doing?"

"Making my princess come. It's what she's wanted all evening and you're all too cruel to give it to her." He squeezes my throat tighter and growls through his teeth, "Aren't I nice?"

"You're so fucking nice," I whimper, my back arching. Lorenzo's going to make me come so hard and I don't even care that two other men are listening to me moan and someone might catch a glimpse of me through the window.

Cassius swears some more in Italian but I'm too focused on Lorenzo's fingers working my clit faster and faster to be able to translate what he's saying. I glance from Lorenzo, his face just inches from mine, savage with desire, to Salvatore's blue-green eyes in the review mirror, to the man in the white SUV next to us.

All of them. I want all their eyes on me. If Vinicius was here, I'd want him seeing me and hearing me, too.

Fuck being the mayor's good little daughter.

"Please don't stop, please don't stop," I sob, clutching Lorenzo's muscled arm and staring into his pale eyes.

He shakes his head.

He wouldn't.

He won't.

He's as hungry to see me come on his fingers as I am to climax.

"Baby, you look so fucking good pinned to that seat,"

Salvatore breathes from up front. His eyes flick from me to the road and back again. Salvatore has never seen me with any of the others before.

"*Bambina*, come so I can hear you."

I haven't got a choice. The pressure Lorenzo's putting on my throat makes me feel like I'm flying, and my climax grips me as hard as he does. My head tips back in a long, loud wail.

"*Bella*, Chiara," Cassius murmurs in an indulgent voice. *Beautiful*. And then in an entirely different tone, "Fuck you, Scava." Then he hangs up.

I open my eyes and lick my lips as Lorenzo loosens his grip and tucks my panties back into place. He's smirking as he rearranges my clothes.

"Is Cassius really mad at you? Is there some rule I don't know about?"

Lorenzo smiles lazily and rubs his hand over his jaw. "Who cares? You looked fucking hot."

"I care. I don't want to get in the middle of you four and cause trouble."

Salvatore's eyes laser into mine in the rearview mirror. "Baby, all we want is for you to get in the middle of all four of us and cause trouble."

"Causing a fight isn't..." I trail off, catching his hidden meaning.

Oh.

Oh.

That kind of "in the middle of all four of us." My face flames again, imagining all five of us naked together. Both Salvatore and Lorenzo's smiles are wicked.

That's so many men. So many hands. So many dicks. How would I even...?

Lorenzo runs a finger down my burning cheek. "You're so cute when you blush."

I'm still staring straight ahead trying to figure out the mechanics of something like that—all at once? One or two at a time? —and feeling pretty squirmy about it when we pull into a driveway.

Squirmy, but not in a bad way. A fluttery, restless sort of excitement. Is that even allowed, all five of us? I went to Catholic school. I was raised with so many "a young lady doesn't so and so" rules that surely a sinkhole will open up before me if I so much as go down on my knees with a cock in each hand.

I haven't even done *that*.

My gaze flicks between Salvatore and Lorenzo, vividly imagining it.

Yet.

My inner muscles pulse at the thought. I thought being corrupted by bad men would be a guilt-ridden experience, but apparently my pussy is eager to dive in the deep end.

Cassius is there to help me out of the car and he kisses me hard. "Your moans. I nearly drove off the road."

I open my mouth beneath his. I *need* kisses right now. "You're not mad, are you?"

"With Salvatore," he growls. *Kiss.* "For making plans." *Kiss.* "When all I want to do is fuck you." *Bite.* His teeth sink into my lower lip and my knees nearly give out underneath me.

"With Lorenzo, I mean."

Cassius makes an irritated noise but goes on kissing me.

Out of the corner of my eye I see Lorenzo watching us, amused. I guess Cassius' bark is worse than his bite. Unless he gets it in his head to spank me, and then damn, he bites deep.

He finally pulls away and runs his thumb under my lip, correcting my lipstick. "Your mouth is fucking delicious, *bambina*."

A smile tugs at my lips. Cassius has definitely softened around some of his harder edges. My mother was always affectionate with me. So were Francesca, Violette and Stephan, the people who worked for us. I'm used to affection. I *need* affection.

I turn to look at the house. It's more like a mansion with white columns, huge windows, and a garden of sculpted hedges, all lit up in the dark. It's stylish, formidable, and beautiful.

Just like Salvatore.

The man himself slips an arm around my waist and walks me toward the front door. "I organized this surprise for you. I thought you might need it after the week you've had."

"Is it a party for the five of us?"

"No, it's just for you. The four of us will be in the house, but we'll leave you alone."

"I don't understand..." I begin, and then break off as we cross the threshold and Salvatore leads me into the sitting room.

There are three girls sitting on the sofas. Beautiful girls wearing cocktails dresses and jewelry, their hair in loose curls and their nails manicured.

Three familiar girls.

An olive-skinned girl with long, dark hair jumps to her feet and squeals, "Oh my God. *Chiara!*"

Rosaline, a friend I made at school last year after my previous best friend dumped me. If it weren't for making new friends, I don't think I would have survived last year. The other two girls getting to their feet are Sophia, a curvy and petite brunette with tanned skin, and Candace, a tall, slender blonde.

Rosaline's father is the head croupier at Salvatore's biggest casino. She's energetic and irreverent, and a breath of fresh air in any room. Her long, dark hair hangs down to her waist and she's wearing a tight red dress. Sophia's mom is the head of PR for Salvatore's restaurants and she's one of the kindest and sweetest girls I've ever met. Finally, Candace's father is a financial manager who works for Salvatore, and she's as ambitious as she is stunning. She has her sights set on a first-class college and marrying a wealthy man, preferably one who works for Salvatore.

They took me under their wings when I was bewildered by the world. They all love Salvatore. Adore him, in fact.

And they're staring at me like I'm back from the dead.

They cluster around me, hugging me, kissing me, and tearing up, exclaiming that they thought they'd never see me again after I was kidnapped from my wedding. I find my eyes getting blurry and a lump forms in my throat as I hug and kiss them. I didn't realize how much I'd missed my friends.

Sophia is nearly sobbing. "When Mr. Fiore invited us here, we thought it was to tell us bad news, and then he said to wear cocktail dresses. We didn't know what to think. And then the *news* tonight. This is all so crazy! I'm so happy you're safe. Where have you *been*?"

Before I can answer her, Salvatore speaks up. The girls fall silent under the force of his severe gaze. "Don't make me regret inviting you all here. Not a word about Chiara being here tonight. Not to your parents. Not to any of your friends. *No one.* If it gets back to me you've spoken about Chiara to anyone..." He trails off, his blue-green eyes glittering with menace as he glares at each of the girls.

Even Rosaline looks solemn. "We wouldn't Mr. Fiore."

"You can trust us, Mr. Fiore."

"Thank you for inviting us, Mr. Fiore. We won't break your trust."

Salvatore holds each of their gazes, and then nods. "See that you keep your word."

I step closer to Salvatore and place my hand on the lapel of his jacket, smiling in delight. "You invited them here for me?"

His severe expression finally melts away as he gazes down at me. "We thought you could use a girls' night."

Vinicius, Cassius, and Lorenzo have come into the room, and Salvatore introduces them to the girls. "Ladies, these are my friends, Vinicius Angeli, Cassius Ferragamo and Lorenzo Scava."

Vinicius gives them a broad, winning smile and Cassius nods politely. Lorenzo ignores them. He has his head tilted to one side and he gazes at my dress, as if he's wondering if I'm still wet underneath. I smooth my hands down my dress and edge my ankles closer together, trying not to blush.

Rosaline has her mouth hanging open and Sophia is swallowing nervously. I forgot that the last time they saw these men they were kidnapping me from my wedding, and for a year they believed that they and Salvatore were sworn enemies. Candace has taken her cue from Salvatore and greets them with a smile.

"It's wonderful to meet you all. I've heard so many...interesting things about you."

It's not like she could say *good* things.

Salvatore takes my waist in his hands and plants a kiss on my mouth. "Have a lovely time."

I glance at the other three over his shoulder. "And what about you guys? Are you going out?"

Cassius raises a severe brow. "And leave you unprotected? Of course not. We'll be playing poker in the next room."

Salvatore kisses me again, and then heads through the door. Each of the men file past me, telling me to have a good time. Vinicius drops a lingering and heated kiss on my lips, and Cassius' kiss is brief, awkward, but hard. Lorenzo captures my jaw in his hand and puts his face close to mine like he's going to kiss me—and my heart races—but then he moves on, and closes the door behind him.

There's stunned silence behind me, and I know what I'm going to see. My three friends with their jaws on the floor.

I turn around, and I'm right. Salvatore didn't tell them anything. Not about the four of them being friends "again," and not about him sharing me with said friends.

Thanks a bunch, Salvatore. I guess I know what we're going to be talking about on girls' night.

To delay the inevitable and give myself time to think, I glance around the room. There's a long side table covered with canapes and jugs of iced cocktails, and I make a beeline for it. All the drinks are fruity, and when I taste a few, I find they're alcoholic. What's a little underage drinking when your boyfriends are in the mafia? Is this vodka? Tequila? I have no idea. I choose one that's sweet and delicious, pour four glasses and take them over to the girls.

"Drinks!" I say brightly, handing them out. I think they need them for the shock of the last few minutes. "How have you all been? What are you doing with yourselves? How's work and college?"

Since school finished, Candace and Sophia have been attending Coldlake University and Rosaline has been training as a croupier.

They all stare at each other, then at me.

Rosaline waves my questions away. "Babe, you have ten thousand questions to answer. What the hell is going on?"

I sink down onto the sofa, my smile fading. I barely understand the events of the past year myself, so how do I explain what's been happening between Salvatore, me, and his three friends? Maybe they'll think I'm cheating on Salvatore. Or I'm slutty. Or I'm just plain weird.

I gesture to the sofas. "Sit down and have a drink with me, and I'll tell you everything. You're going to need a drink for this."

The girls sit, and we all clink glasses and take a mouthful of our cocktails.

"Damn that's good," Candace says, and takes another sip. She gazes around the living room with huge, admiring eyes. "Mr. Fiore's home is beautiful, isn't it?"

The sofas are richly upholstered and the furniture is edged with gold. Ornate brass light fittings hang over us, and the painted ceiling soars high overhead. Every vase and oil painting seems like a family heirloom, and I remember what

Ginevra once told me about family being everything to Salvatore.

"This is the first time I've been here," I murmur, gazing around the room. "Isn't that strange?"

"Babe, that's low on the list of things that are strange right now," Rosaline says. "First of all, you're alive. We've been hearing all sorts of rumors about you getting shot. Second of all, you're with Salvatore when we thought you were kidnapped. Third, he's with his friends, and you're, like, *with* his friends? Are we reading that right? And then your Dad's press conference tonight—this is all so crazy."

"What's the last thing you know? I have no idea what's been said about me since my wedding day."

Sophia says, "We were about to walk down the aisle behind you when that scary blond man charged into the church, hurling smoke bombs."

"Lorenzo Scava," Candace supplies. "We ran outside just in time to see you being shoved into car by a big man that we figured out later was Cassius Ferragamo, and you drove off with Vinicius Angeli at the wheel. We were so scared for you. You looked *terrified*."

Sophia draws out her phone, taps it several times and hands it to me. "I took a video. Here."

I hit the play button, and see the taillights of Lorenzo's 4WD disappearing down the street with Salvatore running after it. My heart twists as I remember gazing out the back window at him as I was pinned between Cassius and Lorenzo.

Then I spot something parked on the other side of the street. Salvatore's gray Maserati. It's right there and he could have jumped in and given chase instead of fruitlessly running after us. How good it looked, though, the groom desperately trying to save his bride. Quite the performance for everyone at the church. And my father.

My stomach lurches as the camera finds Dad, his jaw tight with anger and his face a mask of fury as he marches toward Salvatore. They talk, but Sophia's too far away to record anything that's being said. Outside the church is chaotic as all the guests mill about. Rosaline and Candace have tears running down their faces. Smoke pours out the doors. Everyone's in uproar as they try to understand what just happened.

Dad looks right into the camera and shouts, "Turn that off," and the screen goes black.

I pass the phone back to Sophia, who tells me, "The mayor instructed all the guests not to breathe a word of what happened and not to call the police. The only way he could get you back was if we all did exactly what he said. Mr. Fiore backed him up."

"There wasn't anything in the news about you," Candace says. "No missing persons reports. It was so scary."

"Dad expected a war on the streets after you were promised to Mr. Fiore and the Coldlake Syndicate fell apart," Rosaline says, "but everything stayed quiet. Eerily quiet. Then after you were kidnapped everyone braced themselves again, but still nothing happened."

"It was quiet because Salvatore and the others never stopped being friends," I explain.

"But they kidnapped you!"

"Salvatore was in on it."

All three girls stare at me in shock.

"I'm so sorry you didn't know. I was trapped in Cassius'

penthouse. To me, the kidnapping was real and I was Cassius' prisoner."

"Did they hurt you?" Sophia asks.

Rosaline shakes her head. "We just saw them all *kiss* Chiara. The kidnapping was fake, remember?"

"But still..." Sophia says, her huge eyes worried.

I hesitate, wondering how much to tell them and how to tell them. "Not hurt, but there were moments that..."

Terrified me.

Shocked me.

Turned me on.

"They're dangerous men, even Salvatore. Especially Salvatore. I know your parents all work for him and this doesn't reflect on them or you, but you've heard the rumors about him. They're not just rumors."

Rosaline and Sophia nod, but Candance looks uncomfortable. If she wants to marry one of Salvatore's powerful men, she'd better get used to the idea of getting into bed with a criminal. Fast.

"They're all like Salvatore. They all do shady, dangerous, and criminal things."

Sophia takes a thoughtful sip of her drink. "All last year you were miserable at the thought of marrying a criminal, and yet I think you like these men. What's changed?"

I think about this carefully. Last year I was struggling to reconcile who I was with the fact that my father was a murderer. "I admire their loyalty to each other. They would die for each other. Their bond is like nothing I've ever known."

"But why is it so strong?" Sophia asks.

"Because of the Black Orchid murders," Rosaline says

right away, and a chill goes down my spine. "They took control of this city from Salvatore's father when old Mr. Fiore became senile, and one by one their sisters were murdered. Everyone thought their hold on the city would fall apart, but in the end their bond was stronger than ever."

Sophia nods sadly. "I heard the same thing. Their poor sisters."

"That's how Coldlake works," Rosaline says, topping up all our glasses. "Everything seems bright and sunny, but when you look beneath the surface, it's all blood and murder and darkness."

"You don't know the half of it," I say bitterly.

"What do you mean?" she asks.

So far I've only told the girls things that are secret, but not life-threatening. If I want them to truly understand why I'm with these men, they have to hear the whole truth. "You really can't speak about any of this because it could put you in horrible danger. I'm a witness to a vicious murder, and someone very powerful might hurt you if they find out that you know the truth."

"We already swore to Salvatore, and we would never break that promise, but I'll swear to you, too," Candace says. "Whatever you tell us, I won't breathe a word to anyone."

Rosaline and Sophia nod in agreement.

I take another mouthful of my cocktail for courage. "The night of my seventeenth birthday, Dad murdered Mom. I saw him do it with my own eyes. He took Lorenzo's knife from him and slit her throat."

The girls' faces are rigid with shock. Finally, someone else knows truth about what happened to Mom. One day, everyone will know. I won't rest until the people of Coldlake hear the truth about their mayor.

I swear it.

"I have been carrying around this horrible secret for a year. Salvatore, Vinicius, Cassius, and Lorenzo all saw it happen as well. We've all lost someone we love in horrible, brutal circumstances, and those loved ones have never been avenged."

It's romantic, in a twisted way, that they'd kill for me, but what we share is dark and brutal.

"The mayor murdered his wife right in front of you?" Candace asks. "That's *horrible*. I'm so sorry, Chiara."

The other two tell me how sorry they are, too, and my heart feels lighter already. Their words mean more than the thousand empty platitudes I heard at Mom's funeral.

I fill them in on my attempt to avenge my mother by killing my father and Salvatore reuniting with his friends. "Dad figured it out and put a price on all our heads, and that brings you all up to date."

"Wow. What a crazy time you've had lately," Candace says with a shake of her head.

"Are you still going to marry Salvatore?" Sophia asks.

Murder and vengeance is one thing, but how the hell am I going to explain this part? "Not really. I mean, we're not engaged anymore and there's no wedding planned."

"But you're wearing an engagement ring. Who gave it to you?"

I touch the ring on my finger, angling it this way and that so it sparkles in the light. "All of them. They all chose it."

"You're going to marry all of them?" Candace asks.

"They all want me to be with them. This ring is meant to

represent that. It's been a crazy few weeks. It's been a crazy *year*. I like them all in different ways, but I'm only just getting to know them."

"This is so crazy and hot. I love it." Rosaline leans forward with a conspiratorial smile. "Who's the best kisser?"

Candace hits her arm. "Don't be nosy. That's private."

"I haven't kissed them all yet," I confess, thinking of Lorenzo.

Rosaline's face falls. "Oh, really? I was going to ask who's got the biggest dick next, but I guess you don't know if you haven't got past kissing."

My face flames and I take a gulp of my cocktail.

Rosaline sits up. "Oh my God. Look at her face! Who have you slept with?"

Candace gasps, "Rosaline, you are *unbelievable*. Chiara has been dealing with grief and revenge and unprecedented circumstances. She hasn't been jumping into bed with four men."

"Well…" I say, and trail off.

Rosaline grabs my hand and pleads with me like I'm a faith healer and she got an incurable disease. "I'll never ask for anything ever again. Please tell me who you've banged. They're all so gorgeous. You're such a lucky bitch."

Candace is red-faced with shock and outrage. Sophia is torn between laughing and telling Rosaline to shut up.

"They're all pretty sexy," I agree, and trail off.

Rosaline reaches for the jug and tops off all our glasses. "Seriously sexy. If it were me, I would have fallen to my knees in front of all of them by now. Please tell me you've at least let Mr. Fiore take you to bed."

I can't help myself. I nod, fighting a smile.

"Was he your first?"

I shake my head.

"No *way*. Who was the first? I bet it was Vinicius Angeli. He's so freaking handsome."

"He tried. But no."

"The big muscly one? Cassius?"

"Nearly, but no."

Rosaline's eyebrows shoot up in surprise. "The crazy tattooed psycho? Wow, I didn't think he was your type. So, just the two of them, or...?"

As my face burns harder and I cover my grin with my hand, Rosaline screeches like a pterodactyl, *"Oh, my God, Chiara. You've fucked all—"*

Candace lunges for her friend and claps her hand over her mouth, hissing, "They're in the next room. Are you trying to get us all killed? We're not supposed to be gossiping!"

I fall back on the sofa, laughing. If Salvatore didn't want a bunch of eighteen-year-old girls to start discussing their dicks, he shouldn't have given us enormous quantities of liquor on empty stomachs and left us in his huge, luxurious living room. "It's fine. It's their faults we're talking about them like this. Just be sure that none of this leaves this room, okay? Remember, I'm supposed to be missing. Or was it dead? I can't keep up."

Sophia takes a sip of her drink and licks her lips, smiling mischievously. "Dead girls can't ride four dicks."

"Four dicks," Rosaline says with an envious moan. "Four super-hot dicks."

"What's it like, really?" Candace asks, ever the practical one.

I think about it, swirling the drink in my glass. "Really? It's all been happening at breakneck speed. This is the first chance I've had to sit down and talk with anyone who's not them. It's confusing. But it's really, really hot."

Just thirty minutes ago, Salvatore and Cassius were listening to me moan in the back of the Maserati while Lorenzo was fingering me and whispering filthy things in my ear.

Candace runs a finger around the rim of her glass. "Are you in love with them?"

I don't know if you can be in love with four men at once, and they with me. Are these four broken, brutal men even capable of love? Can I love four corrupt men who are keeping me their prisoner in a luxurious, invisible cage?

None of the men have said anything about loving me. Obsessed, tick. Horny, tick. Insanely overprotective, tick. "I don't know if love is even on the table."

"I can't even find one hot, tattooed boyfriend and you have four," Rosaline says.

"Only Lorenzo has tattoos," I point out.

"But they're all hot."

She's not wrong there. They're so sexy it short-circuits my brain.

"Do they have any single friends?" she asks hopefully.

"I have no idea. I've never met any of their friends." No wait. I have. Acid. He's ridiculously good-looking even when he's covered in blood, but he's not boyfriend material for polished, high-maintenance Rosaline. He'd eat her alive. Though she'd probably enjoy that in the short-term.

"Can we meet them?" Sophia asks, nodding at the door.

I hesitate. Salvatore they know a little, and I'm sure

Vinicius would be more than happy to charm them, but I'm not sure that Cassius and Lorenzo have the patience to field a dozen nosy questions from a group of tipsy teenage girls.

But they're my friends. If the men mean what they say and what's between us isn't just about sex, they should make an effort with them.

"I'll go and see if they're between poker hands," I say with a quick smile, and then head into where the boys are playing, closing the door behind me.

Vinicius catches my eye and winks, smiling broadly, like he knows we've been talking about him, and he loves it.

I place my hand on Salvatore's shoulder. He's in the middle of a hand and he throws chips into the center of the table. "Baby. Give me a kiss for luck."

I lean down and kiss his cheek, before darting looks at the other three to see if this has annoyed them. Am I showing Salvatore too much favoritism? Are they going to be mad at him or me if he wins this round? No one's frowning, though, as they finish placing their bets. Cassius is even smiling faintly as he glances at me.

"No more bets. What have you got?" Vinicius asks them.

Salvatore turns his two cards over and smiles broadly. It must be the winning hand because the others all mutter and pass their cards back to Vinicius as Salvatore scoops in the chips.

"That's my girl," Salvatore says with a smile as he reaches around to squeeze my behind.

"Aren't you all going to share what cards you have?" I ask the others in surprise.

"So they'll know if I was betting high on a strong hand or

if I was bluffing? Never show your hand if you don't have to, *bambina*."

They obviously take this seriously, but to me, half the fun would be seeing who got the next best hand and who was just pretending. "The girls were wondering if you'd like to have a drink with us before your next hand of poker."

Cassius stands up right away and buttons his jacket. "Of course, *bambina*."

The other three get to their feet as well, and I blink in surprise. I expected them to dismiss my request and say they're too busy.

Lorenzo and Salvatore follow Cassius into the lounge. Vinicius slips an arm around my waist and pulls me into his side. His other hand is casually in his pants pocket and he walks me into the room. He walks me slowly, though, and leans down to my ear to murmur, "I didn't get the chance before to tell you how beautiful you look." His teeth find my earlobe and he bites down. "Stunning, kitten. And I heard about you coming all over Lorenzo's fingers. I'm glad you're feeling more like yourself again."

They must have discussed it over poker hands. Vinicius looks totally normal as he escorts me over to a sofa, but now my face is flaming and I don't know where to look.

I sit between Lorenzo and Vinicius and let Salvatore do most of the talking, and I'm happy to see that Vinicius and Cassius ask the girls about themselves. Lorenzo sits back on the sofa in silence, his gaze occasionally running up my bare legs.

"Have you got any friends you could set us up with?" Rosaline asks with a smile at the four men.

Lorenzo says flatly, "No. We don't."

"You've got plenty of friends," Vinicius says, mischief glinting in his eyes. "What about Acid?"

"The gang member who nearly died of gunshot wounds in my basement a few nights ago? Is that the kind of asshole you want to set a nice girl up with up with?"

"Acid?" Rosaline asks with interest.

"Oh, um. One of Lorenzo's...friends," I say. Friend? Subordinate? Minion? The only clue I have is that Acid called him *boss*.

Rosaline's gaze slips over Lorenzo with interest, taking in his handsome face, his tattooed hands, his sharp suit, clearly wondering if Acid is anything like the man sitting in front of her.

"Acid's not good for any woman's well-being," Lorenzo says, with finality that stops all other questions. He reaches out and strokes my back. Lorenzo hasn't been good for my well-being, either, with all his threats and kidnapping, but here we are.

After about an hour of sitting together and talking, the girls are all tipsy and it's getting late. Salvatore arranges cars to take them home, and I hug them goodbye in the hall.

"Let's do this again soon," Rosaline says, and looks hopefully at Salvatore. His face reveals nothing, and he won't let me go outside and wave goodbye to the girls.

"I'll be in touch as soon as I can. Be safe. I'll miss you." I give them all one more hug and watch as the front door closes behind them.

Salvatore and I are alone in the hall. "Thank you for the surprise. That was thoughtful of you."

He angles my face up to his and frowns at me. "If you cry, I won't invite them back."

I swipe at my eyes. One too many cocktails and seeing friendly faces has made me emotional. "I'm not crying. There's mascara in my eye."

He leads me back into the room where he and the others have the card table set up. "Do you know how to play poker?"

"I'm fine. I'll just watch." Not only do I not know how to play poker, but I also don't want to be eaten alive by four poker sharks.

Cassius pulls another chair up to the table and the others move theirs to make room. "Sit down. Our woman must know how to play poker."

"Winning at poker means winning at life," Vinicius tells me as he starts to deal cards. "If you can learn the killer instinct, when to bluff and when someone's lying to your face, then you're set."

Lorenzo takes off his jacket and tie and rolls his sleeves back, revealing his tattooed forearms. His eyes are gleaming with excitement as he places a stack of chips in front of me.

"You're going to absolutely murder me, aren't you?" I say, staring from the chips to him.

"I know how to have fun," Lorenzo replies.

Cassius has lit a cigar and fragrant smoke curls around his head.

Salvatore pulls off his tie slowly, showing me his teeth in a predatory smile. "You wouldn't want us to go easy on you, baby. How will you learn?"

I'm so screwed. Thank goodness it's only poker.

Vinicius deals two cards to each of us, face down. "These are your pocket cards. You can look at them, but don't show them to anyone, kitten. Now, we bet."

I take a peek at my cards. Ten of clubs and two of diamonds. I make a face, and Lorenzo snorts with laughter.

"She's got a shit hand."

"*Bambina*. Poker face," Cassius chastises me.

We all put red chips in the middle and Vinicius deals three cards face up in the middle of the table. One of them is a ten and I perk up. Two of a kind. That's something, isn't it?

"Princess, your fucking face," Lorenzo growls.

"I can't help my *face*," I mutter.

"These three cards in the middle are the flop," Vinicius says. "The cards next to those are the turn, and the river. We're all going to bet again now, and then twice more as I reveal the turn and the river." Vinicius watches me for a moment, and a smile breaks over his face, foxlike and heated. "How about we make this interesting? Whoever wins gets the pot, but they also get a favor from anyone at the table."

"I love when things are interesting," Salvatore says with a smile at me.

"I can already guess what *you* want," I say to Vinicius.

A smile is dancing around his lips. "Place your bets, ladies and gentlemen."

I keep throwing chips into the middle of the table and trying to keep my face straight, but by the end of the round all I have is the pair of tens. Cassius has three kings, and swears loudly in Italian and scatters cigar ash everywhere as Lorenzo reveals a full house.

I take a sip from Salvatore's glass of vodka, trying to act like I'm not apprehensive and turned on by whatever Lorenzo's going to order me to do.

Something twisted, or something sweet?

Finally, he gives a dry smile and nods at the man sitting next to him. "Give Cassius some sugar, princess. I think he needs it."

Cassius shoots an annoyed look at his friend, still smoking his cigar, but he leans back in his chair as I stand up and walk slowly around the table toward him. All their eyes are on me. The room is huge and decorated as richly as the living room where the girls and I were sitting, but I sense we're totally alone in this house.

All alone with my men. I can do whatever I want.

Smiling, I straddle Cassius' lap, hug his hips with my knees and press a kiss to his bristly cheek. Lorenzo watches me with narrowed, hungry eyes as I stroke my fingers through Cassius' dark curls. The way I'm touching his friend is so innocent, but from his expression you would think I was doing something hardcore and depraved. Lorenzo can't tear his eyes away from me.

I turn and look at Vinicius. The golden-haired devil riffles the cards between his fingers, his head to the side as he watches me with his lower lip caught between his teeth.

"*Bambina. Guardati. Così carina,*" Cassius murmurs, squeezing my bottom. *Little girl. Look at you. So cute.*

I wriggle higher in his lap and wrap my arms around him. While the others are watching I put my lips against his ear and whisper, "Is that another cigar in your pocket?"

I get up and go back to my seat. They're still watching me. I bet if I felt in each of their laps they'd all be hard. Maybe I'm a betting woman after all.

Vinicius deals another hand and this time he bets so aggressively that I fold after the turn. Only Salvatore is left at the end, and he pushes all his chips into the table. Vinicius goes all in as well.

"You're bluffing. What have you got?" Salvatore says.

"You first."

I recognize the exultant expression on Vinicius' face. "He's not bluffing."

Salvatore raises a brow at me. "How do you know?"

"That's the way he looked when he was tricking me into having sex with him. Is that his tell?"

"It's not a tell if you're already fucked," Lorenzo deadpans.

True.

Salvatore has three jacks but Vinicius wins with a straight flush. He doesn't even bother collecting his chips before he's turning to me, and my stomach swoops.

"I have some questions for you, kitten."

My eyes narrow. "Only questions? What's the trick?"

"No trick. I want answers, and I'm sure the others do as well. Who among us is the best kisser? Who has the biggest—"

"Cassius," Salvatore and Lorenzo say in unison. Cassius casts his eyes to the ceiling and I start to laugh. If the question was who has the biggest dick, then of course it's Cassius. He's big all over.

Vinicius grins. "Alright, we know the answer to that. Who's the best kisser, and who licks you best?"

I take a sip of Salvatore's drink again and shake my head. "You want me to rank the bedroom talents of four insanely competitive men? Blood will be spilled."

"So there *is* an answer. Interesting," Salvatore says, his eyes alight.

"No, there's not. Only two of you have gone down on me for any length of time and not everyone's kissed me, so I couldn't compare."

I cast a furtive look at Lorenzo, and I'm not even sure why. To check if he's angry I mentioned it? Because I hope he'll lean over the table and press his lips against mine? His flat expression doesn't change, and he doesn't move. Disappointment settles over me and I look away before the others notice.

Salvatore takes his drink back from me. "I'll save you from answering the first one. It's me who's the best kisser."

I roll my eyes, but I don't argue. His kisses are pretty amazing. One of his kisses even brought me back to life.

He points at Lorenzo and Vinicius. "Who licked you best out of these two?"

"I'm not going to—"

"It's fine," Lorenzo drawls. "You can say Vinicius. I know the way he gives head."

I sit up in surprise. Lorenzo wasn't anywhere near me the night Vinicius went down on me. "You know? What have you seen? What have the two of you been up to together?"

Vinicius smiles, showing his pointed canines. "Let's play another round."

Hm, interesting. I bet they've screwed another girl together, just like they had sex with me the day I lost my virginity. I'll come back to that another time.

I sit up and concentrate as he deals the cards. I have a few questions of my own and if I win this hand, they have to give me answers.

But I suck at poker.

Lorenzo wins again.

He watches me in silence and then pats the table in front of Vinicius. "Get up here and let him show off."

That's the second time Lorenzo has won and he's given his favor to the others. Slowly, I get to my feet and walk around the table toward Vinicius. He puts his hands around my waist and sits me on the table in front of him, his eyes glimmering with desire.

"Thank you, Lorenzo," Vinicius murmurs, running his fingers down my hips to my thighs. "I've missed touching you, kitten."

He places each of my feet in his lap, hooks his fingers into my underwear, and pulls them slowly down my legs. My breathing picks up and I caress his cheek.

"I've missed the way you look at me," he says, easing my dress up my thighs and pushing my legs open. "I've missed the way you taste."

The first slow lick of his tongue against my clit has me moaning. "Has it been that long?"

"It's been eons. Fuck, you're wet, baby," he groans.

Out of the corner of my eye, I see that Lorenzo is gripping his thigh and his eyes are dilated. I guess Cassius isn't the only one who likes to watch. Come to think of it, all three of them are watching like they can't tear their eyes away.

I guess I'll have to put on a show.

I fall back, stacks of chips clinking, and arch my body. I turn my head and open my eyes. Cassius is sitting back in his chair and watching me intently. I reach up and pull down one straps of my dress, and then the other, and as I cry out from the way Vinicius is working his tongue, I take hold of the bodice of my dress.

Do I dare?

Letting them all watch me get eaten out on their poker table is one of the least messed up things we've done together. What are murders and kidnappings compared to reveling in the way these four men make me feel?

I do dare. I pull my dress down, exposing my breasts, and then tug slowly on each of my nipples, loving the sensations that go chasing through me.

Cassius swears in Italian.

"Princess," breathes a voice in my ear. I turn my head and see Lorenzo hovering over me. He runs two fingers over my lower lip and then pushes them into my mouth.

"Suck," he orders.

My toes curl as he commands me, and I suck hard on his fingers. He breathes in sharply and his eyes lock with mine. He pulls his fingers from my lips and a moment later he pushes them deep into my pussy. Firm, slow thrusts of his fingers that curl around a sensitive spot deep inside me. Vinicius goes on licking me and heat floods my body.

I lick my lips and arch my back. God, I'm such a harlot. "Are you going to make me come on your fingers again?"

"Salvatore," Lorenzo says, still staring into my eyes. "Think she can manage any more?"

I feel Vinicius smile against my pussy.

On my other side, Salvatore sits forward in his chair, and he sucks slowly down his middle finger. "I know she can."

I sit up on my elbows and watch as his finger joins Lorenzo's at my entrance and works its way inside me. It's a lot, and it feels tight and delicious at the same time.

"Good girl," Salvatore purrs, and heat flashes through me as they both fuck me in unison.

Vinicius glances down at their fingers and groans, "Oh,

fuck yes," before redoubling his attention on my clit. His tongue feels like heaven. I start to breathe faster and faster, and hug one of my knees to my chest.

I know where we're headed if I keep letting them all watch me come and make me come at the same time. There are four of them and they all love to fuck. These two-on-one and three-on-one sessions are getting crazy. Soon I'll be pinned mercilessly between all four of them. I picture it vividly, and the mental image is so daunting and delicious that it drives me over the edge.

Vinicius sits back and swipes his lower lip with his tongue. Salvatore and Lorenzo keep thrusting with their fingers and the aftershocks of my orgasm coalesce into something deeper, something powerful, and my back arches off the table and my head flies back as I come again.

"Damn, your pussy baby," Salvatore says admiringly as he and Lorenzo withdraw their fingers.

I stretch my arms over my head and take a deep breath. "I think I won that round."

Someone helps me up off the table and when I open my eyes I see that it's Cassius. My arms lock around his neck with my fierce, post-orgasm need to be held. I hope he doesn't push me away because his arms feel like heaven.

Cassius sits down and pulls my legs across his lap, and I practically purr with victory and happiness as he plants kisses on the side of my neck and slides the straps of my dress back up my shoulders. Beneath my thighs, I can feel how hard he is.

"Do you only like to watch? Do you never join in?" I whisper.

Vinicius collects all the cards and distributes the mess of

chips back to the rightful players. "Cassius loves to play. Don't you, Cassius?"

Cassius settles me more securely in his lap and taps the table in front of him. "Come on. Deal." Then he murmurs in my ear, "*Bambina*, you can help me with this hand."

As Vinicius deals the cards, I gaze around at the others. I think I could get addicted to the content expressions on their faces. Even Lorenzo is almost smiling.

Cassius tilts the corners of the cards up so we can see what they are. The king and queen of spades.

I put my lips against his ear and whisper, "It's us."

"These cards? You and me?" he murmurs. I nod, and he laughs softly. "Then shall we bet high?"

I lay our bets each round, and then finally push all our chips into the middle of the table. Vinicius and Salvatore both fold.

Lorenzo jerks his head at our cards. "Show me what you've got."

I turn over the king and queen. With the cards in the middle of the table, we have two pairs.

Lorenzo shakes his head. "You got me."

"Really? What's your hand?" As cutthroat as he is, I wouldn't put it past him to throw a hand just to see what I'll ask for.

But he's already passing his cards back to Vinicius. "I'll never tell, princess."

Cassius strokes my hair back. "You win, *bambina*. You get to ask for anything you want."

What *do* I want? I gaze at each of the men in turn. Dangerous sex with Lorenzo? To sleep in Cassius' arms while he whispers cute and sexy things in Italian? For Vinicius to go down on me again with that insanely hot tongue of his, or Salvatore to deck me in diamonds and rail me senseless on this poker table?

If I ask for any of that even when we're not playing poker, they'll give it to me. I want something more, and they have to say yes because those are the rules.

"I want to know why I'm here."

Salvatore frowns. "You already know why you're here."

No, I don't. There's something they're keeping from me. It's huge and painful and I sense it in their anger, in their brutality, in the way they pull away from me. Right now, they're happy because they're distracted, but it won't last.

"I want to know what you all sacrificed to make me yours. I want to know *everything*."

All their expressions turn blank and cold. Suddenly I'm not playing fair, but I don't care. They know my misery and pain. I need to understand theirs.

6

Cassius

The mood changes from happy to glacial in a mere second.

Salvatore gives Charia a tight smile. "It's no sacrifice making you ours, baby."

If that was meant to reassure or distract her, it fails.

Chiara wriggles in my arms. "You're hurting me."

My muscles have locked tight around her. I pick her up and put her back on the empty chair before striding over to the bottles of liquor at the side of the room. I need a fucking drink.

When I bring the bottle back, Chiara is sitting bolt upright, clasping the arms of the chair. "You spent all last year pretending that you four weren't friends anymore. You pretended in front of me, but it wasn't me you were pretending for. Was it?"

I look from Salvatore to Vinicius to Lorenzo. How little can we say to stop her asking questions? "*Si.* It wasn't for your benefit, and it's not your business, either. You know what happens to you when you stick your pretty little nose in places it doesn't belong, *bambina.*"

I'll put her over my knee and spank her right here if I have to.

"I won that hand," she says. "I get to ask for anything I want. Those are the rules of the game."

This isn't a game anymore. "Now's not the time. You've been drinking. We're trying to relax. It's been a long year for all of us and now you're ours, we just want to forget."

Chiara looks slowly around the table at the others, her eyes liquid with sympathy. "I know it's hard for you all to talk about, but I need to understand. You were pretending for my father's benefit, weren't you? I just want to know why."

"Baby, you know why," Salvatore says, reaching out to caress the nape of her neck. "Remember the night of our engagement? You threw it right in my face. The four of us united were a threat to your father, and we needed him to believe that the threat had passed."

"Yes, but *why* did you need him to believe that?"

Vinicius pushes his hand through his hair and sighs. "Maybe we should just tell her."

I widen my eyes at him. Everything, Vinicius? *You* want to tell her the whole truth?

Vinicius closes his mouth and falls silent.

I thought so. We barely speak about Evelina, Ophelia,

Amalia, and Sienna among ourselves, let alone with someone else. I top off my glass with vodka. "You have your answer, *bambina*. We don't want to tell you, and we're not going to."

Chiara gazes at me steadily. "As I was part of your plan, I think I deserve to know."

Deserve. My woman thinks she deserves to know whatever she likes about me. "You don't. It's got nothing to do with you."

Spots of color burn in her cheeks. "So, you do what you like and say what you like, and I just have to take it? Screw you, Cassius."

Fury erupts in my chest and I lean forward with my hands flat on the table. "Watch your mouth. You're forgetting your place."

Salvatore shoots me a look, telling me silently to get a grip. I fucking won't get a grip, not when we're talking about our sisters.

"My place?" she asks, her eyes narrowing. "Oh, please, tell me about my place."

"You're our captive and our lover," Salvatore tells her. "Where you go and what you do is up to us, not you. Stay within your boundaries and you'll be perfectly happy."

Chiara's eyes flash and her cheeks turn even redder. "Screw you as well, Salvatore. I'm not an unthinking piece of meat. You told me weeks ago that I'm not a sex slave and you didn't want one, so stop treating me like one." She looks at Vinicius and Scava. "What about you two? Anything to add?"

Scava glances at her with a flat, bored expression, and then away again.

Vinicius shakes his head, smiling. "Kitten, you don't want me to answer that. I'm the nice one and I'd like it to stay that way."

"We all feel the same," I tell her. "You already know that you can't play us against each other. We took you, and we'll keep you, and you don't get to ask questions. That's final."

"If I get up from this table without hearing some answers, I'll never let any of you touch me again."

"You're threatening us?" I ask in a quiet, dangerous voice. "You're in Salvatore's home wearing an expensive dress with an enormous diamond on your finger, and you're threatening us? You could just as easily be locked up in a dirty basement."

"Let's lock her up," Scava says with a cold smile. "A week or two in the dark with the rats will improve her personality."

Locked up, she'd be safe from everyone's eyes but ours. How Scava would love that. He might get his wish before the night is over.

Chiara glares at him, and turns back to me. "You were so kind to me when I was living with you. You agreed to let me try and kill my father even though you didn't like it. What happened to that Cassius?"

"It suited us to allow you to try," I tell her. "If you thought that made us equals and you could ask for whatever you like, then you're wrong. You're not our equal and you never will be. You may be the Princess of Coldlake, but we are its kings."

Lorenzo told me what his injured man called Chiara the night she helped save his life. It suits her. She grew up as

Coldlake royalty, and now she belongs to the men who are truly in charge.

"Kings should rule with benevolence, not cruel, iron fists."

I've let Chiara talk back to me again and again. I've tried to be gentle with her even though it goes against my nature. I've upended my entire fucking world for her, and she still isn't grateful. Maybe a cold, dank basement really is the only solution.

"The truth is crueler than silence, kitten," Vinicius says. "Be careful what you wish for."

"I lived a lie all my life with Dad and if you four are going to lie to me as well and stay silent about things that matter, then you can find some other girl to torment."

Anger and defiance ripples through the others.

Some other girl?

We don't want *some other girl*. We want Chiara. We want to pass her among us. We want to watch her with each other. We crave to pin her between us all at once. Protect her to our dying breaths.

Fuck being soft. I just remembered why it's so important to stay hard.

"You think you want to know what we're keeping from you? Fine, I'll tell you a little piece of our story, and when it gives you nightmares you can cry alone in your bed."

Chiara's eyes flash with hurt, but I'm too far gone to rein my temper in.

"You're not—" Lorenzo says, sitting forward.

I hold up my hand. "I'll tell her my secrets, not yours."

His eyes burn but he closes his mouth. I glance at the

other two, and their expressions are tense, but they say nothing.

A few weeks ago, I cradled her in my arms as she sobbed against my chest in the dark. I'd never been that man for a woman before. The one she turns to when she's filled with despair. The last thing I want is to give her more reasons to cry in the dark, but she's not going to let this go.

And the Ferragamos are meant to be stubborn.

"Are you sure you want this?" I ask her, leaning over the table my face close to hers.

"I already said that I do."

Then we're doing this.

I sit down, watching her with narrowed eyes. "You know who ran this city before we divided it up?"

"Vinicius told me that the whole city used to belong to Salvatore's father, Francesco Fiore."

"That's right. I was one of his *capos*. Captains. The Fiores and the Ferragamos go back generations together."

"Two fancy fucking families with their heads up their asses," Scava mutters.

Salvatore nods at Scava. "In my father's day, the Fiores wouldn't sit at the same table as Scava riff-raff."

"In your father's day, I would have ripped the gold fillings from his teeth if I got within ten feet of him," Scava shoots back.

"It was Francesco Fiore's dearest wish that Salvatore marry my sister, Evelina." I rub my hand over my eyes, remembering the day I introduced them to each other. "My little sister and the boss' son, meeting for the first time in the boss' bedroom. Francesco was bedridden by then. Barely clinging to his wits. He smiled and tears poured down his face as Salvatore took Evelina's hand. Tears, from one of the most ferocious men I'd ever known."

"Old Fiore cut off his best friend's hand for touching his wife," Vinicius says with a grin.

Salvatore isn't laughing. "A fitting punishment. No one touches what doesn't belong to him, no matter who he is."

I stare at the glass of vodka in my hand. There's so much to say, about Evelina, about Salvatore, the city, but the words are acid in my mouth. I'll just get to the point.

"Salvatore and Evelina never got the chance to get to know each other. She was abducted from her school and murdered. A caretaker found her body on a rooftop in the city. There was a black flower shoved into her throat, her eyes had been ripped out, and all her organs were laying around her feet."

Chiara's face slackens in shock.

I swallow hard and reach for my cigar, the scent of blood and death thick in my nostrils. "And she was impaled on a spike."

I see the blood and rain running down her naked corpse. Her empty eye sockets staring up at the sky. Her mouth open wide in a silent scream. If I close my eyes I can walk around that rooftop in my mind and see her from every angle.

Some nights I fucking hate closing my eyes.

Had enough yet, *bambina*?

"We're an old family. It's a medieval form of torture. The spike missed all the vital organs, traveled up through the body and out her shoulder. She could have been like that for hours, maybe days, before the *bastardo* finally killed her."

"You mean when...she was still...?"

"Alive," I say without mercy. "Yes. She was impaled while she was alive. Being gutted was what killed her."

Salvatore pushes a hand through his hair and takes a deep breath. Vinicius is staring blankly into the middle of the table. Scava has taken out his knife and is twisting it over his knuckles like he isn't listening.

He's fucking listening. That knife. That's his tell. Whenever he gets it out he's thinking about revenge. At the mayor's house on Chiara's seventeenth birthday, he couldn't stop playing with it. We were closer to our goal than ever.

"Evelina was taken before I realized she was in danger and she was dead before I knew where to start looking for her. And that's why you—" I point a finger right in Chiara's face "—need to do what you're fucking told. Her killer is still out there. He hates the four of us and he loves to cut up pretty girls. So don't pout and tell us we're cruel. When we tell you what to do, you do it and say fucking thank you."

Chiara swallows, looking pale and sick. "But *why* were your sisters killed? And what has this got to do with my father?"

All that I've told her, and she still has questions? She should be begging me to stop.

Vinicius sits forward with the air of a man wanting to get things over with. "You've heard of the Black Orchid Murders. The most notorious unsolved murders in the city. Four pretty young women all dead, some of them wealthy and well-known. The police should have been scrambling to solve the crimes of our dead sisters, but the police don't like us, kitten."

"They *hate* us," Scava says. "Guess why."

"Because you're a bunch of criminals?" she guesses.

"A bunch of murdering, stealing, lying criminals who make them look like a pack of idiots at every turn," Vinicius says.

"What's more," Salvatore says, "my father murdered the chief of police twenty years ago for putting one of his *capos* in prison. The Coldlake cops are still angry about that."

"The police spent about two minutes investigating how our sisters died and then let the cases go cold," I say bitterly. "Nothing was done. *Nothing.* The evidence they collected has been sealed up tight and left to rot. The only person who could have forced them to reopen the case was the mayor himself."

Chiara sits bolt upright. For the past few minutes her expression has been horrified, but she's realized what we're getting at. "You're right, Dad could do that in a heartbeat. The police adore Dad and do everything he—wait."

She leaps to her feet, her chair flying out from beneath her. "But he knows Salvatore was never on his side. He'll never help you now."

"*Si*. Sit down, Chiara."

Chiara's expression is horrified and she stays on her feet. "You let me try and kill him when I could have persuaded him to help you. I should have married Salvatore and then Dad would have done a favor for his son-in-law. What the hell, Cassius? Why did you kidnap me from my wedding?"

Salvatore points at her chair. "Chiara, sit the fuck down. We all agreed that if we wanted you, we'd keep you all to ourselves. We wouldn't use you to get what we wanted."

"You should have!"

"Our woman is not a pawn," he growls.

"I would have gladly helped you avenge your sisters. How could you be so stupid?"

"Watch that mouth, kitten," Vinicius warns her.

Chiara ignores him. "You should have told me what was at stake instead of letting me ruin your whole plan. Your sisters deserve justice. Don't you understand how terrible I feel?"

I slam my hands on the table, making her and all the chips jump. "How *you* feel? How you fucking feel?" Rage is boiling through me. I haven't been this angry since Evelina was killed.

"We don't want you mixed up in that, kitten," Vinicius says, his voice gentle and his hazel eyes filled with worry. "You're small. You're weak. Just thinking about you at the same time as our sisters makes us insane with worry."

"Stop calling me weak. Maybe I'm not armed and dangerous like all of you, but I can be clever. I can be useful." Chiara's torn between fury and sympathy, her gaze flickering around the table at each of us.

"Sit down or I'll send you to bed."

She rounds on me. "I'm not a child and you won't talk to me like that."

With two long strides I walk around the table and pin her arms behind her back. With my lips close to her ear, I snarl, "Don't tell me *can't*. I can do whatever the fuck I want with you."

Her body makes me insane. With her pulled against me her ass is pressed tight against my cock. Spanking her until she cries in front of the other three would be humiliating for her, but I've been aching to fuck her all night.

She wriggles against me, trying to escape, but I've got her. I've got her at my mercy.

"Get *off* me."

"She never wants to behave." Salvatore says. "She'll keep talking back until you shove something in her mouth. This is exactly what she used to do with me."

I'm usually so good at pulling women back into line before I lose control, but talking about Evelina has shredded my restraint. "You have three seconds to sit down, say sorry and behave."

Chiara gazes up at me and runs her tongue over her top lip. "I'll never behave."

What I hear is, *Make me.*

I force her face down over the table, grasp her skirt and yank it up.

Chiara's eyes open wide and she wriggles in my grasp. "Cassius—"

Cassius nothing.

I'm done with her shit.

She's not wearing any underwear and her pussy is so wet from the games we've been playing. I pin Chiara in place with one hand and grasp her hair with my other hand, pressing her cheek into the table.

Chiara is fighting hard to get away from me. "Get off me, you asshole."

"You've forgotten all your rules. Do you think they don't apply anymore? What are they?"

"But that was before when I was locked up in your penthouse."

Scava has settled back in his chair to enjoy the show.

"You're locked up in mine, now. What made you think you could do whatever you like?"

"I'll remind you, *bambina*. No talking back. No trying to escape. Do as you're told. Remember now?"

"*I said get off me.*"

"We give you presents and indulge your every need, but don't forget who's in charge. Us, not you."

It's supposed to feel satisfying, laying down the law. It's sorely tempting to fuck my misbehaving girl back into line, but all I can think about is picking her up in my arms and cradling her against my chest.

I was soft with Evelina. So fucking soft, and look what happened to her. A pang goes through me. The last thing I want is to make Chiara hate me.

I let her go and stand back. She slowly peels herself up off the table, her cheeks burning with humiliation, and she tugs her dress down.

We stare at each other, breathing hard and glaring at each other. Both of us open our mouths at the same time.

"All right, the poker game is over." Salvatore stands up, grasps Chiara's elbow and steers her toward the door. "Come on. Move."

I watch them go, fists clenched at my sides.

"If Salvatore is staying, someone has to be my ride," Scava taunts. "Want to drive me home?"

"*Zitto.*" *Shut up.* But instead of heading for the front door, I'm compelled to follow Salvatore and Chiara further into the house. They don't notice me walking quietly down the hall in their wake.

Outside his bedroom, Salvatore grasps Chiara by the

shoulders and pushes her against the wall. I step into a doorway and watch them from the shadows.

"What do you think you're doing, talking to Cassius like that? He spilled his guts about his sister to you. Could you have been more ungrateful?"

"He forced me down on that table and you all *let him*."

"You fucking deserved it. You understand better than anyone what it's like to have someone ripped away. How dare you tell Cassius he was wrong for choosing you over revenge."

She tries to move away but he shoves her back against the wall.

"He chose *you*."

Chiara glares up at him, seeming like she's ready to start another fight. Then, all the fight goes out of her and her shoulders slump. "I kept thinking about Mom and how I'd feel if I lost a chance to tell the world who murdered her. I lost my temper."

"No kidding. You're a firecracker, baby. Try not to explode when we're dealing with sensitive shit, okay?"

"You can talk," she mutters, and the corner of Salvatore's mouth quirks.

"Hey, what did Cassius just tell you about talking back?" he chides gently. Then he takes her face in his hands and leans his forehead against hers. They stay like that for a while, breathing each other in.

"You wanted to help us. I understand that. Cassius will understand that too when he calms down."

Chiara's breath hitches with a sob. "It would have meant so much to me to help all of you. Why didn't you tell me why you were marrying me? I would have been on your side in a *second*."

"This isn't about you. This is our past. Our misery. Our pain. You're our future and we don't want the two getting tangled up."

Chiara's eyes glimmer with tears, and she wipes them away as they spill down her cheeks. "I feel sick at the lost opportunity. Dad will never help you now."

He gathers Chiara into his arms and holds her close, rocking her slowly. "The four of us talked about the kind of girl we wanted many times. A beautiful girl. Someone with courage. Someone who's soft and sweet. You know what we never thought to hope for?"

"What?"

He draws away and runs a forefinger down her cheek. "Someone who would fight for us as much as we'd fight for her."

Salvatore dips his head and presses his mouth to hers.

Envy courses through me, thick and ugly. I want to be the one kissing her, but I know that if I go to Chiara and she utters one word about what we talked about, I'll lose my temper all over again.

As Salvatore and Chiara disappear into his bedroom, I groan and rake my hands through my hair. Did we make a mistake not considering whether Chiara would help us? A Ferragamo hasn't made a mistake in four hundred years.

I turn and head back the way I came. When I reach the room with the poker table, there's only Scava still sitting in his seat.

"Where are you going?" he asks.

"Getting the fuck out of here. Are you coming?"

Wordlessly, he gets up and walks with me out the front door and toward my Porsche. Before I get into the SUV, I pause. "That's the first and last time we'll ever discuss our sisters with Chiara. If she brings them up again, I'll make her wish she'd never been born."

His cold eyes meet mine over the hood of my car. "If she brings them up again, I'll help you."

7

Chiara

I stand under the jets of hot water, steam billowing all around me. I was clean five minutes ago, but the pounding of the water against my body is soothing my aching heart. I keep picturing Cassius' furious face as he told me to get out of his sight.

The dark and violent descriptions of what happened to Evelina slash through my mind. Did he see her like that, impaled and brutalized? Did he collapse to his knees in front of her, knowing it was all his fault she'd been tortured to death?

Did he beg for forgiveness from her corpse?

I turn off the water, pull on a bathrobe, and head back into the darkened bedroom. Salvatore is standing at the window, staring out into the garden. The moonlight washes over his handsome face and turns his eyes to silver.

He carries a story just like Cassius' in his heart. A story drenched in blood and pain. He's never even spoken Ophelia's name in my hearing.

"Thank you for inviting the girls here. It was lovely seeing them again."

He turns to me with an expression so bleak that I wonder if Ophelia is on his mind right now. "You're welcome, baby. I'm glad you had a good time."

I was having a wonderful time until the end of the night. I was so proud to show off my handsome men to Rosaline, Candace, and Sophia. For a few minutes, I was happy.

After the first time we had sex, Cassius held me close and managed to speak a few words about his little sister. I thought that was the beginning of our conversations about Evelina, but for Cassius it was the beginning and the end.

"Will you please tell Cassius I'm sorry?"

"I'm not your messenger. Whatever you have to say, tell him yourself."

I turn toward the door, but Salvatore grasps my hand tighter and pulls me back. "Not tonight. He's gone now, anyway. I heard his car drive away."

He didn't even say goodbye. I guess I deserve that after losing my temper. "Do you think he's really angry with me?"

"Yes."

Don't bother to sugarcoat it, Salvatore. "I'm sorry I upset him, but I can't be sorry that he shared a little bit about Evelina with me. Maybe if you told me about Ophelia—"

Heat flashes through his eyes. "Chiara, don't. I barely discuss her with the others, or with Ginevra. Did Lorenzo tell you much about Sienna? Has Vinicius talked about Amalia?"

"Lorenzo's never even told me her name. Vinicius told me a little about Amalia, but I could tell he didn't really want to."

"Precisely. Just leave it alone. We don't want to talk about them, and especially not with you."

Especially not with me. My heart sinks even lower.

"Did you love her?"

Salvatore frowns. "My sister?"

"Evelina. You were engaged."

"We were never engaged. She was promised to me when she was a schoolgirl, just like you were. I barely knew her."

Jealousy flashes through me. Was he repeating with me all the things he did with her? "Did you show up at the school gates and kiss her in front of all the girls?"

A smile slides over his face. "Baby, the idea never even occurred to me. I can't imagine anything worse than marrying the female version of Cassius."

I laugh tiredly and rub my hand over my face.

Salvatore takes off his tie and starts to unbutton his shirt. He's going to get into bed with me, and because he's being kind and I feel so awful, I'll probably burst into tears.

"I'd like to sleep alone tonight, please."

Salvatore freezes, and glares at me. "This is my house. This is *my bedroom*."

"I can sleep in a guest room. Just show me where it is."

Salvatore grabs a pillow from the bed and a blanket from one of the wardrobes. He dumps the bedding on the carpet and lies does with his back to me, muscles rigid with fury.

I clamber between the sheets and pull them up to my

chin. When I close my eyes, I see a pretty, dark-haired girl with eyes just like Cassius. Only they're being torn out of her skull and she's screaming.

My eyes fly open and nausea rushes up. I take a few deep breaths, trying to dispel the ghastly image, but the horror of her death is overwhelming. I demanded to know everything, and Cassius punished me with the truth.

The truth is crueler than silence.

I picture Cassius all alone in his pristine penthouse. Who holds him when he wakes up covered in sweat and shaking from head to toe, his head full of blood and horror? He's probably pacing the floors like a wild animal locked in a cage, tormented from the inside out.

Because of me.

I scramble out of bed and stand there in the dark, breathing fast.

"Baby?" Salvatore murmurs sleepily at my feet.

"I can't stop thinking about Evelina."

Salvatore reaches up for my hand and pulls me down on the floor beside him. He wraps me in his arms and pulls me tight against him.

"But Cassius," I whisper against his chest. "I made him relive all that horror and now he's alone."

"Cassius is fine. Promise me something," Salvatore murmurs, cradling my head in his hand and stroking his fingers through my hair. "Don't bring this up again. What Cassius has seen, what Vinicius and Lorenzo have seen, what I've seen, it's not for you. We don't want any of that horror touching you. Now go to sleep."

But sleep evades me for a long time. I watch Salvatore as the tension on his handsome face melts away and his breathing evens out. Vinicius is probably asleep too, and Lorenzo, assuming someone hasn't come to his compound, riddled with bullets. Only Cassius is awake. I can feel it, and so I lie awake with him for many hours.

I wake to daylight streaming through the curtains. Salvatore must have carried me back to bed while I was sleeping as I'm tucked beneath the blankets once more. I roll over and feel another warm body in bed with me.

Salvatore.

I reach out and stroke his cheek. There's fine, dark stubble on his chin. He smiles against my palm without opening his eyes and kisses my fingers.

I wriggle closer to him and he wraps two big arms around me and cuddles me. Pleasure pours through me like sunshine and I rest my cheek against his chest.

"Four boyfriends, and this is the first time I've woken up with a man."

He opens his beautiful blue-green eyes, the color of the sea, the color of peacocks. Wild and proud.

"Do you know why this is so hard?" I whisper.

"Why?"

"Because I think I really like you. All of you."

His brow raises sardonically. "That's supposed to make things easier, not harder."

"It's hard because I want to make you happy, and you all seem to have decided that happiness isn't important."

Salvatore strokes my cheek and throat, his gaze slipping down my body. "I'm happy now."

Horny isn't the same thing as happy.

"Lorenzo told me I should be happy I'm still breathing."

"Lorenzo has seen a lot of death and violence. He knows what he's talking about."

"What's your idea of happiness?"

"Your tits in my face as you slide your pussy down my cock. Come here." He grasps my waist and tries to pull me astride him.

I put my hand against his chest and laugh. "I'm serious. When are you happiest?"

He gazes around his bedroom. It's as beautiful as the other rooms I've seen and reeks of old money and rigid customs. This was the house he grew up in and where Francesco Fiore grew old and died. Ginevra was a little girl here, and so was Ophelia.

"When I'm here. In this house, I learned what it is to be a man. My sisters were raised to be dutiful and obedient daughters and wives. My woman should feel at home in such a place."

Salvatore's idea of the perfect woman is someone who does what she's told. That's probably what his house wants, too. No wonder I feel like these walls are rejecting me this morning.

"I hope you've had some rest, and some time to think. You have all your answers. It's up to you to decide what happens next."

I see the finality in his eyes. Just like that, he's done talking to me about the past.

Salvatore sits up and stretches his arms over his head. "Come on. I'll take you back to Lorenzo's."

"Why am I staying with Lorenzo?"

He finds some sweats and a T-shirt in a drawer and passes them to me. "This house isn't secure enough. Cassius' penthouse was the perfect place to keep you in. Lorenzo's compound is the ideal place to keep others out."

I sit barefoot in Salvatore's Maserati as we drive through the streets of Coldlake, the top up to keep me hidden from view. When I get out in Lorenzo's underground garage, Salvatore pulls me down through the window for a kiss, turns the car around, and drives away.

There's no sign of Lorenzo when I head upstairs to my room. I take a shower and put on a new pair of jeans and a silk shirt, and then wander restlessly around the house.

I'm in the kitchen trying to get the sliding door open when a voice speaks sharply in my ear.

"What are you doing?"

I press a hand against my pounding heart and turn and see Lorenzo. "I want some fresh air. I was going to sit in the garden."

Lorenzo's wearing black sweats, a black T-shirt, and runners, and his blond hair is swept back and sweaty as if he's just been working out. He steps forward, digging in his pocket for a key.

I search his face, wondering if he's got anything to say about last night. "Are you angry at me as well?"

Lorenzo glances at me as he unlocks the sliding door, his face impassive. "When I'm angry, people don't usually have to ask."

He shoves the door open. A guard with a German Shepherd is on the far side of the garden. Lorenzo catches his eye and jerks his chin at me.

Watch her.

I open my mouth to ask him if he's going to enforce my rules like Salvatore and Cassius do, but Lorenzo turns and marches out. Things felt different here at Lorenzo's house, but nothing's changed. No talking back. No trying to escape. Do as you're told.

And my new rule. *No asking about our sisters.*

I sit down at a glass-topped patio table and gaze around the garden. Well, the lawn. There are no plants. The only decorations are the CCTV cameras mounted everywhere. The man in military fatigues has drawn closer with his dog and is standing just a few feet away.

"How long have you worked for Lorenzo?"

The man glances at me, and then away again. Not a chatty person. I hold out my hand to the dog, beckoning it closer. "Who's a good dog? Would you like a pat?"

The dog stares at me with as much interest as the guard. I drop my hand with a sigh.

I crave the company of the girls again. They'd know what to say about the disaster that was the rest of last night. Rosaline would help me blow off steam, Sophia would ask if I was okay, and Candace would talk some sense into me.

I wonder what a true outsider would make of this situation. Someone like my best friend Nicole who has her morals pointed true north at all times. She's been the good angel on my shoulder, but she hasn't made a peep since I tried to kill Dad.

"Well, Nicole," I whisper. "What do I do now?"

If she were here, I would imagine she'd give me a hug and smile crookedly at me as she promised that we'd think of something. Then we'd go and get donuts, walk in the park, and talk about other things for a while, just like we did when she was fourteen and she thought her parents were getting divorced. Her Dad isn't the best at expressing his emotions, and he and Nicole's mother could have some terrible fights, usually about the medical conferences in other cities he was always attending. Nicole was so scared, but after a few donuts she'd cheer up and remind herself that even if her parents did get divorced, it's not like she'd never see them again.

But Nicole hasn't got anything to say about my current situation. It seems she's completely out of her depth.

I watch the guard walk the dog around the high perimeter wall, that keeps me in just as much as it keeps everyone else out. "Me, too. Nicole. Me, too."

WHEN I RUN into Lorenzo over the next few days he's writing in his blue notebook like he might suffocate if he stops even for a second. Every time I approach him, he flips it closed and glares at me until I walk away again.

There's no sign of the others. I'm being punished for speaking my mind. I hate that.

I'm wandering restlessly through Lorenzo's house when I round a corner.

And walk right into a solid wall.

Of muscle, not of brick.

Cassius' expensive cologne washes over me, and I look up into his severe expression. He's doubly handsome when he's frowning, those thick brows of his drawn together and his eyes dark and forbidding.

I feel a lurch as I gaze up at him. I don't know what to do with my hands so I tug the hem of my T-shirt. I want to touch him, but I'm still mad at him for losing his temper and shoving me face first down over the poker table. But I'm sorry for him, too. I pushed and pushed to hear about Evelina and made him relive that horrible experience.

"Stop looking at me like that," he snaps.

I blink. "Like what?"

"Like you pity me. No one feels sorry for Cassius Ferragamo." He steps slowly toward me, crowding me against the wall. My heartrate picks up as the big Italian man glares down at me.

"I'm annoyed with you as well," I say. "Are people allowed to be annoyed with Cassius Ferragamo?"

He captures my jaw in his hand and turns my head to the left and then to the right.

"What are you doing?"

"Looking at your pretty face. Scava says you've been behaving. Good girl."

"Oh, shut up," I say, pushing his hand away, but my fingers twine through his and hold on tightly.

Touch me, oh my God, touch me.

"All that punishment, and I didn't forgive you yet. You know how I love to forgive you, *bambina*."

His heated words twine through me and my toes curl. How I love receiving Cassius' forgiveness. And his punishment, come to think of it.

"You have to tell me sorry, *bambina*. Then I can give you what you need." He kisses my throat and along my jaw.

My heartrate picks up. "You say sorry first."

"That's not what you need."

God, he's so bossy. I smooth my hands up the muscles of his chest. "What about what you need? My heart hurts for you. My heart aches for you."

Cassius covers my mouth with his hand and kisses my throat again. "*Bambina*, stop that."

I pull his hand away. "But—"

"I want you to be my sweetness. I want you to be our future. Don't let yourself be polluted by the past." He backs me against the wall, unzips my skirt, and lets it fall to the floor. Then he drives his hand down the front of my underwear, groaning softly as his fingers slide through my wet pussy. "Are you going to be my good girl? I'll make you come if you swear you'll be good."

Say, *Yes, Cassius.*

Just say it.

My eyes are closed and I lick my lips, trying to cling to my scraps of sanity as his expert fingers work my clit. "I don't want to be your mindless prisoner. I want—I want—"

Cassius hoists me up in his arms, sliding me high up the wall until my legs are hooked over his shoulders and I'm spread wide. He pulls my underwear aside and runs his tongue up my slit.

I yelp in surprise and pleasure and grab his strong neck. "Cassius, oh God—"

As high up as I am, I feel secure on his broad shoulders as he continues to work his tongue against me. He's giving Vinicius a run for his money with the way he's massaging my clit. I can feel my orgasm approaching as I whimper his name.

"You want to come, don't you, *bambina*?"

Yes, by all the gods I want to come. This is torture. I'm so close and his tongue is right there.

"All you have to do is say, *Yes, Cassius*, and I'll give you everything you want. You're my whole world. Let me make you come, *bambina*." He coaxes me with his deep voice between licks until I can't even remember what we're fighting about. "You have all my protection. You're my only woman. You're everything to me. Just say two little words. *Yes, Cassius.* You'll make me so happy."

When I don't answer, he slides me back down his body, carries me over to the kitchen bench and sits me on it. With a furiously determined expression in his eyes, he slides two thick, long fingers deep into my pussy and rubs that spot hard until I'm shouting. I hold tight to his shoulders, my orgasm barreling down on me.

"Are you my good girl?"

I'm going to come so fucking hard. This is wrong. This is all wrong.

He presses a hand to the middle of my chest and pushes me onto my back. As he slams his fingers into me, his tongue circles my clit. "Chiara. Are you my good girl? I won't let you come until you say yes."

I open my eyes and reach down to cup his cheek. I can barely form the words I'm so close to the edge. "No, Cassius."

"What?" He lifts his mouth and his fingers still inside me.

I pull myself up onto my elbows. "I can't pretend like nothing's wrong and say, *Yes, Cassius* like some mindless idiot."

Fury blooms on his face. "I make these rules for your protection."

All I know is Cassius is used to people shutting up and doing what he says, and I'm not going to do that when it's hurting both of us. "If we could just talk about—"

Before I've even finished what I'm saying, he rips his fingers from my pussy and stalks out of the room. A few minutes later, I hear the roar of an engine as a car disappears out of the front gate.

Well, fuck.

Now things are really screwed between us.

I pull my underwear and skirt on, wondering if I've made the biggest mistake of my life. My future is uncertain and I've just made it even more so by pissing off one of the most powerful men in Coldlake. I can only imagine the text messages that are flying around their group chat right now.

We need to get rid of her.

I agree.

Yeah, I'm tired of her, too.

Shall I kill her or do we just throw her out?

The compound is quiet for several days and nights. I hear only Lorenzo in the kitchen or walking up and down the stairs. When we pass each other in the hall he gives me a baleful look—though heavy-lidded, unfriendly gazes are his norm and maybe I'm just reading too much into them.

When I can't stand the silence anymore, I go and find Lorenzo. He's in the living room sitting crossways in an armchair, his legs over the arm. I can see over his shoulder and there is reams of writing in the notebook propped against his knees.

Does that say *princess*?

I step closer. "Lorenzo?"

He slams the notebook closed, jumps to his feet and rounds on me. "What?"

His expression is so ferocious that I take a step back. What kind of work is he doing that he has to be so secretive about? The expression in his pale blue eyes is almost fearful.

No. Guilty.

I glance at the notebook. "Was that me you were writing about in your book? I was wondering what you were doing."

"No, and none of your fucking business. Why do you keep wandering around my house? Are you bored or something?"

His handwriting is such a scrawl that maybe it wasn't *princess*, but I feel like it was. "Of course I'm bored. Where's your TV? Where are all your books?"

"I don't watch TV. And I have books."

"Medical textbooks and journals."

"That's all I read."

"That's not what *I* want to read."

"If you're that bored, I'll find something for you to do."

The savage glint in his eyes makes me nervous. "Actually, I don't—"

But it's too late. Lorenzo is already grasping my arm and steering me down into the basement.

"Put some gloves on. The autoclave needs stacking."

I pull a black latex glove over my left hand, but it immediately shreds on my diamond ring.

Lorenzo taps a shelf. "Take that rock off, princess. You can put it up here."

I do as he suggests, and as I put on gloves, he explains that the autoclave, a squat metal box that opens at the front like a microwave, sterilizes his instruments. There's an array of bloody scalpels and clamps in a kidney dish. "Who got shot?"

"No one. Two of the bounty hunters who work at Strife got stabbed. Nothing serious."

Only Lorenzo would describe two stabbings as nothing serious. By the amount of bloody gauze in the trash, I'd say that a lot of bleeding went on in this room. "Bounty hunters?"

"Yeah. Like hitmen, but their services are more diverse. Not just killing. You can hire a bounty hunter for a bit of torture. Couriering hot gear. Stalking. Beatings. That sort of thing." He shrugs like what he's saying is actually quite dull. "Hit *people*, I should say. All sorts of crazies work out of Strife. Women can be just as insane as men." He thinks for a moment and adds in an admiring tone, "Sometimes more so."

Could I do any of that? I wonder what would happen if these four men threw me out and I showed up at Strife looking for work. Actually, I'm pretty sure I know what would happen. Acid would mock me for being the Princess of Coldlake and laugh in my face. "Do you know many women bounty hunters?"

"A couple."

Of course he does. I bet they're all hot, too, and wear tight leather pants and winged liner, and they're fierce. The sort of women who would walk right up to a dangerous man like Lorenzo and tell him to buy her a drink. They wouldn't even care that he doesn't like to kiss because they're far too badass and busy to be bothered by that sort of thing.

"Do you hang out at Strife often?"

"When I have time." He glances at me, eyes narrowed as he smiles. "Why? Jealous, princess?"

"No," I say, but far too quickly. To distract him from taunting me, I ask, "Would I make a good bounty hunter?"

He slides his fingers up the nape of my neck. "Why would you want to be a bounty hunter and carry out someone else's orders? I want to see you giving orders of your own one day."

I glance over my shoulder at him in surprise. "You do?"

Lorenzo slides his other hand down my stomach and cups my pussy. "That would be so hot, princess, seeing you walk into Strife and telling Acid and his bunch of assholes what to do."

My head falls back against his shoulder as he works my clit through my clothes. "But Strife is in your quadrant."

"*Mi casa, su casa*. Same with the other three."

Me, give orders in their world. The idea is alluring. My mind goes wandering over the possibilities—and then crashes back to earth. "That's never going to happen. Salvatore and Cassius want me to do nothing except what I'm told. I said no to Cassius earlier and he detonated like a nuclear bomb."

Lorenzo must know about this thanks to their mafia group chat, but it doesn't seem to bother him. "They're old fashioned, but they'll come around soon enough. Show 'em what you're made of, and their dicks will be so hard they'll forget about everything else." His teeth nip my neck.

Speaking of dicks, with Lorenzo pressed tight against me I can feel how turned on he is. "You never stop surprising me, Lorenzo."

He smiles against my throat. "I wouldn't want to get boring." His head lifts as we hear the grinding of the gate opening out front. "That'll be the others. Come on. Let's go eat."

"The others?" I ask, following upstairs.

"Yeah. We still owe you Chinese food on the sofa."

I smile at Lorenzo's broad back. He remembered. Maybe eating together will reset things between the five of us.

But when I enter the living room, only Vinicius and Salvatore are there with the bags of takeout.

"Where's Cassius?"

Vinicius is laying out boxes of noodles and dumplings on the coffee table. He hesitates, and says, "Something came up, but he wanted me to give you this."

He stands up, rests his hands on my shoulders and presses a soft kiss to my lips. It feels heavenly from Vinicius, but I doubt that Cassius is thinking about kissing me right now.

"Your kiss is a pretty lie," I whisper.

Instead of answering, Vinicius takes my hand with a frown. "Kitten, you're not wearing your ring. Why aren't you wearing your ring?"

Salvatore whips around and stares at my hand, his expression filled with alarm.

"I left it downstairs when Lorenzo and I were working. I'll be right back," I call over my shoulder as I hurry back downstairs.

The ring is where I left it on the shelf. As I wriggle the ring back onto my finger I walk toward the door, brushing against Lorenzo's desk. Something is sticking out from one of the drawers and it drops to the floor and falls open.

The battered notebook with a blue cover.

The notebook that I thought I saw he'd written *princess* in.

I glance at the door. I can't even hear the others from down here. What was with that guilty look on his face earlier? I could have sworn that whatever he was writing had something to do with me, but he claims it's work. So which is it?

I stare straight ahead, telling myself not to look. If I find Lorenzo's confessed to the page how much he hates me in his house, or that he regrets kidnapping me, or that he and the others are this close to throwing me out, I'll feel terrible. No one ever finds out something they want to know when they snoop.

I bend down to pick the notebook up and put it away, but my eyes lock on a paragraph that he's written.

...VIVID RED SPLASHED AGAINST COLD, white flesh. Her lips are blue, open and inviting. No talking back with breathless lungs. The needle in her arm has drained the fight out of her and now she's perfect, perfect, perfect. Cold flesh so vivid against my hot skin. I'll sweat for both of us, princess.

MY MOUTH FALLS OPEN. I slowly turn the page.

A DEAD LITTLE doll with perfect, golden curls. So fucking pretty as she sits there on a shelf with glassy eyes. Safe forever now with chemicals in her veins and lips sewn shut. I take her down and play with her anytime I like. All mine.

Ready for another game?

Let's play doctor.

. . .

I FEEL my chest tightening and bile creeping up my throat, but I can't tear my eyes away. Lorenzo has written pages and pages of sadistic, blood-soaked fantasies. The girl he's playing violent games with is described over and over.

She looks just like I do.

He calls her princess.

He even does things to her that Lorenzo has done to me. Sticking needles in her veins and drugging her. Leaving bitemarks all over her body while she screams. Tying her up and shoving her into the trunk of his car, and then dropping her in the desert and hunting her down like prey, just like he once threatened to do to me.

The most recent entry, he has this girl in his bed and he's screwing her until there's blood coating his cock and she's bleeding out all over him. There's a gun to her head and she's whispering *thank you* over and over as she's dying. Then he pulls the trigger, and it makes him come to watch her brains spatter over his headboard.

"What are you doing?" A tattooed hand swipes the notebook from my hand.

I stare from the notebook to Lorenzo's furious face. I was so absorbed in the blood and horror on the page that I didn't hear anyone come into the room.

He wrote those things.

About *me*.

Lorenzo fantasizes about killing me and screwing my corpse.

"I asked you what the fuck you think you're doing. *Answer me.*" He advances on me, a solid wall of bunched muscles and fury.

His shouting draws Vinicius and Salvatore. They run

into the room, and then stop short when they see the notebook brandished in Lorenzo's hand.

"Why...why are you writing those things about me?" I whisper. My heart races, sick and fast. Are those his fantasies, or his plans? I thought I had Lorenzo figured out but he's tricked me before.

"You always wanted your skin to crawl when you thought about me, didn't you, princess?" he says savagely. "A million tiny insects burrowing into your flesh. Horror prickling up your spine. Did you get your wish? Do you hate me yet?"

I back away slowly as he looms over me, my jaw working. I don't even know what I'm trying to say.

"I said, *did you get your fucking wish?*" he roars, his face suffusing with blood-red rage.

Salvatore and Vinicius seem to be rooted to the spot, their expressions hard and closed. But they're not glaring at Lorenzo.

They're glaring at me.

"Well, guess what?" Lorenzo brandishes the notebook. "Not everything's about you, princess. If I'd wanted you to read it, I would have fucking invited you, you sneaky little bitch."

Blonde hair. Blue eyes. Petite. *Innocent.* It's exactly how he'd describe me. The needle draining my blood. Drugging me. The gun to my head as he fucks me.

Not about me?

We've *done* these things together.

"Lorenzo," I say quietly, swallowing my emotions and trying to keep my voice steady. "I know you're...different. There are things about you that scare me and I'm accepting that." I thought I was, anyway. "But please don't lie to me."

Salvatore calls across the room, "I know you're upset, but don't call him a liar. If he says it's not about you, then it's not about you."

I don't take my eyes off Lorenzo. There are so many blades in this room and he's barely clinging to sanity. "I will call out lies when I hear them. Read his notebook if you don't believe me."

"I don't need to. I know what's in it," Salvatore says.

"What?" I risk a glance at him, and then at Vinicius. There's unease on his face, but not shock.

"We all know," Vinicius says.

Even Cassius? Cassius who has a meltdown at the idea of me getting hurt even a tiny bit or put in the slightest bit of danger? Lorenzo's fists are clenched so tightly that his biceps are bulging.

I take a step toward Lorenzo. "*I'll sweat for both of us, princess.* That's not about me? Drugging this girl. Kidnapping her. Biting her. Screwing her with a gun to her head."

Salvatore and Vinicius glance at Lorenzo in surprise.

He lied to them, too.

Now it's three of us staring at him. Lorenzo's gaze flicks between us.

"Fuck you all to hell." He shoulders his way out of the room, slamming the door behind him.

"What did you all think was in this notebook?"

Salvatore and Vinicius don't seem like they want to answer. I pull open the door and hurry down the corridor, calling Lorenzo's name. He's taking the steps two at a time. "Lorenzo, wait. Please."

I catch up with him in the kitchen. I almost run right into him because he stops short, and rounds on me.

"You sure you can stand to look at me, princess?" he mocks, arms flung wide. "Be careful, get too close and you might throw up."

There's a hard, bitter edge to his voice, but if anyone's going to be sick, I think it's him. The notebook is squeezed so tight in his fist that it's bent double.

"I'm sorry. I didn't mean to read it. It fell open and…" I only looked at the end of the notebook. Maybe the earlier pages *are* about another girl. One who was tortured and killed. One Lorenzo loved. Maybe writing down what happened to her is the only way he knows how to cope, and then I came along and things got complicated.

I step forward slowly and put my hand on his arm. "I think the last few dozen pages are about me, but maybe it's about someone else, too? She must have looked a little bit like me."

Blonde. Blue eyes like Lorenzo's. Like mine. Younger than him and smaller.

Do I dare say her name out loud? Someone has to. "Were you writing about Si—"

Lorenzo grabs me by the throat and slams me against the wall. All the breath is knocked out of me. I clutch his wrist, trying to pull his hand away, but his fingers tighten mercilessly. His hot breath fans my face and rage is rolling off him in waves.

I whimper in his grip. Cassius hates me, and now Lorenzo does, too. This is all falling apart.

"You were warned what would happen if you ever brought this up again," he snarls, his face less than an inch from mine. "I can thrash you just as easily as Cassius, and you won't like it half as much."

"I won't say her name," I gasp, my chest heaving in panic as I grasp his wrist. I can't lose it, or he will, too. A tiny bit tighter and he'll strangle me to death. "But please, can we talk about this?"

"You shouldn't have looked. I could fucking kill you."

I make myself let go of his wrist and press my hand against his heart. His wildly beating heart. It pounds against my hand, full of malice. Full of anguish.

"Is that what you really want? You're not a monster, Lorenzo."

He looks down at my hand and then back up at me. "You don't know what I'm hiding, princess. You don't know shit about what I've done."

Salvatore and Vinicius have come into the room. I can see them out of the corner of my eye, but I don't look away from Lorenzo. His heart is thumping against my palm. I reach up with my other hand and caress his cheek. Lorenzo has the face of a killer. Of a man any woman would be afraid to see behind her in a dark alley. The savage beauty of an apex predator.

"Please tell me. I'm not afraid."

He lets go of me with a growl and stands back, his head bowed and his tangled blond hair falling around his face. I take deep lungfuls of air, trying to get my breath back.

Both of Lorenzo's fists are clenched at his side like he hasn't decided if he wants to walk out or beat me senseless.

"Fine. But when I'm done, you'll wish forever that I hadn't."

8

Lorenzo

N*ine years ago*

"Are you going to point that gun at my head all day?"

I'm straddling a chair backwards with a Glock 19 aimed at the pretty blonde's head. She's sitting on the floor of my bedroom, surrounded by my dirty T-shirts, medical textbooks, and empty cigarette packets. She's small. Blonde. Cute. Her wrists tied in front of her. And she's absolutely furious with me.

"For the rest of my life if I have to, Sienna."

My sister twists her wrists and swears, but she only succeeds in digging the zip tie more savagely into her flesh.

"I have a life, you know! I have things to do. My boyfriend's expecting me."

"Boyfriend?" I sneer. "That married piece of shit who fucks you in secret and buys you handbags to keep you quiet?"

Her mouth opens in shock.

"Yeah, I know all about him. Why are you letting him touch you when you're so much better than him?"

"What, you think we're hot shit now you're running with rich assholes?"

Salvatore Fiore and Cassius Ferragamo, she means. "I'm not running with them. They're running with me."

They know they can't control massive parts of Coldlake without me. I'm the only thing keeping the Geaks and the Blood Pack from running riot over half of this city. I'm the only one who can keep the Strife boys in line.

Besides, I like those two assholes. They're smart. They don't take shit from anyone. Add in Vinicius who runs the north, and the four of us will soon have Coldlake in the palm of our hands. It's perfect.

"All I know is that since you got involved with those morons, they've made you paranoid."

I grab a photo from my desk and shove it in Sienna's face. "Who's that?"

She screws her eyes up and turns her face away. "Don't."

"I said look at it, or I'll fucking make you," I growl. I mean it. I'll prise her eyelids open with my fingers until I'm satisfied she's seen every grisly detail of this photograph.

Sienna takes a deep breath and opens her eyes, and takes a fearful glance at the photo.

"Well?" I ask.

"It's Ophelia Fiore. Salvatore's little sister."

"And what's she doing in this picture?"

Sienna swallows hard, as if bile has risen up the back of her throat. "She's...she's dead."

She's more than dead. This seventeen-year-old girl has been ripped to pieces, and some sick fuck has played with her entrails. A smile has been cut into her face and you can see her teeth all the way at the back of her jaw.

"Do you know how she died?"

"Please stop," Sienna whimpers.

I angle the grisly photograph of the naked and tortured girl toward me so I can look at it. "She hemorrhaged from her face. You wouldn't think it would be possible, would you? Those cuts in her cheeks severed the external maxillary arteries. My guess is he slashed her face first and then got on with torturing her and she screamed herself to death. If you look closely—"

"Lorenzo, shut up!" Sienna buries her face in her knees and screams and screams to drown out the sound of my voice. When she looks up her face is furious and blotchy. "You think I'm not already afraid of this? Women walk around vividly imagining all the ways we might get raped and murdered every day. It must be lovely being a man and thinking about tits and beer instead."

With my free hand, I reach for my pack of cigarettes and light one, still with the gun pointed at my sister. "Then you already get it. I'm not letting you out of my sight until Salvatore has hunted down whoever killed Ophelia."

She eyes my cigarette. "Those things are dangerous. You should know better seeing as you're going to be a doctor."

"Oh shit, seriously?" I deadpan. I need to smoke. I need something to do with my hands.

"Ophelia Fiore's death has got nothing to do with me.

Ophelia and I don't even know each other. God, you're such a control freak."

I take a drag on the cigarette and exhale slowly. Maybe I'm overreacting. Maybe not. Francesco Fiore hands the city over to his son. Salvatore Fiore agrees to divide it among himself, me, Cassius, and Vinicius. Salvatore and I start kicking the gangs back into the shitty southwest corner of the city, and the next thing, his sister is kidnapped and murdered. The gangs hate us right now. You hate a man, you go after his women and you make them bleed.

Though the way Ophelia was murdered has been bothering me. It's not your typical gang-rape and beating. It's more clinical. Precise.

It seems...gleeful.

"You can be mad all you like with me. I don't care, princess. I'm not letting you out of my sight."

"How many times do I have to tell you? I'm not in any danger."

I lean closer. "Oh, really? So where's Amalia?"

That shuts Sienna up. Amalia, Vinicius' twin sister, vanished from the brothel she worked in just a few days after Ophelia was snatched off the street.

"I don't know. She's a junkie. She ran away," Sienna mutters.

No one heard anything or saw anything, but I know, and Vinicius knows, that she wouldn't just run off. She might have been miserable and strung out, but she had every reason to stay. *Every* reason.

"Yeah fucking right."

Sienna rubs her forehead, her brow creased with frustration. I get why she's fighting with me. She doesn't want to believe that she's in any danger. It's too horrifying for her to imagine that she might show up as a mutilated corpse as well.

But I can imagine it. All too fucking vividly.

"It's not just me taking precautions. Cassius is driving out to his sister's boarding school in the mountains right this second to fetch her home."

"He's bringing her back to Coldlake? Isn't he better off leaving her where she is?"

I shake my head. "First thing in the morning, he's putting her on a plane to Naples and she's flying out to stay with family. Come to think of it, how do you feel about a trip to Italy?"

"I'm *not* staying with the Ferragamos. They all have massive sticks up their butts. I don't think any of them have cracked a smile in four hundred years."

I pass my hand over my mouth, trying not to grin. I mean, she's not wrong. "You'd be safe with the Ferragamos, and I wouldn't have to hold a gun to your head to keep you safe."

"You wouldn't have to hold a gun to my head if we just left Coldlake."

This shit again. I'm not leaving Coldlake. This city is in my blood and I'm going to mold it into what *I* want it to be.

"I don't get you, Lorenzo. If this life is so dangerous that I'm not safe anymore, why are you diving into it headfirst? You were nearly out, and now you're going to end up like Dad, dead before his fortieth birthday."

I gaze at the medical textbooks and notebooks piled up on my desk. Another six months and I'd be graduating and starting a surgical residency. Who knew I had the brains to do a medical degree when Dad told me I'm a dumb fuck my whole childhood? Mom was so proud when I enrolled, but... I scrub my hand over my face and sigh. "I don't know. I'm not cut out to be a doctor. You have to care, and people are fucking annoying. It's all about putting people back together, and I spend more time taking them apart."

"You're going to be a *surgeon*. You have to be hard as nails to cut people open and mess around with their insides. Your bedside manner totally sucks, but no one will care when you save their life."

And what will the Geaks and the Blood Pack do to Coldlake while I'm dicking about at a teaching hospital? Every time some kid comes in with a stab wound or a bullet in his stomach, I'll wonder if it's because he ran into a piece of shit that I didn't kick back into the hole it crawled out of.

I grew up on these streets. They're *my* fucking streets, not theirs.

"Let's just get out of here. Leave Coldlake. We'll go to California and start fresh."

I reach out and flick my cigarette ash into an empty coffee mug. Sure, we'd be safe and we could have a normal life, but what would I do with a normal life? "I don't know. Maybe."

Sienna just looks at me. She knows what *maybe* means.

"Listen, when this shit has blown over and I know there's no one coming after you, I'll give you as much money as you want and you can go to California. I'm loaded now we've formed the Coldlake Syndicate. I get a cut of all the business done in my quadrant."

She gazes around at the bedroom of my shitty apartment. "Then why are you still living in this dump?"

"There's no place like home, I guess."

"So I go to California and you stay here where you can play at being a tough guy until someone puts a bullet in your head? You're an idiot."

I glare at her. Even tied up on my bedroom floor while I have a gun to her head and she dares to talk to me like this. "You're lucky you're cute."

She rests her chin on her bound hands and blinks her lashes at me. "I'm so cute you want to untie me."

"You're not that cute." My phone rings. I stab my cigarette out and answer it without looking. "What?"

"There's trouble in paradise, boss," says a deep, sarcastic voice.

Acid.

This fucking asshole.

I presume he means there's been another shootout at Strife, the bar that his gang hangs out in. "Can't you deal with it?"

"I wouldn't like to step on your toes, *boss*."

The line goes dead. His bar is on my turf and he answers to me now. I take a cut of what his gang brings in, and in return, I make sure he has everything he needs from the other three to make his money. No one hosts underground poker games without Salvatore's permission. The only fake bills being laundered come from Vinicius' factory. Illegal prize fights, brothels, and strip clubs have to be approved by Cassius. And we keep the gangs off their backs. We provide, and we take a cut. This is how I like my crime, nice and organized. It's a perfect arrangement and everyone's happy.

More or less. The Strife gang loves all the money I'm helping them make, but they're pissed off that they don't own their neighborhood like they did under Francesco Fiore.

I get to my feet and shove my gun in the back of my jeans. "Get up. We're going out."

"Just leave me here. I promise I won't go anywhere."

Hell no. This apartment is only safe when I'm in it to protect her, and as soon as I turn my back she'll run off. "From now on, where I go, you go."

I cut through the bindings on her wrists. She needs to be able to get out of a bad situation if shit goes down. For a second she's delighted, and then I grab her by the scruff of her denim jacket and march her outside to my car, a beat up 1989 Dodge Challenger.

"Where are we going?" she asks as I start the engine.

"Strife."

"Oh? Will that goth punk guy be there? The tall, black-haired one?"

She must mean Thane, one of the four men who run Strife. "Why, do you like that creep?"

She shrugs, finger combing her hair. "Maybe. He's all mysterious. You know, the strong silent type."

"He never says a word because he's dumb as mud," I snap. Actually, Thane is insanely intelligent and can crack open anyone's computer or bank account given enough time, but I don't want my sister getting mixed up with the Strife assholes.

Sienna turns to me with a teasing smile. "Shame. He's so gorgeous with that jawline and those muscles. Such cool clothes. Makes me want to help him out of them."

"Shut up or I'm going to lose my breakfast," I mutter.

It's a short drive from my apartment to Strife. Ten

minutes later, I make a left-hand turn and pull up by a chain link fence.

Strife sits on a corner, a three-story brick building painted black with neon signs in the windows and fixed above the door, exclaiming about beer and strippers. It's not yet noon and the bar's still closed, but there are two men out front.

Acid, who's sitting on a beer keg in ripped jeans and a tank top, his arms folded, and Thane, leaning against a wall wearing head-to-toe black with his hair falling into his eyes and a shotgun over his shoulder. Those creepy, dark eyes wander over to my sister.

Don't you even fucking think about it.

I get out of the car, dragging Sienna with me as I cross the street toward the men.

"Let go of me. I can walk by myself," she hisses, her face flaming. I keep a tight grip on her upper arm.

Acid gives me an ironic salute but he doesn't get to his feet. "Nice to see you again, boss."

There's no blood on the pavement. No broken windows. If Acid's dragged me down here for no reason, I'll burn his place down. "What's happened?"

Acid gestures toward the front door. "Go and see for yourself. But I wouldn't take the lady in there."

He smirks, giving Sienna the up-and-down. Thane towers over my sister, and she's giving him her brightest smile.

"Inside," I say to Sienna, leading her toward the entrance. "But stay by the door."

Inside, the bar is cool and dark and smells of whisky and stale cigarettes. The carpet is so dark you can't make out the stains. A silent jukebox flashes in the corner.

Sienna wrinkles her nose. "This place looks even worse in the daylight."

It's a dive, but there's more to Strife than meets the eye. "You're underage. You shouldn't know what this place looks like at night."

"My big brother, always so concerned with the law."

Through a door I can see the empty poles of the strip club and the main bar. Nothing seems out of place. Then we move further into the room, and I see it.

Actually, Sienna sees it first. She grabs my shoulder and gasps. "Oh, my God. What's that?"

A woman is lying on the floor, her limbs haphazardly arranged. Blood streaks her thighs and face and has matted her hair.

That is a body. I'm guessing it's one of the strippers who work here. I can't tell which one. I doubt her own mother would recognize her anymore.

"What happened to her?" Sienna whispers.

"Don't look." Sienna is rooted to the spot, so I turn her around and shove her back the way we came. The stench of blood follows us outside.

Sienna stumbles on the broken sidewalk, her hand over her mouth and her shoulders shaking. After a moment, she straightens up and stares at me. "That woman was dead. Doesn't that make you sick? Aren't you horrified?"

I shrug. It's not that I like looking at shit like that but you get used to it. I've seen bodies on the streets. Cut up corpses in labs. There's not much that turns my stomach anymore.

Acid steps forward, his thumbs dug into the waistband of

his jeans. "So, what are we doing, boss? Are we calling the cops, or are we taking her out to the woods?"

He doesn't want cops crawling over this place any more than I do. "Do you know who she is? Who her family is?"

"Sure, I do. Her name's Astrid. Lives with her mom and little sister down on Fernwood."

Lives with her mom. Christ, she must be young. "When it gets dark, take her body to an empty lot and then call it in, anonymously. In a couple of days, go see her mom and sister and give them fifty grand."

"Fifty? I don't have that kind of cash to blow on a dead stripper."

"I'll give you half. You pay the rest, and from now on, don't let your fucking strippers get killed."

Acid glares at me like he wants to punch me in the face. He needs to get serious about keeping our enemies away from this place. If they're working for him, these girls are his responsibility. Cassius hates dead girls and he will shut the stripper room down if this happens again.

Thane's been lounging against the wall but he suddenly comes to life and flips the shotgun from his shoulder and points it at an approaching car. There are two men inside, and the driver, a mean looking asshole with a buzzcut, is staring at me like he can't believe his luck.

Lorenzo Scava himself. I've just made his morning.

He goes for his piece at the same time I reach for my own gun, but before either of us can get off a round, Thane steps forward and blasts a shell into his face. The windshield explodes and there's a screech of tire rubber and a horn blast as the dead driver hits the steering wheel. The passenger side door opens and a man scrambles out, but Thane has taken three long strides around the car and is lifting his shotgun to shoot the guy in the head.

"Don't kill him," I shout.

Thane lowers his aim and blasts the guy in the stomach. Then he stands there, staring at the man writhing on the ground, casually reloading the weapon.

Sienna is clutching my arm, her nails digging in. "We need to leave."

"Get inside."

"I'm serious, Lorenzo. We need to get out of here. This city is tearing itself apart and it's going to tear *you* apart, too."

"You'll do what you're told and stop giving me a fucking headache," I snarl at her, grabbing her wrist and dragging her back inside. Guilt slashes through me as she whimpers in pain, but I harden my heart against it. Better that she's with me and alive than out there alone where she could be turned into mincemeat at any moment.

I glance at the stripper's corpse, and shove Sienna toward the stairs. "Go upstairs and barricade yourself into the office. Shove the furniture against the door and don't come out until you hear my voice."

"But—"

"*Do as you're fucking told.*" I head back out and over to where the man is dying in the middle of the road. His midsection has been blasted open and a river of blood is running across the blacktop.

My guess is their dumbass plan was to cause trouble at Strife and then cruise the joint in the hopes that I might appear. They were shitting themselves so hard when they saw me standing on the street that they didn't see Thane with his shotgun. Morons. It's insulting.

I kneel by his side. "Did you kill one of my strippers?"

"Go fuck yourself," he seethes through gritted teeth.

I shove my fingers into gaping wound in his stomach, and he screams. "I said, did you kill one of my strippers?"

"It was on Jax's orders."

"What's he planning next?"

It takes several minutes of me persuading the man while he screams and I get blood up both my arms before I discover that Jax plans on throwing Molotovs through the windows of Strife tonight.

"Where's Amalia?"

There's genuine confusion on the man's face. "Who?"

Worth a try. I stand up and pull the gun out of the waistband of my jeans and aim it at the man's head. He puts up both his hands.

"Don't, pl—" His words are lost as I pull the trigger and the sound of the gunshot ricochets off the buildings.

I walk back over to Acid and Thane and explain about the Molotovs. "For the next two weeks, there'll be men searching every car that tries to get within a mile of this place."

I've got a couple of guys free and I'll borrow a few men each from the other three. Acid stares at the blood all over my T-shirt and hands, and for once, he hasn't got anything sarcastic to say.

"If any Blood Pack or Geak steps foot in my territory, drop their bodies back in the southwest gift-wrapped with a big fucking bow. They're not welcome here. Send a fucking message." As I head inside, I call over my shoulder, "And get those bodies into the cool room and wash the blood off the road before the cops roll by. You're opening in thirty minutes."

I head upstairs and knock on the office door. "It's me. Come on out."

Silence.

"Sienna?" I try the door handle, and it opens. The office is empty.

Fuck.

Fuck.

I run back downstairs and outside to the other two. Thane is dragging the Geak off the street by his ankle and Acid is trying to start the smashed up car.

"Where's Sienna?"

Acid turns the key again and the engine makes a choking noise. "I don't know. I think I heard the back door open and close while you were busy with our friend here."

I grab a fistful of his tank top, panic slamming through me. "Are you kidding me? Why didn't you go after her?"

"Because I'm not her babysitter! If you're so worried about her, why the fuck did you bring her here?"

I race into the bar, blow through the back door and into the alley. There's an overflowing dumpster and boxes of empty beer bottles. "*Sienna.*"

A kid with a basketball under his arm is staring at me from the other end of the alley, and I jog over to him.

"Did you see a blonde girl out here a minute ago?"

"Yeah, she came out of the bar, and then a big black car pulled up and she was dragged inside."

Ice floods my veins. "Who was in there?"

The boy shrugs. He can't be more than eight but he's

already seen so much that a woman being kidnapped is no big deal. "Don't know. Windows were all dark."

Big car. Tinted windows. Could be a gang, but might not be, either. It could be fucking anyone. "Which way did it…"

But my eyes land on something lying on the sidewalk, perfect and lustrous. A black flower.

An orchid.

I sink down onto my heels and groan, my hands to my head. "No, no, no."

She's gone.

I took my eyes off her for one second and she's gone.

My phone buzzes in my pocket and I dig it out. Vinicius' name is on the screen. "They've taken Sienna. That fucking asshole has taken Sienna."

"Not her, as well."

"As well?"

"Cassius didn't make it in time. Evelina's gone." There's a smashing sound in the background and a great howl of rage and pain.

Cassius.

"I'm so fucking sorry, Lorenzo. Where are—"

There are muffled sounds and exclamations, and then a thick, Italian voice comes on the line. "Scava? Where the fuck are you, Scava? You take your sister and you get out of Coldlake. If I see your face I will kill you myself. *I will wring your fucking neck, do you hear me?* Take Sienna and get out of here."

Cassius is raving like a man possessed. I can hear Vinicius shouting at him that it's too late, that Sienna's already gone. Cassius finally falls silent and harsh breathing fills my ear.

"Salvatore and Vinicius didn't know their sisters were in danger, but you and me, Scava? We deserve to die." His voice breaks, and the line goes dead.

EVELINA'S BODY is found first on the roof of a building that Cassius' penthouse overlooks. I thought he was going to break the entire city with his bare fists when he heard the news. He punched a dozen holes in the walls of his apartment before Salvatore and Vinicius physically restrained him.

They should have let him get on with it. Smash the entire city apart. Turn it all to dust. Maybe then we'd find Amalia and Sienna because I sure as fuck couldn't. Every man under me was searching derelict warehouses, abandoned apartment buildings, deserted shopping malls. Vinicius and I put on vests and carried guns into the southwest a dozen times, certain that our sisters were being held somewhere in enemy territory. I broke the fingers of every Geak and Blood Pack gang member I could find. No one knew anything about our sisters, but they were all fucking delighted that we were miserable.

Sienna was found on a cool, breezy Tuesday morning, sitting on a bench. Not a scratch on her, that anyone could see at first glance. The jogger who found her thought she was an incredibly detailed mannequin, until they got closer and saw the tiny blood vessels in her dead, staring eyes. When the medical examiner cut her open, all her innards were gone and she'd been filled with feces and dead insects.

Finally, Amalia, a week later, tangled up in trash and

bushes down at the edge of the lake. Thrown away like garbage. Most of her, anyway. It was hard to tell. She was in so many pieces.

Salvatore tells me through my locked front door. I sit with my back against it, a bottle of vodka in one hand, a gun in the other. He knocks his fists bloody as he tries to get me to open up but I'm not leaving this apartment ever again. As soon as I've finished this bottle, I'm putting a bullet in my head.

"Vinicius just lost his sister. He's your best friend," Salvatore snarls, his voice raw with grief. "Open this door right now, you selfish prick."

He lost his sister?

He's not fucking special.

I take a swig from the bottle, and it burns down my throat. Every knock of Salvatore's fist ricochets through my skull. "Fuck off, would you? Let me kill myself in peace."

Salvatore lets loose a string of expletives and harsher pounding, calling me every name under the sun. "This is our city. We own these streets and the men who did this are going to pay with their blood. With their sanity. *With their fucking souls*. Are you going to let Sienna's killer get away with this?"

My fierce little sister who used the charred bones of her enemies as eyeliner and gave the finger to the world. My throat burns with rage and grief so powerful that I can't see. Can't breathe.

I curl up on the floor and scream at the top of my lungs. I can hear Salvatore yelling and pounding on the door over the sound of my rage.

I scream so long that I pass out.

Several days later, I'm still not dead, and my phone is ringing.

I see myself from above, lying on a filthy bed in a stupor, surrounded by cigarette butts and empty vodka bottles. There are burns in the sheets. I keep dropping cigarettes hoping that I go up in flames.

The ringing goes on and fucking on. I glance at the screen. It's Vinicius.

I swipe the screen to answer. "What?"

There's the sound of uneven breathing.

"Say something or fuck off."

"It's me," says a thick voice.

He sounds weird, like he's been throwing up or crying. Or both.

"Did you get anything in the mail this morning?"

"How should I know." I reach for a pack of cigarettes on the nightstand and light one, and draw the smoke deep into my lungs. The nicotine washes over me, and I can finally sit up. I passed out in my dirty jeans. I stink.

"Go and see."

There's an open bottle of vodka on my nightstand and I take a swig. Warm, cheap vodka, that tastes more like chemicals than a proper drink. The burn is all I want. The burn, and the numbing fog of alcohol in my veins.

I walk through my apartment with the phone pressed against my ear, the vodka bottle in my other hand and the cigarette hanging from my lips. The mailboxes are by the front entrance and I walk downstairs and through the lobby, still smoking, barefoot and bare chested. One of the asshole residents opens his front door and starts whining at me about the cigarette. Like this hole is too good for a bit of smoke.

He sees its me and quickly closes his front door.

I stick the bottle of vodka on top of the mailboxes and open mine. There are about fifty letters inside. I haven't cleared it out since before Sienna was taken. "What am I looking for?"

Before I can finish asking, I see it. A pristine envelope, right on top of the pile, and it's thicker than the other envelopes. In the middle, anyway, like there's something small but chunky inside. There are only two words printed on the envelope. Lorenzo Scava.

"A hand delivered envelope printed with your name," Vinicius says. "No return address. Lumpy."

Well, fuck me.

"You've got one, don't you?" Vinicius asks when I don't reply.

I drop the cigarette on the carpet and crush it under my bare foot, tendrils of apprehension curling through me. I couldn't even say what's causing it. The strangeness of a hand delivered letter just a week after my sister's death. Vinicius acting so weird. Or maybe it's the envelope itself radiating evil.

I stare at it and take another swig of vodka. "Yeah, I've got one."

Vinicius breathes in sharply. "Lorenzo, don't watch—"

I hang up, and take my envelope and the vodka back upstairs. Inside the envelope is a flash drive, and I stick it in my laptop. There's only one file, a video, and I open it and press play.

A second later, I get to my feet and stagger backwards, the chair tipping over behind me.

What the fuck.

What the fucking fuck.

I'm still staring at the screen when I hear my front door crash open. Someone's calling my name, but I can't tear my eyes away from the screen until my laptop is slammed closed.

"I told you not to watch it," Vinicius yells. He's breathing hard like he's been running. He must have been on his way here when he called.

I point a finger at my computer. "What the fuck was that?"

Vinicius sinks down onto the bed and sits among the overflowing ashtrays and empty vodka bottles.

"Did you get one? Did you watch it?"

He nods, his hand shaking as he passes it over his face. "Just a few seconds. Then I threw up."

I reach for the vodka bottle, but it's empty. There's a fresh one on the floor and I crack it open, and I drink until my heart stops pounding.

Vinicius gets slowly to his feet. "Come on. I'll take you to Salvatore's. Cassius is already there."

"Why?" I don't know why I'm asking when I already know the answer.

Because they got them, too.

I pull on a T-shirt and some high tops and follow him out. Vinicius tries to close my front door but he broke the lock as he forced his way in and it won't shut.

I wave him away. "Leave it. No one will steal my shit."

"Why do you live in this place? You're making more than

enough money to move out," Vinicius mutters as we walk down the corridor.

I take another swig of vodka. Sienna and I grew up in shitty apartments like the one I'm living in now. It's what I'm used to. "I'm waiting for my dream home. White picket fence. Two golden retrievers. One of those Live, Laugh, Love cushions."

Vinicius looks like he came from money, but his background is as rough as mine. Rougher, even. These days he looks like he stepped out of a Gucci ad, so you wouldn't know it.

"Where's Ginevra?" I ask. The last sister the four of us have, just eleven years old.

"She flew out to Naples with her mother last week. They're staying with one of Cassius' cousins."

Fucking good. I hope she never comes back.

At Salvatore's, Cassius sits at the kitchen table with eyes that are bloodshot and red rimmed. He rampaged all over Coldlake looking for his missing sister, and he still lost her. Salvatore's had some time to get used to Ophelia's death, but for the rest of us, it's so raw it's still twitching.

"Here." I hold out the bottle to Cassius.

He takes the vodka from me, gets up and pours it down the sink.

"Hey!"

"I'm not drinking that shit." He opens the freezer and there's a bottle stashed among the frozen vegetables. His lip twitches, like he doesn't approve of Salvatore's vodka, either. "*Che cazzo è questo?*" *What the fuck is this?* "You know what? I don't care."

Salvatore has placed four glasses on the table and

Cassius pours the vodka. The four of us take our seats and sit in silence.

I throw the flash drive I was sent into the middle of the table. One after another, Salvatore, Vinicius, and Cassius reach into their pockets and add three more.

Sienna.

Ophelia.

Amalia.

Evelina.

We stare at the small black and silver objects, each one containing the same thing, or so I assume from their faces. Our sisters' torture and murders, in graphic, full-color high definition video. I push a shaking hand through my hair. Graphic in every fucking sense.

"Why did they do it? That's what I want to know," Salvatore says. "They never even demanded anything from us."

I take another mouthful of vodka. "He doesn't want anything. He just wants to punish us."

Cassius raises his red eyes to me. "I think you're right."

"But who?" Salvatore growls.

"Someone who wants what we have," Vinicius says. "But they're not strong enough to take it, so they took them instead."

"He's a fucking coward," I growl.

Cassius looks like he's on the verge of flipping the table and howling with rage. Vinicius is staring out the window. Salvatore seems like he wants to hit something.

I scoop up all four flash drives and put them in my pocket.

"What do you think you're doing?" Salvatore asks.

"I'm going to watch them all."

Cassius stares at me. "You want to watch them, you sick fuck?"

Of course I don't want to watch them. I want to gouge my eyes from my skull and pour scalding water into my brain, anything to make those images disappear, but someone has to. We have no idea who murdered our sisters and there might be clues in the recordings.

"Either one of us watches these videos, or we hand them over to the police."

Now they all look like they want to punch something. The cops don't give a damn about our sisters. The detectives who took our statements were all laughing up their sleeves at our misery.

Vinicius gets to his feet. "I'll watch them with you."

"No, you won't. Everybody fuck off and leave me alone for a few days. No. A week. Don't call me for a week."

All three of them stare at me with a mixture of worry and gratitude. They want to say they'll watch their own video, but they'd rather shove red-hot needles under their nails.

"Can I do anything for you, Scava?" Cassius asks.

"Yeah. Send me some vodka."

An hour later, I'm sitting in front of my laptop and staring at the flash drive marked Ophelia, turning it over and over in my hands. She was such a beautiful girl. Tall, like her brother. Long legs and a big smile. I saw the crime scene photos and what this psycho did to her body. I have no fucking interest in seeing how she got that way.

I shove the flash drive into a port and open the video. Ophelia Fiore is tied to a chair in an empty room with moisture-stained concrete walls. She's shivering and hunched over, her eyes darting left and right.

There's the sound of a door opening. Ophelia whimpers and starts to struggle. Someone steps into the shot holding a knife in a gloved hand. She takes a deep breath, preparing to scream or beg for mercy. I slam the space bar on my keyboard and lean forward, clenching my head between my hands.

I don't want to do this.

I don't want to see this.

I don't want any of this.

I want to die.

I fumble for a pen and one of my notebooks. On a blank page after my notes about the endocrine system, I write OPHELIA in block letters.

I take a deep breath, and I write down everything I saw. The floor. The walls. What she was tied up with. How she looked. Every cruel, stomach-churning detail. I watch another five seconds of the video, pause it, and write that down, too. I fill half a page with my scrawl from just those few seconds.

As I finish writing, I hear a knock. I get up and find a delivery man gazing in bewilderment at my broken front door. He has a heavy cardboard box for me, and I shove it into the kitchen with my feet and open it.

A crate of Grey Goose. Cassius has sent me the good stuff. I stash three bottles in the freezer and carry another one back to my computer and crack it open. After a few long swallows and a deep breath, I hit the space bar again.

Three days later, I'm finished with Ophelia's video. I watched the entire thing at least a dozen times. Some sections I watched more than others. When the man's hands and body were in the frame, I was searching for tattoos, brand names, jewelry. Anything distinctive. When he spoke, I listened to his words over and over again.

And I drank vodka.

I drank so much fucking vodka.

I can't stomach another swallow, and I can't bear to stick the flash drive marked Amalia in my computer and find out what they did to Vinicius' sister. Not yet.

In the corner is a box of Sienna's things. I rummage through them and pull out one of her sketch books. Sienna loved to draw, mostly fantastical and mythological creatures that never existed. Wolves with seven eyes. Goats that live in shells like hermit crabs. Trailing vines with clusters of eyeballs instead of berries. Psychedelic patterns.

I trace my fingers over a fire-breathing dragon. I want to escape my head and crawl into hers.

I pull on some clothes, and ten minutes later, I walk into the tattoo parlor down the street. I throw the sketchbook down in front of the tattoo artist. "I want these."

He starts flicking through the pages. "These are cool. Which ones?"

"Any of them. All of them. I want them all over me." I pull off my T-shirt and turn around. He glances at the handful of tattoos that are inked into my arms. Most of my chest is bare. All of my back. There's plenty of space.

"I'll make up some stencils. Come back tomorrow."

The first piece the tattoo artist inks into my flesh is the dragon on my back, wings spread across my shoulder blades, its tail curling around to hug my ribs. I go back for another tattoo every time the videos get too much for me. The pain and rhythm of the needle even me out.

Soon, I have four full notebooks and my upper body is

covered in tattoos. I've scoured every frame in three videos. I've watched Ophelia, Evelina, and Amalia scream, cry, vomit, bleed and die too many times to count.

There's only one video left.

I stare at the flash drive in my hand and take a swig of vodka. Every nerve is screaming at me to call one of the other three and make him watch it. I watched their sisters suffer. One of them should watch mine.

But I don't because I deserve this.

I open the video—and immediately slam the space bar to pause it and squeeze my eyes shut.

I took my eyes off her when I knew she was in danger. I showed her those pictures of Ophelia's mutilated corps. She knew every bit of pain and terror that awaited her when she was taken. She must have fucking hated me at the end.

I reach for a cigarette, but Sienna's voice fills my head, reproaching me. I grab a garbage bag from the kitchen and throw out every pack of cigarettes and empty all the ashtrays. When there's not even a trace of ash left, I sit back down in front of my computer.

"I'm fucking sorry, princess."

I don't know how she'll forgive me. I'll never forgive myself.

I hit the space bar on my laptop.

And I open my eyes.

9

Chiara

"You watched the video?" I ask in a whisper.

It's been five solid minutes since Lorenzo stopped speaking. He drains his glass, and then sets it down and pours himself another two inches of vodka. He stares at the drink, his eyes black and hollow.

I glance at the other three around the table. We're sitting in Lorenzo's kitchen, and they all look as shattered as he does. For the last thirty minutes, we've listened to Lorenzo relate the whole blood-soaked, miserable story of what happened to his sister, and what he did for the four of them. I wonder how much of his sanity he sacrificed to protect the others. How many sleepless nights has he suffered, and how many sweat-soaked, heart-pounding nightmares has he been tormented by.

Cassius showed up not long after Lorenzo started talking, and he hasn't said a word. We meet each other's eyes, and there's no anger in his face. Only bleakness and sorrow.

I reach for him at the same time he reaches for me.

"I'm sorry—" I start to say, gripping his fingers.

He holds my hand even tighter. "No, *bambina*, no. I'm sorry. I'm ashamed of myself. Scava sat here calmly and told you everything and showed me what a disgrace I am."

Lorenzo picks up his glass of vodka, salutes Cassius ironically and drains it down.

"I made that night all about me," I whisper. "I wasn't thinking about what you've all been through." They relived their pain for me the night we played poker, and I just made them relive it again. A hurricane has blown through this kitchen, leaving us all dazed and bruised in its wake.

"She was surgically...She was alive when he..." Lorenzo glares down at the glass in his hands, his jaw flexing. His voice is a husky whisper. "It is you. Everything I wrote in that notebook since we met is about you. Every sick, twisted thing. My head is full of those videos, every day. The harder I try to push those memories away, the louder they scream. I can't make them stop. The only thing that helps is writing everything down."

Lorenzo slams the glass onto the table and pushes anguished hands through his hair.

"You're all I think about these days, princess. I didn't want to write that shit about you, but I couldn't stop myself."

I reach out with my other hand and slip my fingers into his. He looks at our hands in surprise. Me holding him, but him not holding me back.

"You don't have to touch me. I know your skin is fucking crawling."

I get up and go to Lorenzo, slip between his knees and sink down to the floor. I rest my cheek on his thigh and close my eyes.

One by one, the others stand up and leave the room.

"How can you bear to touch me?" he whispers between gritted teeth.

Between his thighs, I feel the safest I've ever been. There's nothing Lorenzo wouldn't do for the others. There's nothing he wouldn't do for me. Without him, there isn't a chance for us. "Please touch me."

We sit like that for a long time, Lorenzo's body rigid as iron. Then his forefinger touches my hair and slides through the tresses.

"You're fucking pretty," he says hoarsely. "You're so pretty it hurts. I'm scared what could happen to you."

His hand traces lightly down my face and his thumb caresses my lower lip. I reach out with my tongue and lick it, and he groans. The wet pad of his thumb rubs back and forth. I open my mouth and suck slowly up the length of him.

Lorenzo groans again. He reaches down and scoops me into his lap. Holding me like his princess. His pretty doll that fell on the floor.

I take his hand and press kisses to his palm, gazing at him with half-lidded eyes. "You can play with me. I won't break."

"I don't play nice."

I drop his hand and plant slow kisses on his jaw. "I can be nice for both of us."

"You really are killing me, princess," he says in a strangled voice. "I don't want you like this."

"Softly, you mean? Sweetly?"

He shakes his head, not even daring to look at me.

"How do you want me?"

"Stop tempting me," he growls, fisting my hair tightly. I stroke his face. The softness to his rage. "You won't like it and I don't want to hurt you. I already feel like shit enough as it is."

He *feels*.

He pretends to be so cold, but there are scars in his soul and they throb with pain.

"How, Lorenzo?" I whisper, pressing fluttering kisses to his jaw. "How do you want me?"

Lorenzo stands up suddenly and puts me on the table. There's a belt around his hips and he unbuckles it and loops it around my neck. With his other hand he pulls my underwear and my skirt roughly from my body.

Every breath drags against the leather around my throat. He squeezes it tight. "Are you starving for breath, princess?" He chokes me tighter as he explores my body, keeping me on a knife's edge. Looking me dead in the eye, he pushes one thick finger deep inside me, and then out again. "Or are you starving for me?"

Only for him.

He looks down at his hand and suddenly lets go of the belt, his eyes widening. "Oh, princess. You didn't say. Did you want this to be a surprise?"

"What?"

He holds his finger up, and it's covered in blood.

Oh, shit.

Oh, *shit*.

He turns his hand back and forth in the light and his middle finger glistens red with blood. I lost track of the days. God, this is so embarrassing. I think I'm going to burst into flames and blow away in the wind.

Lorenzo puts his finger in his mouth. And sucks.

I actually feel my soul leave my body. "*Lorenzo—*"

He pulls his finger from his lips with a wet pop. "What? Quit squealing in my ear."

He scoops me up in his arms and carries me toward the stairs, shouting to the house in general, "Nobody get stabbed or shot for the next hour, or you can just fucking die."

I bury my face in his tattooed neck as he carries me, half moaning in horror and embarrassment, half laughing. The next thing I know is I'm being dumped on my bed and Lorenzo is standing over me while he takes his clothes off. T-shirt. Jeans. He's barefoot and he wasn't wearing underwear. With his hair falling into his glittering eyes, he palms the length of his cock and squeezes the swollen head.

"Should I tie you up again? No, fight me harder this time. I want some scratches." He grabs my T-shirt and pulls it off, his smile wicked. "But first I'm going down on you."

I slap his hands from my legs. "You are *not* going to do that."

"Perfect," he breathes, slipping between my thighs and pushing them apart with his knees. I'm on my back and completely naked. "You're fighting already. You can hit me if you want."

"I'm not going to hit you."

He braces a hand by my head and taps his cheek. "Come

on. After all I've done to you, you must be dying to smack me in the face."

I reach up and shove his shoulder. "There, are you happy?"

Lorenzo's grin is devilish. "Come on, slap me. Like in the old movies. A good, sharp crack like I'm lowlife scum who's just manhandled the pristine mayor's daughter."

"And you'll be satisfied with that?"

"Fuck, no. But it's a start."

"You shoved a knife between my thighs the night of my seventeenth birthday. You deserve more than a slap."

His eyes glint with malice. "I should have shoved the whole fucking handle right inside you. I should have fucked you with it until you—"

I pull back my hand and slap him hard across the face, and his head snaps to the side.

Lorenzo turns back to me with a hiss. "Hell yeah, princess. Now we're getting somewhere." He holds a fist in front of my face. "Make your hand into a fist, like this. Punch with your first two knuckles and hit me. Hard. I want to bleed, too."

"You're crazy. I'm not going to punch you in the face."

For starters, I've never punched anyone in my life. Second of all, he's gorgeous. What if I break his nose or give him a black eye?

Knowing Lorenzo, he wouldn't care. He'd probably wear an injury like a badge of honor.

"Do it. Punch me in the face."

I grab his shoulders. "How is this foreplay? I thought you wanted to have sex!"

"Come on, hit me! Just fucking hit me! If you don't punch

me right this second then I'll call Cassius in here to punch my teeth out. So, it's either he does it, or you do it."

We glare at each other with narrowed eyes. He wouldn't. One hard punch from Cassius would fuck him up and he's the only damn doctor here. I picture Cassius calmly rolling up his sleeve, drawing his arm back and smashing his massive fist into Lorenzo's mouth.

Lorenzo takes a deep breath and shouts, "Cass—!"

Panic shoots through me. I pull back my arm and let him have it. My knuckles sink into the middle of his face.

"*Jesus, fuck!*" he roars, reeling back and grabbing his nose. Blood spurts between his fingers.

I clap my hands over my face. "Holy shit. Are you okay?"

Lorenzo sits on his haunches, my legs around his thighs. He lets his head fall back as blood drips down his lips and chin and over his chest, decorating his tattoos, his eyes closed in bliss. His dick is hard, and a drop of blood lands on the shiny head.

"Lorenzo? Are...you okay?"

Lorenzo cracks one eye open. "Fuck, yes. That was the hottest thing that's ever happened to me." He smiles like a devil and dives down between my legs. "Let's get this blood everywhere."

The first swipe of his tongue against my clit has me forgetting all about telling him not to, it's gross, he shouldn't. It's hard to be squeamish about my blood getting on his face when he's already covered in his own.

I reach up and grasp the headboard, my eyes closing and my thighs wrapping around his head. "Doesn't your face —*ah*—hurt?"

He thrusts two fingers deep inside me and groans.

"Aching. Fuck, princess, I can't tell what's blood and what's you getting wet."

Lorenzo sits up and swipes his forearm over his face, smearing blood across his cheek. Fresh blood trickles from his nose and over his lips as he grasps his cock, smacks it once, twice on my clit, and then sinks into me.

I yelp at the shock of his first thrust and grab the sheets. "Am I allowed to touch you this time, or will you blow my brains out if I lift my hands?"

He grins, showing bloodstained teeth. He looks absolutely feral. "Why don't you find out?"

I run my fingertips up his chest, tracing the tattoos. Across his Adam's apple. His jaw. His perfect lips. I pull my hand back and slap him again. Hard.

Lorenzo squeezes his eyes shut and groans. I can't tell if it's in pain or pleasure. Every few thrusts, a fresh drop of his blood spatters onto my breasts, and he drags his fingers through them.

He flips me over, slides an arm under my hips and hauls them up. "Arch that back. I want to fuck you deep."

I brace my forearms on the bed and spread my knees wide. He plunges into me, gloriously deep and fast.

I hold up my arm and show him my wrist. "That bite mark you gave me has faded."

Lorenzo leans over me and his heated tongue slides against the side of my throat. "You asking for another, princess?"

I want his mouth on me. I want him to give me marks and wounds like I've been into battle so I can wear them with pride.

His teeth sink into the flesh between my neck and

shoulder as his hand reaches down between my legs to work my clit with his fingers, fast and rough.

I scream as loud as I can, and the pain and shock tip me over the precipice I've been riding. My head arches back and I press back into his cock as I climax hard, his teeth sinking deeper and deeper.

With a growl, he releases me. Lorenzo flips me face up, sits back, and runs his tongue over his bloodstained teeth as he pumps his cock up and down with his hand. His gaze fastens on my bitten throat. "That's going to last. I'll freshen it up any time you like."

My eyes drop to his cock. It's covered in blood. So is his hand. So am I, and the sheets. We're both a sticky mess and the scent of blood is heavy in the air. "You look really hot when you do that."

"Yeah? Wait till you see me nut." He walks his knees up my body until he's straddling my waist. "Hold those pretty tits together, princess. I'm going to shoot my load all over them."

I do as he says, scooping my breasts together watching the thick head of his cock as he works it up and down in his fist. He's so close that his body is radiating heat and his cheeks are flushed red.

"Lorenzo. The next time we fuck, I want all four of you."

Lorenzo's eyes suddenly open wide and he tries to say something, but then groans and thick ribbons of cum shoot all over me.

I arch my back and smile in satisfaction as his hand slows on his cock.

Lorenzo grasps my jaw, still breathing hard. "Do you mean that? All of us?"

I glance down at the creamy cum covering my breasts, mingling with his blood. "You seem to like the idea."

He collapses down next to me on the bed. "It's all I've been jerking off to for months. Salvatore sent us an essay about spanking your pussy in his car, and I couldn't stop thinking about the pretty girl who soaked right through her panties on her seventeenth birthday."

Those goddamn group texts. I need a phone so I can gossip about their dicks to each other and see how they like it.

I roll my eyes. I bet they'd love it.

Lorenzo has one of his arms flung over his head and his eyes are closed. I edge closer and drape an arm lightly over his belly. Immediately, he sits up and tries to get out of bed, but I tighten my hold on him.

"Please, stay here. Just for a few minutes."

Lorenzo looks at the bitemark on my shoulder. There's blood all over me and my hand is aching. "Go shower. Get a hug from Cassius or something."

I don't need Cassius right now. I don't need Lorenzo, either.

He needs me.

I remember what he said after I couldn't kill Dad. That I should be grateful merely for going on breathing, but that isn't a life. I trace the tattoos decorating Lorenzo's chest. "If I die tomorrow, I want to know that I lived today, even if I do end up buried in a shallow, unmarked grave."

"If you talk about dying one more time I really will lock you up in a cage," he growls.

"It's not your fault," I whisper, stroking his hair back

from his face. "It's not Vinicius', or Cassius', or Salvatore's either."

"I can't keep up with you. Are we talking about you, or me?"

"We're talking about everything."

Lorenzo presses the heels of his hands to his eyes. He stays like that a long time. "After I finished watching those videos and getting tattooed, I bought my knife. I swore to Sienna that I'd use it to kill whoever murdered her."

He drops his hands and stares at the ceiling.

"That was nine years ago, princess. I watched those videos and I didn't learn anything. Whoever killed our sisters is still walking around, and it's my fucking fault."

10

Vinicius

"Wow. You look like shit." I cast my eyes over Lorenzo as he steps out of the elevator at Cassius' penthouse. There's a black bruise under his left eye and the bridge of his nose is swollen. He has an arm draped around Chiara's shoulders. She's wearing a scoop necked top that reveals a bitemark between her neck and shoulder.

Lorenzo grins lazily at me. "Fuck you, pretty boy."

I hold out my arms to Chiara and she comes over to me for a kiss. "Did you mess him up, kitten? I'm proud of you."

She glances at Lorenzo with a bashful smile. "It was either I punch him, or he was going to make Cassius do it."

Behind us, Cassius comes over with glasses of white wine

and passes them out. "What's that? I get to punch Scava?" He cracks his knuckles. "Let's do this."

Chiara laughs and covers his fist with her hand. "Leave him alone. He's had enough."

The elevator pings again, and Salvatore emerges with bags of takeout. Chiara finally gets her wish for Chinese food on the sofa, and we're doing it at Cassius' penthouse, just like the first time.

A few minutes later, Chiara is snuggled in Cassius' lap while he feeds her slices of beef and peppers with his chopsticks.

Salvatore helps himself to kung pao chicken, shaking his head. "You two are adorable."

"Yeah, it's disgusting," Lorenzo says around a mouthful of Singapore noodles.

Chiara turns to him with a smile. "Don't be jealous. I'll sit in your lap next."

I'm expecting that to draw another sarcastic remark from Lorenzo, but he glances at her, all cute and snuggled up in Cassius' lap, and then glares down into his box of noodles. Like he's disconcerted. Even flustered.

"But I'm not done with you, *bambina*," Cassius says, slipping a possessive arm around her waist.

She turns back to him and plants a kiss on his nose. The two of them didn't speak for days, but since hearing Lorenzo's story and Cassius' stricken apology, she seems to have forgiven him. It's hard to stay angry with someone when you understand their pain.

I guess that's all she wanted. To understand him. I shove a dumpling into my mouth and chew moodily. Who would have thought that Cassius and Lorenzo would ever spill their guts to a woman? Salvatore hasn't told her much about himself, either, but I have the uncomfortable feeling of being left behind. Is this what Cassius felt like when he saw Lorenzo taking Chiara's virginity when he thought he had more time?

Yeah. I hate it.

As we're eating, Cassius announces, "I have some news. I have a new gentlemen's club opening tomorrow night."

"I thought City Hall said you couldn't open any more strip clubs," Salvatore says. "You're lowering the tone of Coldlake, I hear."

Cassius makes a disgusted noise. "My girls raise the tone of this city. The prudish *bastardos* down at City Hall can shove their permits up their asses. Anyway, let's all go."

"Me as well?" Chiara asks in surprise.

"Of course, *bambina*."

Salvatore pauses, his chopsticks halfway to his mouth. "No. Out of the question. Cassius, go by yourself, or take Vinicius. Lorenzo and I will stay in and look after Chiara."

Cassius' nostrils flare. "You think I can't keep my woman safe in my own club? Security is going to be tighter than the assholes at City Hall. With the four of us surrounding her, what's going to happen?"

A new club opening means the best and brightest of the criminal underworld will be there. People who want to stay in our good books because it's good for business. Cassius' clubs are always stunning, and he wants to show them off to his girl. I'd love to see her there, too, all dressed up. All ours.

"I'll happily go with you, Cassius, but I don't see any reason why Chiara can't come, too."

Salvatore sits up and glares at me. "No reason? No reason? The mayor put a price on all our heads."

I shrug. "Since when do we care about things like that?"

"We care about Chiara," Salvatore growls. "Or we're *supposed* to."

I put my box of noodles down. "Salvatore, don't be an asshole. We all care about Chiara, but it's going to be a long, boring life for her if we never take her anywhere or do anything because we're afraid of someone snatching her away from us."

"Didn't you all discuss this before you agreed to share one woman?" Chiara asks. "I thought that was the whole reason we were doing this. We get to live our lives because I have four insane bodyguard boyfriends."

I smile at her. "Exactly, kitten, and we agreed that we wouldn't let our overprotectiveness stop us from doing what we always do."

"That was before we snatched the Princess of Coldlake from right under her father's nose," Salvatore snarls. "We thought we were going to try this with an ordinary girl."

"What would we do with ordinary?" Cassius says, wiping noodle sauce from the corner of Chiara's mouth with his thumb.

Salvatore glances at Lorenzo. "You're not saying anything. What do you think about this?"

Lorenzo seems more interested in the food and rips a plastic lid from a box. "I haven't been out in forever. Chiara looks hot as shit in her cute dresses. Let's go and show her off, and we'll rub the mayor's nose in how much we don't give a fuck about his bounties. Princess, I've got your soup dumplings here."

He passes them over and watches her eat them. A weight has been lifted from him the last few days. Putting himself through hell for her has changed him. Cassius has softened up like butter since he unburdened himself as well. Whereas Salvatore is tense and snappish, and I feel a prickle of guilt every time I remember the lies I've told Chiara. A prickle that's quickly becoming a stab.

Salvatore sits back and folds his arms, scowling deeply. "Fine. But she's taking a weapon."

"I already thought of that." Cassius reaches over to the side table and picks up a box tied with a ribbon. "I got you this, *bambina*."

Inside the box is a small, pearl handled revolver. She takes it out and turns it over in her hand. "It's actually quite pretty. Thank you."

"It's small enough to put in your purse," Cassius points out. "This way, you'll be armed wherever you go in my club."

"Oh, I don't have a purse. Vinicius and I forgot to buy any."

Cassius lifts a carry bag from next to the sofa that reads Balenciaga, and gives Chiara another kiss. "I thought of that, too."

Lorenzo rolls his eyes. "You're so fucking soft it makes me sick."

I kick his leg. "You're just jealous no one ever buys you presents."

"I'll buy you presents, Lorenzo," Chiara says, smiling in delight as she takes out a small red handbag. Lorenzo digs in his box of noodles like he's hunting down the last prawn, but there's a smile tugging the corner of his lips.

You're his present, kitten.

You're all our presents.

Cassius' new club is called Topaz. It's in a popular new area of the city that until recently was the meatpacking district. From the outside, it looks like a nightclub, with a rope in front of the door, bouncers, and a long queue of people waiting to get in.

The five of us pull up in a limousine and step out onto the opening night red carpet. Is it arrogant to show up so ostentatiously in public when there's a price on all our heads and news of this will spread all over the city in the morning? Yes.

Do we care?

Not a fucking bit.

I hope the mayor interprets this as the *fuck you* it's meant to be.

Cassius leads the way and loops Chiara's arm through his. "I've wanted to walk into one of my clubs with you since we met, *bambina*."

Tall, imposing Cassius draws enough stares of his own, but with Chiara on his arm in that stunning red dress, everyone is looking at them. The three of us are close behind them, watching anyone who gets too close to Chiara and sending them back with hard looks.

Inside, the décor is upscale, more like a five-star hotel than a strip club. Girls in long, tight dresses carry trays of drinks and Cassius' acquaintances—rich businessmen, rich criminals, their girlfriends and sugar babies—sit clustered in booths and at tables. Cassius leads us to a room decked out in shades of topaz, chandeliers dripping from the ceiling, and even more tables and booths. A catwalk runs down the center of the room where three stunning women perform.

They are athletic and flexible, at the top of their game in nothing but G-strings and smiles.

We head up to the VIP bar, where Cassius and Salvatore are quickly swamped by business associates wanting to talk to them. They stay close by while I find a table for Chiara, Lorenzo, and myself that overlooks the main room.

"Drink?" I ask her and Lorenzo.

"Just lemonade for me," Chiara says, and Lorenzo shakes his head. He's glaring at everyone in the bar like they're about to attack his woman. When he's satisfied that no one's secretly an assassin, he goes and strikes up a conversation with the bouncer by the door. They seem to know each other, so perhaps Cassius hired some extra muscle from Strife for tonight.

Once I have a Negroni and Chiara has a lemonade, I ask, "So what do you think of your first strip club?"

Chiara's eyes are wide and shining as she gazes down at the catwalk where the women are dancing. "It's incredible. I didn't think strip clubs were like this. I thought they all had sticky carpet and served nothing but beer."

"A lot of them do. I should take you to the stripper room at Strife sometime. It's downscale, but it's fun as hell."

She leans forward and whispers, "But Salvatore wouldn't like that."

Then she winks at me.

A smile spreads over my face. Little minx.

Chiara plays with the straw in her drink. "But seriously, I hope it didn't upset Salvatore too much to hear Cassius and Lorenzo talk about their sisters. The two of them seem so much more relaxed now." Her eyes flick up to me. "What about you?"

"What about me?" But I say it too quickly. Suddenly I can feel my pulse beating in my throat. I glance around, wondering if it's Chiara making my stress shoot through the roof, or whether my subconscious is picking up on something.

My gaze lands on a man downstairs sitting in a booth next to the catwalk. He's watching the dancers and throwing bills onto the stage, saying something to the people he's sitting with that I'm too far away to catch. But I hear his voice just the same. *Smile, you dumb bitch. No one wants to screw you when you look so fucking miserable.*

Oh, I get it.

It's both.

I take a large gulp of my Negroni, still staring at the man. After all these years, he's still breathing. He dares to go on fucking breathing.

"Vinicius? What's wrong?"

I open my mouth, close it again, and then look away. It's my fault. After Amalia was killed, I forgot all about him. I guess he forgot about me, too, or he wouldn't have dared to come to one of Cassius' clubs. I glance at Lorenzo standing a few feet away. One text message to him, and he'd go down to that booth and cover the dancefloor with that piece of shit's blood. I know he's got his knife on him.

Lorenzo's the best friend I've ever had. He'd do that for me in a heartbeat.

But that would ruin Cassius' opening night and upset Chiara. Now I know he's still in Coldlake, Lorenzo and I can follow him home and murder him in private.

"Nothing. I don't want to spoil our evening. You look beautiful, kitten."

She puts her hand out and covers mine. "You couldn't ruin it by telling me what's on your mind. I feel like we never get to talk properly."

She wants a *proper* talk, about all the ugly things that I could polish away with a few untrue words and a smile. Isn't it better this way? Why speak of darkness and despair when I could make everything sound perfect as easily as snapping my fingers.

I gaze into her lovely face. Those wide blue eyes that don't hold an ounce of guile.

She knows.

Maybe not that I've been lying to her, but that I'm holding something back.

I run my thumb over the ridges of the crystal cocktail glass. "Kitten, do you know why I tell lies?"

Her brow wrinkles at this abrupt change of subject. "I presume it's so you can get ahead in business. You don't like using muscle or threats, so you trick people."

"But why do I lie to you?"

Her face falls slightly. She didn't know I did until just now.

"Habit?" she guesses with a sad smile.

Not exactly.

I gesture at myself. My clothes. My grooming. My carefully cultivated air of arrogance and indifference. "I didn't always look like this."

"Vinicius, were you an ugly duckling? That's nothing to be ashamed of, and looks aren't everything."

"Oh, no. I was an adorable little boy and a cute teenager before growing into the Adonis that you see before you today."

Chiara rolls her eyes and smiles. "I bet you never even had a zit. I hate you."

"A zit wouldn't dare appear my face." The smile fades from my lips. "I mean I was hungry. Dirty. Invisible. What Lorenzo described about his own childhood? That was luxurious compared to mine."

"So the story about you and your sister being rich kids from an old crime family...?"

"I lied a lot that day. And then I lied about lying to you. Do you hate me, yet?"

Chiara gazes at me for a long time. "I don't think it's fair to ask me that when you haven't given me an explanation, and you haven't said sorry. Is it because you're ashamed that you and Amalia grew up poor?"

How I wish it were that simple. I stand up and take her hand, helping her to her feet. We step onto the mezzanine overlooking the catwalk.

"I've just seen an old friend," I say softly, but with malice. I nod at a man downstairs at a booth in a tuxedo with thinning hair, an oily smile, and a gold ring on his pinkie.

Lorenzo steps closer to see who we're looking at, and he makes a hiss of anger and starts toward the stairs.

I put my hand on his shoulder and stop him. "Not now. Not yet."

Lorenzo gives me a long, hard look, and then draws back and leans against the mezzanine and folds his arms, his expression cold and furious.

I put my arms around Chiara and stand behind her. "I'm going to tell you a story, kitten, and while I do, you and I are going to keep an eye on that man down there."

"Who is he?"

With my lips against her ear, I whisper, "That's what my story is about. Once, long ago, in a faraway city called Cold-lake, lived a brother and a sister. You with me so far, kitten?"

She nods and places her hands on the mezzanine rail.

"They were twins, and they did everything together. Sometimes they felt like they could read each other's minds. The home they lived in was scary and volatile. Their parents fought. Their father was brutal, but they had each other. That's all that mattered until they were old enough to go to school. When the teachers noticed bruises on the brother and sister, everything changed. The twins were taken away from the parents and split up."

Chiara gives a soft cry of dismay.

"The boy went to one foster home and the girl to another. The boy searched for his sister all over Coldlake, but he couldn't find her anywhere. Years and years went by, until the boy's best friend, Lorenzo, heard about a very beautiful girl called Angel who was working in a brothel in the southwest."

"Amalia Angeli," Chiara whispers.

"The brothel was owned by a man who wouldn't let Amalia go. She owed him money, and she was going to work for him until she'd paid off her debt. He'd taken her in when she was fifteen and homeless and given her a heroin habit. Isn't that kind?"

Chiara stiffens in my arms and clutches my wrists. "She wasn't made to do sex work at fifteen, was she?"

I give a mirthless laugh. "Kitten, do you know how much money you can make from a beautiful fifteen-year-old who'll do anything for her next hit?"

By the time I found Amalia, she was twenty years old and

had been ravaged by drugs and countless men. She was so out of it that she didn't recognize me when I walked in. She thought I was a client. When she finally realized it was me, she sobbed and pushed me away, telling me not to look at her. She was so ashamed.

"Seeing the hell that Cassius and Lorenzo put themselves through telling you the truth makes me feel like a lowlife piece of shit that I lied to you about anything."

Chiara turns in my arms and takes my face between her hands. "I don't care about the lies. I'm so sorry this happened, Vinicius."

I try to go on but my throat is locked up. How the fuck did Lorenzo get through his whole, horrible story? I didn't even say the worst part yet.

"Amalia...Amalia's head was so messed up with drugs and beatings that she refused to leave with me even though I could pay off her debt. That was the only life she knew and the world was terrifying to her. I went back to that brothel again and again, hoping to convince her to trust me, but all I did was lead the killer to her brothel."

I didn't know that he was watching me. None of us knew. Ophelia was killed, and I was so wrapped up in my own despair that it didn't occur to me that what happened to pristine, perfect Ophelia could befall my wretched, unhappy twin.

A few days later, she was gone.

"Did you love your sister?" Chiara murmurs, stroking my hair back from my face.

I nod, reaching up to cover her hands in mine.

"Do you miss her every day?"

My brow creases in pain and I nod again.

"Then you told me the truth." Chiara puts her hands on my shoulders and presses her mouth to mine. She tastes like forgiveness. She tastes like hope. Her kiss is the sweetest thing I've ever known.

I break away. "Where I came from—who I was—"

She presses a finger over my lips. "You didn't want me to think of you as anything but perfect. I never believed that the Vinicius I held in my arms began and ended there, with a witty remark and a Prada suit."

I groan and my arms come around her, holding her tight against my chest.

Her whisper is so soft that only I can hear her. "I've witnessed Salvatore's savage cruelty along with his honor. Cassius' vicious temper and his sweetness. Lorenzo's brutality and his courage. Whoever you are, I want all of you, too."

"Will you stay up here with Lorenzo? I have to do something."

She gazes at me solemnly. "You're going to talk to that man? Then I'm coming with you. So is Lorenzo."

Behind her, Lorenzo gives a sharp nod.

Downstairs, Chiara and I approach the table with Lorenzo behind us. I recognize the men Flavio Ricci is sitting with. Two of them owe me money. I jerk my head to the side, telling them to get lost, and they scramble out of their seats.

Chiara and I sit down, and Ricci's expression changes from confused, to shocked, to fearful. All of which he tries to mask with a quick smile. He realizes there's someone standing behind him and turns to see Lorenzo. The smile dies on his face. "I thought the syndicate had fallen apart. How...how wonderful it is to see you're still friends."

I gaze at him in silence. I suppose that's why he thought it was safe to come here tonight. Cassius wouldn't recognize him, but Lorenzo and I do.

We'd know him anywhere.

"And who is this beautiful creature?" he asks, gazing at Chiara.

Lorenzo produces his knife from inside his jacket and sticks the point into the side of Ricci's neck, not quite hard enough to break the skin. "Look at her again and I'll slit your fucking throat."

Ricci holds up his hands and turns back to me. His brow is suddenly damp with sweat. "Gentlemen, I meant no offence. Mr. Ferragamo would be upset if we caused trouble."

"Then why don't you leave?" I suggest.

Lorenzo twists the knife a little, and then lowers it and steps back.

Ricci licks his lips. While he's in here, he's safe. Or he thinks he is, anyway. "After all these years, we should be able to be friends. We're both businessmen."

I take a gun out of my jacket and lay it on the table in front of me. "Sure. Best of friends."

Ricci stares at the gun, his jaw working.

"How are you making your money these days, Ricci? We shut your hovel of a whorehouse down years ago, and yet here you are, throwing bills at strippers like you have money to burn."

"I have, ah, business interests."

"My friend Cassius will be interested to know if you're running brothels or strip clubs in this city without his permission." I doubt that Ricci would ever get his permission. Cassius expects working girls to be over eighteen, to work by choice, and to be paid properly, not forced into it with drugs and threats.

I smile and touch my tongue to one of my pointed canines. "Actually, that's a lie." I turn to Chiara. "Sorry, kitten, I just keep telling lies, don't I?"

Chiara is gazing at Ricci like he's something disgusting she's stepped in. "I don't mind if you lie to him."

I turn back to Ricci. "What do you think? Am I terrible person?"

Ricci glances between us, clearly wondering if this is a trick question. He gives me a weak smile. "I don't care if the lady doesn't."

"But I care," I say, pressing a hand to my heart and leaning toward him. "I mustn't tell lies. It's a dirty habit. Cassius doesn't care if you're running a brothel without his permission."

"He...doesn't?" Ricci asks, hopefully.

"Cassius doesn't care what dead men do."

Ricci turns white.

Pure rage floods my veins. How many girls are suffering right now in his whorehouses?

Suddenly, there's a commotion in the front bar. Lorenzo and Chiara turn toward it, but I keep my gaze fixed on Ricci.

The music cuts out and there are shouts of, "Police! Everyone stay where you are."

Someone's called the cops on Cassius' opening night. It's so hard to run an illegal club these days.

A moment later, a dozen uniformed cops burst into the room. Everyone panics and jumps out of their seats.

Ricci tries to flee, but Lorenzo grabs a fistful of his hair and he shouts in pain.

I pick up my gun. "We should go. Lorenzo, perhaps there's a way Ricci could help us get Chiara out of here safely?"

Our eyes meet. Lorenzo understands me perfectly.

He hauls the man to his feet, turns him toward the cops, and drives his knife into the man's throat. I grab Chiara and kiss her so she doesn't see the blood spray all over the ground and the nearby people. It's too much like the way her mother was killed.

Ricci gurgles in shock, and slumps slowly to the ground. Lorenzo stands there for a moment, arm raised high with blood dripping from his knife as the cops stare at him in shock.

There are screams as everyone panics. The cops are on one side and a knife-wielding murderer on the other. The cops seem frozen in place by the unexpected deluge of blood on the club floor.

I take Chiara's hand in mine and whisper, "Run."

There's a side entrance that a dozen people are trying to force their way through, but Chiara has another idea.

"No! This way. Come on, Lorenzo," she says, jumping up onto the catwalk and pulling me up after her. We dash along the stage and through the performer's door. There's a dressing room with half a dozen girls wearing not many clothes and they stare at us as we weave through them.

By a door marked *Exit*, we stop and catch our breath.

"Where's Lorenzo?" she asks, chest heaving.

I don't know, but Lorenzo would want me to get Chiara

safely out of here, not wait for him. I clasp her hand and pull open the door.

Beyond is a deserted alleyway, poorly lit and silent. There are a couple of dumpsters and puddles of water.

I send a text message to the others, and the driver of the limousine. *Back entrance. I've got Chiara.*

I take her hand. "They'll meet us out on the street as soon as they can. Come on."

As I step through, a figure moves in my peripheral vision. Before I can turn and push Chiara back inside, something smacks me up the side of my head.

Hard.

I stagger and my vision goes white.

There's ringing in my ears. My gun goes skittering off across the wet concrete and I fall to my knees with a groan.

My head will clear in a second.

It'll clear.

But my head doesn't clear, and I can't stand up.

"Thought that would work," says a slow, deep voice. "A call to the cops and I've flushed one fancy piece of shit onto the street already."

"Vinicius!" Chiara hurries over to me. I feel my head, and my hand comes away sticky with blood. Where's Lorenzo? Fuck, I'm the only one with Chiara and I'm going to pass out and leave her all alone.

This was exactly what was never meant to happen.

Fuck.

Fuck.

Fuck.

Over her shoulder, an enormous man covered in tattoos holding a baseball bat walks slowly toward us.

"Get away from here. Go. *Now.*" I try to push her away and I leave bloody handprints on her legs. She needs to run or she's going to die with me.

"But I can't leave you here," Chiara says desperately.

"One million dollars for me. My slate wiped clean," says the man. He drags the baseball bat across the ground as he approaches us. His face swims in my vision. All I can make out is his grin, but he looks vaguely familiar. "Dope."

Chiara seems suddenly electrified. She stands up slowly and stares at the man who's spoken. "What did you just say?"

The man steps into the light. He's wearing a muscle tee and there are scars and tattoos across his shoulders.

Oh, shit.

Not him.

Where the fuck are the others?

His brow pinches together. "Do I know you, bitch?"

She shakes her head. "I knew a friend of yours. He was going to introduce us last year."

"Why would a friend of mine want me to meet some little whore who runs with this cocksucker?"

My head is pounding so hard I can barely follow the conversation. I slump to my hands and knees, struggling to keep my eyes open.

Chiara gives him a pitying look. "Some little whore? I didn't think the leader of the Geaks would be so stupid."

How the hell does Chiara know that's Jax?

"Wait. I've got something in my bag that might help you remember me." She digs around in her purse and comes out with her gun. She aims right at Jax's head. Her feet are planted wide. Her hands are steady. She's got her eyes fixed on the target.

She's remembered everything I taught her.

Jax sneers at the tiny pistol in Chiara's hands, and then at her. Idiot. She may be small, but she packs a punch.

"A few weeks ago, you nearly killed Acid. Nine years ago, you beat a stripper to death just because she worked for Lorenzo. Last year you tried to murder me. You've smacked one of my boyfriends nearly unconscious, and to insult me even more, I'm standing right in front of you and you *don't even know who I am.*"

Jax gives a mirthless laugh. "Who the fuck are you?"

"I'm the Princess of Coldlake, asshole."

Chiara pulls the trigger. The sound of the gunshot ricochets around the alleyway. Jax's head snaps back, a bullet lodged right between his eyes. He falls to the ground, his face with wide, staring eyes just inches from mine.

Chiara just killed the leader of the Geaks.

All by herself.

"That's my fucking girl," I wheeze.

And then I pass out.

11

Cassius

Scava, Salvatore and I crash through the door into the alley and skid to a halt as we survey the two bodies at Chiara's feet. My heart thuds in panic as I see her with a gun in her hand. She's all alone in the alley. Anything could have happened.

Salvatore steps forward and examines the blood matted in Vinicius' hair. "I know he can be a dick sometimes, but please tell me you didn't shoot Vinicius."

"He passed out. I only shot Jax," she says, nodding at the other man.

I stare at the other body. She *only* shot and killed the leader of the most notorious gang in the city. There's a bullet hole right between his eyes. That man had nine lives, but I guess he underestimated the petite blonde in a red dress.

I step forward and put my hands on her shoulders. "*Bambina*, are you all right?"

She drops the gun back into her purse. "I'm fine. Is Vinicius okay?"

Scava swallows hard, looking from Vinicius' unconscious body to Chiara. "I was fighting with the cops, and when I looked around, you and Vinicius had disappeared. I should have been with you. I'm so sorry, princess."

She shakes her head and smiles at him. "I wasn't going to let him take Vinicius."

Scava hauls the unconscious Vinicius over his shoulder and carries him down the alleyway. We leave Jax where he is for the police to find and get into the waiting limousine.

I stare at Chiara as we drive, searching for any sign that her hands are shaking or she's going to cry. But she's sitting up straight, more worried about Vinicius than about herself. He has his head in her lap and he's bleeding on her dress as she gently strokes his forehead.

"It was what Jax said," she whispers. "*Dope*. He said it on the phone when I was with Griffin last year, and I recognized him right away."

I pass a shaking hand over my mouth.

"Cassius? Are you all right?"

"No. I'm not fucking all right. If you get into trouble we're supposed to save you. You're not meant to save *us*."

"Don't be angry with Vinicius, please. It's not his fault."

"It's my fault," Scava says. "I got distracted by Flavio Ricci and all I could think about was killing him. Vinicius and I shouldn't have taken Chiara downstairs with us."

Salvatore's eyes narrow. "Who's that? The name sounds familiar."

Does it? I can't place him.

"The asshole who ran the brothel that Amalia was working in," Scava says.

"In my club?" I growl. "Jesus fucking Christ."

Chiara touches my clenched fist. "He's dead now, and I'm fine. I just hope Vinicius is going to be all right."

"Don't worry, I'll get him back on his feet," Scava says, but he's frowning at his friend and takes a deep breath. "If he needs a brain scan, I know a technician I can scare into keeping his mouth shut."

I stroke my knuckles over Chiara's cheek. "You were perfect, *bambina*. But the police at my club opening, *inferno del cazzo*," I seethe. City Hall has never done this to me before, the bunch of pricks.

"Jax called them. He wanted you all to come rushing out so he could claim the reward from the cops." Chiara bites her lip as she gazes at me. "Two dead bodies at your club opening, Cassius. I'm sorry you didn't get to enjoy yourself."

I don't know about that. I've wanted Jax dead for a long time, and from what Scava has told me, Ricci should have been dead long ago.

Chiara gazes down at Vinicius. "Poor Amalia. She was just fifteen when she was forced into sex work. Vinicius told me everything."

I take a deep breath and let it out slowly. Yet another dark and blood-soaked story heaped upon Chiara's shoulders. "You shouldn't have to bear our misery, and you definitely shouldn't have to shoot our enemies when it's our job to protect you."

She smiles at me. "Cassius, don't you get it? Standing up

for all of you feels like standing up to my own father. No, even better than that. It's the best feeling in the world."

We all stare at her. All of us, except Vinicius. He sits up slowly, rubbing his head. "She called me her boyfriend in that alleyway. I win. You can all go home."

We shout over him, telling him we'll smack him unconscious again if he doesn't shut up. Laughing so hard she can barely talk, and relieved that he's awake, Chiara calls over the top of us, "I said you were *one* of my boyfriends, Vinicius."

At Scava's compound, he and I help Vinicius upstairs and lay him out on one of the spare beds. Chiara gets on the mattress with him and lays against Vinicius' side as Scava checks him over. He wipes the blood off his forehead and bandages it up, and then shines a pen light in and out of his eyes.

Salvatore is standing next to me, his arms folded. "Is he all right?"

"No, I'm dying," Vinicius moans.

Scava clicks the pen light out. "Goddamn drama queen. He'll be fine."

"Can I have a vodka?"

"No, you can't. Go to sleep."

Vinicius grumbles, rolls onto his side, and buries his face in Chiara's neck. A moment later, he falls asleep.

Chiara smiles and strokes his face. Speaking softly, she says, "He told me everything. All the things he hid from me because he was afraid I would think less of him if I knew the truth."

"Miserable fucking story," Scava mutters as he gets up off the bed.

"It was," she says. "But I'm still glad he told me."

Not in a million years would have I ever dreamed that Vinicius would tell anyone where he really came from, least of all a woman he cared about. He's never properly told me or Salvatore. We've had to piece it together from little things he's said over the years.

But he told Chiara, the girl he most dearly wants to think the world of him. Looking at the way she's gently stroking his face, I can see that Vinicius had nothing to worry about.

Scava gets to his feet.

I lean down and press my lips to Chiara's brow. "Will you sleep here?"

She nods, and I say goodnight. Then she captures my tie and pulls me back down to her. "I meant what I said in the limousine. Standing up to Jax makes me feel like I'm not so weak anymore. I couldn't have done it without you." She looks past me to Salvatore and Scava. "All of you."

I picture her in that alleyway, undefended, Vinicius nearly unconscious at her feet and Jax advancing on her with a baseball bat.

"Why aren't you saying anything?"

Behind me, I hear Salvatore and Scava leave the room and close the door behind them. Next to Chiara, Vinicius breathes slowly and deeply, his face boyish with sleep.

I take her face in my hands. "Are you ever going to stop trying to save us?"

Chiara smiles and shakes her head.

"That's..." Fuck, that's the sweetest thing I've ever heard. That's insanely hot, too. I picture her again standing in that alley with the gun in her hand, defending Vinicius' unconscious body.

She runs her fingers through my hair. "Cassius, did you like seeing me like that?"

I slant my mouth over hers. "I've never seen a woman look so strong before. I couldn't be prouder."

And it was so fucking sexy.

"Scava told us what you said to him the other day. The next time we have sex, you want it to be all of us."

Chiara covers her face with her hands and smiles. "I knew he'd tell you."

My guess is she wanted him to tell us.

Well, that can be arranged.

I give her one last kiss and then pull the blankets over her and Vinicius.

The other two are waiting outside the door for me. Salvatore raises an eyebrow at me. "You're proud of her?"

"Yes, I'm proud of her. Do you have a problem with that?"

Scava smirks at me. "I knew you would get over your old fashioned bullshit once you saw Chiara isn't a fragile flower."

I shove his shoulder with my fist. "Quit crowing, *stronzo*." I round on Salvatore and hold up a finger to his face. "Listen to me. When you tell Chiara about Ophelia, if you lose your temper with that girl, I'll thrash you so hard your ancestors will feel it."

Salvatore's eyes turn cold and he slaps my hand away. "What makes you think I'm ever going to talk about it?"

I have. Scava has. Even Vinicius, the last man in the world who enjoys speaking the painful truth, has spilled his guts. I'd lay bets that Salvatore will be telling Chiara everything within a week.

"You two quit snarling at each other," Scava says, pushing us apart. "I have to get down to Strife. The Geaks will be going crazy now that Jax is dead. Acid and the others will be the first ones they try and get revenge from."

"We'll stay here," Salvatore promises him. "But call me if you need back up."

"Remember when I used to get sleep?" Scava mutters as he stalks toward the stairs. "I fucking miss sleep."

Salvatore and I take turns through the night to check that Vinicius is still breathing and he's not bleeding from his head wound. We try not to wake Chiara, but she's sleeping lightly and opens her eyes every time I come in. On my second visit, I help her change into an oversized T-shirt and give her a damp cloth to wipe the makeup from her face.

Vinicius sleeps like a baby. He's the only one who does.

It's almost noon when I go into her room and find her still napping. "*Bella Addormentata*," I murmur, stroking her hair back from her face. *Sleeping Beauty.* "Are you going to sleep all day?"

"Mm? What time is it?" She reaches out for Vinicius and then sits up in a panic. "Where is he?"

"He's fine. He's been awake for an hour. He's eaten and he's having a shower. That skull of his is as thick as concrete."

She smiles and sinks back down onto the bed, stretching her arms up over her head as she yawns. Mid-yawn, she freezes, and her eyes open. "What's that music?"

There's a record playing downstairs, a slow, gentle tune. It was my idea. I don't want to hurt her by playing this song. I want to give her something precious, after everything she's given us.

"I can turn it off. We thought it might be a happy memory. Even though it made you cry."

Chiara sits up slowly and listens. Her eyes fill with tears. And then she smiles.

"It is. It's the happiest memory."

I help her out of bed and we walk downstairs hand in hand. Vinicius has wet hair and is sitting on the sofa in some of Scava's sweats and a T-shirt. Salvatore's been home to change into a fresh shirt and pants and is leaning against the door into the kitchen with his arms folded.

Scava is sitting next to the record player. He's had about two hours sleep and he's concealing a bandaged shoulder beneath his T-shirt, but he wouldn't miss this for the world. He glowers at Chiara and doesn't move as she comes toward him. She puts her hands on his shoulders and leans down to kiss his cheek. His eyes widen in surprise. A moment later his expression flattens once more. "What was that for?"

"To say thank you. You remembered."

"I didn't do anything," Scava mutters. "Cassius went out and got the record player this morning. Salvatore found the record. I'm just sitting here listening to a song."

But Chiara isn't fooled. While she was struggling after trying to kill her father, she told Scava about this song while he was watching over her. She smiles, and kisses his cheek again.

I put my hands on her waist and pull her into my arms. Her body sways against mine, and I close my eyes and dance with her.

"I'm sad your opening was spoiled. We didn't have much of a celebration last night."

I tilt her mouth up to mine and kiss her. "That's all right. Let's have it now."

Salvatore nods. "Good idea. I bought a load of old records I want to play. Who wants a drink?"

"Me," Vinicius says.

"Anyone but Vinicius."

"I'll have a vodka," I tell Salvatore, and Scava nods in agreement.

"I will, too," Chiara calls.

"You'll have yours with orange juice and a piece of toast," Salvatore tells her, and disappears into the kitchen.

"Vodka for breakfast," she says with a smile.

She drinks her vodka and orange juice and eats her toast while dancing barefoot around the living room to the records Salvatore plays, old doo-wop and pop hits from the sixties. She knows the words to them all and sings along.

I stand with my back against the wall, gazing at her carefree smile and her golden hair spilling down her back, sipping at her vodka and juice. What is this feeling deep in my chest? It's sweet but painful at the same time.

Chiara is dancing with Salvatore and Vinicius, pressed between them as Vinicius holds her hips and Salvatore her waist.

Why does it hurt to see her looking so happy?

"Cassius? Why do you look so serious?" She's got her cheek against Salvatore's chest and is gazing at me with wide, blue eyes.

"Because he's overthinking shit."

I glance at Scava in surprise. Perceptive motherfucker. "I was thinking how magnificent you looked last night in the alleyway."

Her face relaxes into a smile. It's not a lie. In that moment, we could have lost her. If I let myself fall, and love her with everything I have, it will completely destroy me to lose her, too.

It's not pain I'm feeling. It's an ache so sweet and strong like I've never felt before.

I look from one man to the next. I've been watching them closely these past few weeks and every single one of them feels the same way I do. She's reached inside us and she's holding on tight.

Chiara's laughing and asking Salvatore and Vinicius about the messages they've been sending about her. Salvatore pulls his phone from his pocket, unlocks it and passes it to her, and she reads aloud.

"*Salvatore: Were you two having sex, or were you murdering each other? Lorenzo: It's not sex unless it looks like a crime scene after.*" Chiara leans against him, laughing and looking at Scava. "It absolutely looked like a crime scene."

Vinicius points at his friend. "I've been by Lorenzo's side in a dozen fights and every time he's walked away without a scratch on him. Put him in bed with you and he looks like he stepped into the path of a semi-trailer."

Scava is silent in his armchair, thumbs jammed into his pockets. Anyone else might assume that he wasn't having a good time, but he's focused on Chiara. He's not fidgeting with his weapon or staring out the window. He wouldn't be anywhere else in the world.

Chiara smiles at him. "What can I say? I'm the Princess of Coldlake. A badass bitch with four badass boyfriends."

She disentangles herself from the other two and crosses the room to me. She puts her hands on my chest and smiles up at me, mischief dancing in her eyes.

Then she sinks down onto the carpet at my feet. "I have this fantasy."

Suddenly, the room is electrified.

"What's that, *bambina*?"

"Me. And all of you."

My heart thumps in my chest. "How does it start?"

"I'm down here on my knees. And I'm holding onto two of you. Touching two of you."

Vinicius was on the other side of the room, but via black magic he materializes at my side and smiles down at Chiara. "Hey."

"Hey," she replies, running her hands up both of our thighs. I swear we're both holding our breaths. "Why don't you take your shirts off?"

I unbutton my shirt and shrug out of it. So does Vinicius. Chiara splays her hands over both our stomachs and strokes us down over our belts and our thickening cocks.

Vinicius tips his head back and groans.

On the other side of the room, Scava and Salvatore are watching intently.

I reach for my belt, and undo my pants and get rid of them and my underwear, and Vinicius does the same. Chiara takes us each in her hand and runs her fingers up and down our lengths. We watch her, shoulder to shoulder, our chests lifting and falling with hard breaths.

She reaches out with her tongue and licks the tip of Vinicius' cock. And then mine. She encloses me in her wet, hot mouth and sucks slow and hard. Then she does the same to Vinicius, and I swear that I can feel it in my own dick as her cheeks hollow out around his.

Mio Dio. I'm in danger of losing it like a teenager and she's barely touched me.

With a determined expression, she takes my length in her mouth and pushes me deep. Her throat convulses and she coughs. "How do I do this without gagging?"

"You want me to teach you?" I ask, and she nods. There's a broad, flat ottoman in the middle of the room. "Take off your T-shirt and your panties. Go over to the ottoman and lie on your back."

She does as she's told, and I pull her up the ottoman until her head is hanging off the edge. We all stare at her, naked and bared to us.

I trail my fingers along her jaw. "Open your mouth, *bambina.*"

She does, and I slide my length into her mouth, all the way to her throat, and then out again. "Good girl," I whisper, and then push into her again, the angle letting her take so much more of me.

"Deeper, Cassius," Scava said, his bright gaze fixed on Chiara's arched neck.

I gather her hair in my hands and cradle her head, and then slowly thrust as far as I can.

Scava practically moans, "I can see you in her throat."

Vinicius crouches between her thighs, spreads her open, and takes a long lick all the way up her pussy until her toes curl. Chiara closes her eyes, one hand holding my hip and her other covering Vinicius' on her thigh.

The sunlight spills through the window, painting her body with golden light. I look up at Salvatore, Vinicius and Scava in turn.

Are you fucking see this?

They're seeing this. They can't look away.

Chiara suddenly giggles and pulls my cock from her lips. "Vinicius is licking my ass."

So he is. "Do you like it?"

"It's weird...I think I do."

"Would you like a finger in your ass, *bambina*?"

She runs her fingers slowly up and down my cock and smiles. "Do nice girls ask for a finger in their asses?"

"Ours would."

"Yes, please, Vinicius," she breathes.

Scava reaches behind his chair and throws a small bottle to Vinicius, who catches it and shows it to Chiara. It's lube.

Chiara peers past me to Scava. "Someone came prepared."

"He's a regular boy scout," Vinicius murmurs, applying lube to his finger.

Scava gives her a wicked smile and a three-finger salute.

Vinicius looks like he's rubbing his finger slowly over her asshole. Suddenly, Chiara breathes in sharply and closes her eyes, and goes back to sucking my cock in long, languorous strokes.

Vinicius bites his lip, gazing at her, enraptured, as he pumps his finger slowly in and out of her. "You feel amazing, kitten. Jesus Christ."

Salvatore slowly undresses, and then hunkers down beside Chiara and cups her head with his hand. Her blonde tresses spill over his fingers, and he strokes her throat, her breasts, her stomach.

"Baby, you're so beautiful. Do you love us touching you?"

Chiara doesn't open her eyes, but her brows draw

together and she nods emphatically. Salvatore slowly rubs her clit and then curves his fingers inside her sex.

"We're in your mouth. In your pussy. In your ass. We're everywhere, baby. But this is just the start. You know we love to fuck you."

Vinicius leans forward and works her clit with his tongue, and Chiara sucks harder on my cock and her breathing deepens.

"Cassius is teaching you how to take all his cock," Salvatore murmurs. "Vinicius is showing you how good it feels to give us your ass. I'm telling you how beautiful you look with three men getting deep inside your body. And Lorenzo...who the fuck knows what Lorenzo has planned but I can see from here that his dick is hard and he's not going to be sitting in that chair much longer. Show him how pretty you look when you come with the three of us fucking you in three holes."

Chiara makes an urgent noise, her back flexes and the three of us hammer her fast with our fingers and cock. As she comes, I push myself all the way to the back of her throat. No gag reflex. Just all of me deep in her mouth.

Vinicius groans as he sits up. "I could feel your ass clenching on my finger as you came." He casts a heated glance at Salvatore. "Kitten, why don't you turn over and show us how pretty you look sitting on Salvatore's cock?"

"Let's go up to my room," Scava says, getting to his feet.

"There's plenty of room here," I tell him, pulling out of her mouth.

Scava is already heading for the door. "There's a mirror in my room."

Good point. I scoop Chiara up in my arms and carry her upstairs. I set her down next to Salvatore on Scava's bed, and watch as he and Vinicius cuddle her close and kiss her. Vinicius pushes Salvatore onto his back and grasps Chiara around the waist.

"Let me help you, kitten," he says, his eyes heated and foxlike. He wraps his hand around the base of Salvatore's cock and pushes her slowly down his length.

He kisses her hard as Salvatore grasps her hips and thrusts up into her. A moment later, she's reaching for me, and tips forward over Salvatore so she can claim my cock with her mouth. I run my fingers though her hair, groaning and swearing under my breath as Salvatore thrusts up into her. Her breasts bounce with every movement of his body.

She takes me in her hand and turns to Scava. "Lorenzo? What about you?"

He shakes his head, relaxed back in his chair. "I'm keeping an eye on my patient. Got to make sure he doesn't overdo it and smash his stupid head open."

I cast Scava a suspicious look. Keeping an eye on things?

I doubt that. More like biding his time.

He can do what he likes. I've got my hands full with our girl and I'm going to enjoy myself.

Salvatore bites his lip and watches Chiara working my cock with her mouth. "Baby, you're doing so well. Be a good girl and let Vinicius fuck you in the ass."

12

Chiara

I look down at Salvatore, who's giving me one of his *looks*. Devilish. Alluring. Horny. My ass is tingling from Vinicius' finger inside me and I crave more.

Vinicius produces a tiny, dark bottle that he's brought upstairs and holds it up in front of me. "This might help. Poppers. You'll feel lightheaded for a few seconds, and then you'll just feel relaxed. Would you like to try it?"

"What do I have to do?"

"Just inhale. One deep breath."

I glance at Lorenzo. "Is it safe?"

He nods. "Just this once."

I sit up on Salvatore's cock and let Vinicius pinch off one of my nostrils and hold the bottle under my nose. I take a deep breath of a sharp, cold vapor. A moment later, a warm, euphoric feeling rolls through me.

"Oh, Jesus. I feel fantastic." Drunk and incredibly horny at the same time. I gaze around the room at each of my men, their big bodies looming over me, under me and beside me. So many hands on my body. I'm the luckiest girl in Coldlake. I'm also the horniest girl in Coldlake, and I hold tight to Cassius' thick, veiny cock as I sink further down on Salvatore's. More, please.

Lorenzo is suddenly standing by the bed. He grasps my jaw and makes me look at him, and I run my tongue over my top lip. He smiles and shakes his head. "This is one thoroughly corrupted good little girl. Feeling okay? Want Vinicius to fuck you in the ass?"

I nod, warm sensations rolling through me.

He pats my cheek and goes back to his chair. "Good girl."

I feel Vinicius rub more lube onto my ass and one of his fingers slip inside the tight ring of muscle. My fingers clench on Salvatore's chest. Why does that feel so intensely good? A moment later, he pushes two fingers inside me and pulses them slowly.

Salvatore reaches up to cup my cheek. "You okay, baby?"

I nod and take a deep breath, and let it out slowly. Vinicius withdraws his fingers and the blunt tip of his cock nudges me. Slowly, his hands and his soft words coaxing me, he sinks in by an inch. Then another. Salvatore holds still, his hands stroking my face and throat.

I moan and tip my head back. That feels intense. So stretched out and full. Vinicius starts to move, slow thrusts of his hips.

Then...

"Fuck, I can feel Salvatore's cock rubbing against mine."

I reach out for Cassius and draw him closer

As Salvatore and Vinicius thrust in unison, I drive Cassius to the back of my throat.

Yes.

Perfect.

I feel someone gently caress my hair, and open my eyes. Two burning blue ones fill my vision. Lorenzo. I reach out and grasp his hand. I want him, too. I need all of them. My body needs them. My heart needs them.

"As soon as one of the guys are finished," Lorenzo says, softly, "I'm going to take his place. I'm going to fuck your mouth. Your pussy. And your ass. You're going to be covered in cum. You're going to be tender. Swollen. Wet. Worn out."

I moan around Cassius' cock.

Lorenzo's fist tightens in my hair. "And you're going to be a good girl and give me what I want."

I nod as best I can. I love being a good girl for my dangerous men.

"Yes she, fucking is," Salvatore says in a strained voice. He holds tighter to my hips and starts to pound harder into me. "Fuck, I'm going to nut."

He pulls out and I can feel his hand working up and down his length against my belly.

Lorenzo hunkers down on his heels to watch. "Make sure you shoot your load all over—" He breaks off with a laugh as I feel spurts of hot liquid stripe my belly and Salvatore groans his release.

"Perfect," Lorenzo murmurs, and runs his fingers over my stomach.

Cassius is breathing harder and his hands are fisting my

hair. "*Bambina*, your cute little ass is full of cock. Are you going to swallow me down like a good girl?"

The heat coming off him is tremendous. He thrusts deep in my mouth and groans. His cock spasms, and my mouth floods with his seed. Cassius takes a deep breath and pulls out, and as I swallow he leans down to kiss me and swipes my lips with his thumb.

"*Bella*. Fucking *bella*."

Lorenzo stands up, pulls off his T-shirt and winces. His left shoulder is strapped up in a white bandage.

I stare at him. "Lorenzo! You're hurt. When did that happen?"

He takes off his jeans and palms his cock in his hand. "Doesn't matter. Open your mouth."

I open my mouth to protest, but he shoves his cock into it instead. I glare at him but reassure myself that he's all in one piece and he doesn't seem like he's badly hurt. It's not like I can concentrate on anything when Vinicius suddenly starts pounding me harder and deeper.

"*Fuuuck*," he starts to moan, long and loud.

Lorenzo pushes his fingers through my hair and says, "Vinicius is going to come in your ass, and then you're all mine."

A thrill of alarm and desire goes through me.

With a loud groan, Vinicius thrusts deep, once, twice, and then stills. Slowly, carefully, he pulls out of me. Then he groans again, his head bowed. Not a good groan, either.

Cassius slaps his cheek. "What's wrong? Are you going to faint?"

Vinicius doesn't answer. Cassius hauls his arm over his

shoulder and helps him up off the bed. "Cold water. We'll be in the shower."

For a moment I watch the two of them go, and then Lorenzo cups my jaw. "Are your arms tired, princess? Why don't you turn over?"

I'm a sticky mess. My pussy is gushing. My ass is tender. I'm exhausted. I roll onto my back and wrap my legs around Lorenzo's hips, wondering what he's got in store for me.

He sinks into my pussy, but I can already tell he's not interested in that. He rubs his thumb hard over my lower lip, a menacing smile playing around his lips. "Your ass is full of cum. How about I add to it?"

Salvatore stretches out alongside us, smiling with his head propped in his hand.

Lorenzo pulls out of me, repositions his cock and pushes one of my thighs up to my shoulder, and then sinks slowly into my ass. He hisses in pleasure. "Fuck, that's good. You sore, princess?"

I gasp. "I'm okay."

"We can do better than *okay*. Salvatore, there's something in my drawer for Chiara."

I watch as Salvatore reaches into a bedside drawer and pulls out a vibrating wand.

"I expected a weapon."

Salvatore turns the vibrator on with a grin and applies it to my clit. "Come to think of it, so did I."

I gasp as the vibrations roll through me and I grab Lorenzo's uninjured shoulder and one of Salvatore's as well. "Oh, my God. *Oh, my God.* I've never used a vibe before."

Salvatore raises an eyebrow. "Do you like it?"

My breath is coming faster. I can't look away from Lorenzo's thrusting cock. "Yes, oh, *God*, yes I do."

Out of the corner of my eye, I see Vinicius and Cassius come out of the shower. Vinicius is standing on his own two feet again. As he sees me on the bed with Salvatore and Lorenzo, he makes a beeline for us.

Lorenzo points to a chair. "No. Sit the fuck down."

I moan louder as he thrusts deep and Salvature rubs the vibrating wand slowly over my clit. "You're such a good doctor."

He leans forward and clamps a hand around my throat, his expression savage. "What I am is dying to blow in your ass. Now, come for me and Salvatore like the dirty bitch you are."

I look up at him helplessly.

Oh, God.

If I must.

My orgasm rushes up and consumes me. I'm radiating pleasure from head to toe. Lorenzo clamps his fingers tighter around my throat, squeezing the sides until I'm light-headed and flying high. The rhythm of his thrusts grow disjointed and he swears loudly, his fingers digging into me, until he finally stops moving and Salvatore takes the vibe away.

I lie on my back, panting and floating on a cloud of sex while Lorenzo eases himself out of me.

That was crazy.

I loved every second.

Salvatore and Lorenzo help me into the shower. Salvatore kisses me as Lorenzo washes me down with a loofah, and then himself.

Lorenzo takes my face between his hands. "You like that, princess?"

I nod, too exhausted to form words, but happy.

He presses a kiss to my forehead. "That's my girl."

He leaves us alone, and I wrap my arms around Salvatore's waist under the hot spray. He hums to himself as he washes my hair, and rinses it clean under the water.

Finally, he kisses me and gets out of the shower. I stay where I am, enjoying the water running over me and the scent of shampoo. I feel emptied out, in a good way. My head clear and my body relaxed.

When I come downstairs, the four of them are in sweats and bathrobes on the sofa in a row. All my men. The formidable Coldlake Syndicate. I wriggle in between Salvatore and Vinicius, smiling like an idiot. Both of them put their arms around me and I kiss them both, reaching my hands out to Cassius and Lorenzo.

"That was amazing. You're all amazing."

Cassius strokes a forefinger over my cheek and smiles. "No, you are. I'm going out to get us some dinner. What do you want?"

"Not pizza," Lorenzo mutters. "You never stop bitching if we get pizza."

"The pizza in this city—" Cassius begins with scowl.

"—is disgusting, we agree," Salvatore finishes. "Chiara, what do you want?"

I think for a moment. "Burgers and onion rings. I'm starving."

Cassius gets to his feet. "Burgers and onion rings it is."

When Cassius is gone, I reach out and touch Lorenzo's shoulder. "What happened to you?"

"Nothing," he says, automatically.

I edge closer to him and sit in Vinicius' lap. "Where were you last night?"

"He went to Strife," Vinicius says, and Lorenzo glares at him.

"Please tell me what happened."

Lorenzo grimaces and pushes a hand through his hair. "We shut the bar down and sent the patrons and the girls home. Around three in the morning, a dozen Geaks rolled up and tried to torch the place."

"Because I killed Jax?"

He nods. "They were disorganized and stupid. It was over in less than an hour."

"But how did you get hurt?"

"A bullet grazed me. It's nothing."

A bullet hit a man I care about. It's not nothing. A few inches to the right at it would be a serious injury. A few more inches and he would have been dead. "I'm sorry. You got hurt because of me."

To my surprise, Lorenzo laughs. "Princess, you took out one of the most sadistic bastards in the southwest. Acid asked me if you had a sister. I told him to fuck off."

Cassius returns, and we eat off the paper wrappers. Vinicius and I don't say much, while the others discuss who might take over the leadership of the Geaks. When I finish my burger, I crawl into Vinicius' lap again and we get comfy. His breathing evens out and when I look up his eyes are closed. I pillow my cheek against his chest and listen to his heart beating. A moment later, my eyes drift shut, too.

Sometime later, I feel myself being placed on a bed and the mattress sinking beside me. Vinicius is on one side, fast asleep. Cassius is on the other and he's settling the blankets over us.

"Where are we?" I whisper.

"Scava's bed. With fresh sheets."

"Where are Lorenzo and Salvatore?"

"Scava is in your bed. Salvatore is in one of the spare rooms. We're keeping an eye on him," he adds, nodding at Vinicius. "I am, anyway. You go to sleep."

I wriggle closer to Cassius and reach up and touch his face in the dark. He smiles against my fingers. "*Bambina*?"

"I laid awake all night after the poker game. I could feel that you were awake, and I wanted to stay awake with you."

He wraps his arms around me and cradles me against his warm chest. "I could feel you, too."

Held close to him, I fall into a dreamless sleep.

The sun is up when I awaken, and I'm alone in Lorenzo's bed. I find a robe on the back of the door and pad downstairs.

Lorenzo is in the kitchen, standing by the steaming coffee machine. He's dressed in a tank top and black jeans, the edges of his white bandage visible at the top of his bicep.

I slip into Lorenzo arms and hold him close. His body tenses by reflex, and then slowly, his arms come around me.

"How you are feeling, princess?"

I feel great. I feel even better now I'm close to him. "You were being referee yesterday. I thought that was Cassius' unofficial job, but you wanted to look after us instead."

He scowls, looking past me. "Vinicius had a concussion, and he wanted to give you poppers. It was sensible, that's all."

"I feel very safe when you're watching out for us."

He lifts his shoulders and lets them fall, as if what he did isn't a big deal. Isn't anything.

A few minutes pass, and then he quietly says, "I just wanted to see that you had a good time and didn't get hurt."

I press a kiss to his jaw. "You're lovely, Lorenzo."

He gives me a look like I'm crazy, and pulls out of my arms and goes back to making coffee.

Vinicius comes into the kitchen looking fresh-faced and energetic, and all the color is back in his face. "Good morning, my favorite people. The sun is shining. The birds are singing."

Lorenzo casts his eyes to the ceiling and passes him an espresso. As he pours hot milk into a mug to make a white coffee for me, his annoyed expression melts away and his fingers drift absent-mindedly up to touch the spot on his jaw that I just kissed.

Vinicius wraps his arms around me and puts his lips against my ear. "What are you grinning about?"

"He's cute. Don't you think?"

Vinicius smiles. "Lorenzo? Always. And me?"

I turn my head and kiss him. "You're my angel. You look so much better today. I'm sorry you got hurt."

He takes a deep breath, and lets it out slowly. "I'm not."

"What?"

Lorenzo places a mug of coffee in front of me and sits down at the counter with his own espresso.

Vinicius perches on a stool next to me. "I got so many things I needed the other night. Ricci dead." He clinks espresso cups with Lorenzo.

"Long may he burn in hell," Lorenzo mutters.

"I told you everything, kitten. And then the most beautiful woman in Coldlake saved my life. I knew there were three people who'd save me from certain death, but now there's one more. What's not to love about that?"

I caress his cheek. "You're a glass half full man, aren't you?"

He nips my fingers with his teeth. "Only way to be, kitten."

Cassius comes into the kitchen, fresh from the shower and wearing a crisp white shirt. Lorenzo gets up to make him a coffee.

I shake my head, marveling at him. "Cassius, everyone else is dressed in Lorenzo's sweats and T-shirts and you look ready for a business lunch. How?"

He presses a kiss to my mouth. "I keep fresh shirts in my car, of course. Who do you think I am?" He slips something into my hand. "This is for you."

I glance down in surprise. He's given me a phone.

"It's a burner," Cassius explains, and tells me the passcode. "You can make calls and use the internet, but don't log into any of your email and social media accounts. Your father will be monitoring them. He could trace the...something address."

Vinicius grins at him. "IP address."

"That thing. Anyway. Use it to text us."

"Send nudes," Lorenzo says, his back to me at the coffee machine.

"You first, Lorenzo." I unlock the phone and see that there are four contacts saved. I smile at the names in a neat list. "Thank you. It's a relief to know that I'll be able to contact all of you if I need to."

Salvatore marches in, fury radiating from his face. I

haven't seen him this angry since the night of our engagement and he shoved his cock in my mouth. He takes one
look at the phone in my hand and snatches it away from me.

Here we go. Mr. Control Freak doesn't like the idea of his
precious bride being able to contact the outside world
without his permission.

I take a deep breath and hold out my hand. "Give that
back."

"Have you seen the news?" But Salvatore doesn't say this
to me. He says it to the others, and to my surprise, his voice
shakes and his face has drained of color. Salvatore's not
angry.

He's terrified.

"No, why?" Vinicius asks.

I put a hand on his arm. "What's happened?"

Salvatore gazes down at me, his blue-green eyes stormy
and despairing. "I'm so sorry, Chiara."

13

Salvatore

"You're scaring me, Salvatore. What are you sorry for?"

I pass a hand across my feverish brow. How do I tell her what's happened when I don't want to believe it myself? Chiara is going to be crushed, and my friends... We can't go through this.

Not again.

I grip Chiara's arms, forcing the words out and trying to stay calm at the same time. "Baby, I need you to do exactly what I say. Cassius and I will take you to the airport. He'll fly out with you and stay by your side. You don't have to be afraid." I look up at Cassius. "You can go with Chiara, can't you? I have to stay here."

Cassius stares at me, his brows drawn together. *No. Not that*, I can hear him thinking.

Yes, that.

Exactly that.

Chiara grabs my hand. "Slow down. What are you talking about? Where am I going?"

"Naples. You'll be safe with Cassius and the Ferragamos. I wish I could go with you, but—"

Vinicius interrupts me. "Salvatore. What's happening?"

I hand Vinicius my phone, which is open to a news site. His face goes slack as he reads the article. "No. It's not possible."

"It is possible when we never found out who did it," I say though my teeth.

"But why her?" Vinicius asks.

"Because of Chiara."

"*Fuck*."

Exactly.

Vinicius hands my phone to Cassius and studies the carpet for a moment. "I'll go with Chiara and Cassius, but Lorenzo should stay. You'll need his help with Strife and the other gangs."

That makes sense, and we'll all feel better if there are two of us with Chiara. The Ferragamos will put a security detail on her just like they did with Ginevra nine years ago.

Oh, God. Ginevra. She'll need to leave Coldlake as well, but she's in her third trimester and I don't think it's safe for her to fly. She and Antonio will have to drive, maybe to Canada. Once she's out of the country I'll breathe a lot easier.

There's a sudden explosion on the other side of the

kitchen, and Chiara jumps. Lorenzo has flung a handful of espresso glasses onto the tiles. One of his hands is gripping his hair as he stares at his phone. Then he storms out of the room.

Chiara stares from one of us to the other. "You're all scaring me. Has something happened to Rosaline? One of the other girls?"

I shake my head, and it occurs to me how strange it is that the killer didn't target one of them. Rosaline, Candace, and Sophia, all beautiful girls within my circle. It's as if the person he wants to hurt most this time is Chiara. Or he's trying to hurt us through her, before he finally—

I shut that thought down. It's not going to fucking happen. I'll die before I let that happen.

"I need to call their parents. They should fly with you to Naples." Their parents will never forgive me if something happens to those girls, and I won't, either. I head for the door to make the phone calls in private, but Chiara grabs my arm.

"Salvatore! You're not going anywhere until you tell me what's going on. It's not... Has someone been killed?"

I'm opening my mouth to tell her when Lorenzo strides back into the room and slaps something against Cassius' chest. Then he grasps the edge of the counter with both hands, his eyes full of murder.

Cassius looks at what Lorenzo has given him, and crosses the room to Chiara and takes her face in his hands. Reassuring himself that she's alive. That she's safe. He shows her what he's holding. A passport, which he opens to reveal her picture and a fake name. "Vinicius had this made for you a few weeks ago. I'll call the airport and tell them to fuel the jet. We need to go now."

Chiara pulls herself out of his grasp. "I'm not going anywhere until one of you tells me what the hell is going on."

Lorenzo pulls a zip tie out of a drawer and advances on Chiara. "Cassius, grab her arms."

She backs away from all of us. "Don't you dare. Everyone just calm down. Has something happened to someone I know? If Rosaline and the others are all right then I don't see what this has got to do with me."

I take a deep breath. "Chiara, I'm sorry. Nicole has been taken."

Chiara turns as pale as chalk. She hadn't even considered Nicole, a girl who's so far removed from our world that she should be safe. "My friend Nicole? Nicole De Luca? But why?"

"It happened a few hours ago. She disappeared on her walk to college and when her parents searched the route they found a black flower on the sidewalk."

Everyone in Coldlake knows what a missing girl and a black flower means. Her parents must be losing their minds.

Chiara moans, her hand to her mouth. "But Nicole didn't know your sisters. She doesn't know any of you. I haven't spoken to her in more than a year. I thought the Black Orchid Murders happened because someone wanted to punish the four of you."

"They did," Cassius says, his expression grim. "He still wants to punish us, through you."

"It could be a copycat," Vinicius says. "Some other asshole who doesn't like us."

I consider this. "Maybe. We've made enough enemies. Either way, Chiara isn't safe in Coldlake. Baby, go with

Cassius. We're going to do everything we can to find Nicole, we promise."

Chiara looks from one to the next of us with tears shimmering in her eyes. "You don't think you're going to find her alive, do you?"

I exchange glances with Cassius. He looks as fatalistic as I feel. Wherever the Black Orchid Killer holds his victims, it's a place so unassuming that we didn't find it last time, and we probably won't this time, either.

Chiara swipes at her eyes and shakes herself off. "I'm not leaving Coldlake. That's what he wants and I'm not going to run away with my tail between my legs. She's *my* friend. There could be something I could do."

"Baby, she dumped you a year ago. You don't owe her anything."

"That wasn't her decision. Nicole was only doing what her parents wanted because they didn't like the idea of you getting near her through me. She was obedient. She was—is —" Chiara presses the heels of her hands to her eyes and holds her breath.

Vinicius puts his hand on her shoulder. Lorenzo is creeping closer with his zip tie, an expression of barely controlled rage on his face.

"I'm okay," she whispers to Vinicius a moment later. "Lorenzo, if you try and tie me up I will smack you in the balls."

"I'm not playing, princess. If you don't go with Cassius, I'll do whatever it takes to get you on that jet. I don't care if you hate me for the rest of your life."

Chiara looks from him to me, a mutinous expression in her eyes. I'd rather the last time I saw her for the foreseeable future she wasn't cursing us all to hell. "Let me talk to Chiara alone."

"Fine, but make it quick," Lorenzo snarls, shoving the zip tie in his pocket.

The others nod and draw away into the next room. Cassius is the last to leave, his eyes lingering on Chiara like he can't bear to let her out of his sight.

I hold out my arms to her. If I'm going to be without her for God knows how long, then I need to feel her against me now. She slips into my embrace and wraps hers tight around me. Her body is rigid with fear.

"Please. Tell me everything you know about what happened to Nicole."

"There isn't much more to say. As soon as you're safely on the plane with Cassius and Vinicius, Lorenzo and I will try to learn more and we'll tell you everything we uncover. Between the two of us, we have connections across this whole city at every level. If anyone knows something about Nicole, we'll hear it. You haven't met him, but down at Strife there's a man called Thane who will monitor the police scanners and networks for us. We will tear this city apart looking for her, and we will find her. I swear it."

She pulls away and gazes up at me, her doll-like blue eyes filled with fear. "You must be in turmoil. All of you."

I take her face in my hands. I don't know what I did in a past life to deserve a woman like Chiara. I definitely didn't do anything worthy in this life. "We will stay strong as long as you stay safe. It's simple as that. When it all began last time..."

But my words falter and lock in my throat. When Ophelia was taken, we didn't know what we were dealing with. I feel that same restless panic now. It could be the same killer who took Nicole. It could be a copycat.

"What was it like for you last time?" Chiara whispers.

I hold her tighter and rest my cheek against the top of her head. "Hell."

"Tell me everything," Chiara whispers. "You don't have to bear this alone."

I'm not a burden to anyone. I'm Salvatore fucking Fiore of the Coldlake Syndicate and I don't heap my sorrows at the feet of my woman. I carry them deep inside me where they can't hurt her.

Chiara reaches up and strokes her hand over my chest. "You're the man I was going to walk down the aisle to marry. I decided long ago that whatever's in here, I want it. All of it, Salvatore. Dark and light. Love and pain."

My heart is full of so much darkness and pain that it feels like it will shatter at any moment. The night at the fountain, I heard Ophelia's soft whisper in my ear. *Hasn't she suffered enough?*

I hear her again, the faintest echo in my mind.

Haven't you?

I squeeze my eyes shut. "I imagine losing you like I lost Ophelia and there's so much pain I can't bear it."

"You can tell me," she whispers. "You're strong. You're Salvatore Fiore."

The words crowd together in my throat until I can't hold them back anymore. "The fountain outside the Maxim. That was the last place I saw Ophelia alive. She'd been holding out hope that our father was going to get better, but soon he wouldn't even recognize her and she was crushed. I thought she was going to make herself sick from crying so I took her to the fountain to watch the water and the colored lights. It was her favorite place in Coldlake."

Black mascara tracks down her face. Her smile. The colored lights dancing on her skin.

"The next day, she was gone."

Chiara reaches up and strokes my cheek, her eyes shining with tears. "I'm so sorry, Salvatore. She didn't deserve what happened to her. I wish I could find who did this and make him suffer, for all of you. But I'm going to be all right. You won't let anything happen to me. And nothing is going to happen to Nicole."

I wish I could be sure about that. Right now, my priority is getting Chiara out of here. "Lorenzo and I will find Nicole. The police will be looking for her as well. She's from a good family so the police will actually investigate this time. Meanwhile, you have to leave."

She shakes her head. "I'm not going anywhere. I'm not being chased out of my own city by a madman who wants to make you all suffer, and I'm not abandoning Nicole."

"Lorenzo!" I shout. He comes back into the room. "Tie her up."

Lorenzo advances on her with the zip tie. The other two close behind him.

Chiara holds up her hands. "Stop. All of you, listen to me. I'm not flying to Naples. I'm not leaving Coldlake. I'm going to stay here and I'm going to be cautious and sensible, and I'm going to make sure *you two*—" she looks at me and Lorenzo "—don't do anything reckless and get yourselves killed."

Lorenzo and I glare at each other. We aren't going to be

reckless. We're just planning on leveling this city to the fucking ground.

Chiara turns to Cassius and Vinicius. "They need us right now. We all need to stay together."

The two of them exchange glances, and I can tell that they don't want to leave any more than she does.

She goes to Lorenzo and tugs the zip tie slowly from his fingers. "Do you really want to be without the two of them right now? Do you really want to be without me?"

I can't believe my eyes. A slender little blonde is taking Lorenzo's gear from him and he's *letting* her.

Finally, she turns to me. "I've hardened up, Salvatore. Just like you wanted. Remember? I don't want to run and hide, and I'm not going to cry about it anymore." She takes a deep breath. "I'm staying."

Vinicius glances from Chiara to me. "Is that what you told her to do? Harden up?"

I snarled those words in her face the night she wanted me to kill her father for her. That was when I started to fall for our girl, and I knew she needed to be stronger if we were going to bring her into our world.

"I didn't mean she should do whatever the hell she thinks is right," I say, glaring at her.

Vinicius shakes his head. "Well, congratulations. You played yourself."

14

Lorenzo

"Nice fucking work, Salvatore," I snarl.

I don't know who I think I am. My zip tie is in Chiara's hands. If anyone's been played, it's me.

I point a forefinger at Chiara and advance on her until I have her backed against a wall and my finger is right in her face. "Listen up, princess. If you're staying, then you've got a new set of rules, and you'll be in a whole world of pain if you don't follow them. Cassius putting you over his knee will be a fond fucking memory."

The others crowd around me and I start a list. "One. No running off by yourself, no matter what. Two. Don't answer the door. Don't answer the phone unless it's one of us. Don't talk to anyone unless he's us or you know he works for us.

Three. You're going to text us every hour on the hour with what you're doing."

Chiara looks from my face to each of the others over my shoulders. "Are you done?"

I run the rules over and over in my mind. Is it enough? I thought Sienna was safe and she was taken right under my nose.

At Strife.

"No. I change my mind. Don't talk to anyone but the four of us. Don't go anywhere with anyone even if you know them, like Acid."

Her eyes open wide. "But you saved Acid's life. *I* saved Acid's life. We can't trust Acid?"

"Fuck, no. The only people I trust are in this room." I grasp her jaw and make her look at me. "If you break any of these rules you won't get a sunny Italian vacation. I'll lock you up in the remote Siberian wilderness and you won't see sunshine for a fucking year."

"Fine," Chiara says, her eyes narrowing. "But I have some rules for you all, too. You're going to tell me everything you learn about Nicole and who took her as you discover it. No keeping me in the dark about anything. No lying to me to spare my feelings. If you break any of *my* rules, your dicks will be in the remote Siberian wilderness, also known as nowhere near my pussy ever again."

My mouth twitches. Sassy little bitch. "Deal."

I plant a hand on the wall by her head and scoop her against me, burying my face in her hair as I inhale her sweetness. My heart won't be easy in my chest until I'm back by her side, and that won't be for some time.

I push away from her and call over my shoulder. "I'll be back later. Who's staying with Chiara?"

"I will," says Vinicius, and Cassius nods.

Good. Vinicius won't let her get away with anything sneaky and Cassius will lay down the law if she tries.

Salvatore kisses Chiara and we head downstairs together. He turns to me when he reaches his Maserati. "I'm going to speak to my security teams and get them out there looking for Nicole. What about you?"

"Zagreus."

"Good idea." Salvatore gets in his car. "Meet back here later."

I wait for him to pull out of the garage and then follow behind. Before I head out, I roll down my window and speak to the guard on the front gate. "No one gets in or out of this compound unless they're with the four of us. No exceptions. Not Chiara. Not Acid. Not Ginevra Fiore. Not *anyone*. Is that clear?"

He nods sharply. "Yes, boss. We saw the news."

I grasp the steering wheel and stare straight ahead. "Chiara's inside. If this gate opens before Salvatore or I get back, heads will fucking roll."

I roar down the drive and turn left, heading south. The streets grow seedier and the houses shabbier. Groups of boys stand on street corners, eyeing my Mercedes. A man in a singlet with a bulldog on a rope crosses the road in front of me. Ten minutes later I pull up next to a chain link fence. Across the street, a building stands on the corner, painted black.

Strife.

The front door is open and there are a few patrons out

front having a cigarette and shooting the breeze. I can hear the clunk of pool balls being sunk into pockets, and the distant pounding of R&B from the stripper room.

Before I head inside, I create a group chat with the five of us and type, *It's five minutes past the hour. Where's my update, Chiara?*

Chiara: *I'm watching the news with Vinicius.*

Cassius: *And I'm about to turn the news off and put on a movie.*

I grin at my phone. With Cassius there to daddy her, he'll be able to take her mind off things. *I'm going dark for a while. I'll be back in a few hours with takeout. Stay put.*

I see Chiara typing a reply, and something pops up in the chat that I've never been sent in all my life.

A pink heart emoji.

"What the fuck?" I mutter to myself as I get out of my car. There's a warm feeling in my chest as I cross the street.

It disappears entirely as I cross the threshold into the dingy interior of Strife. There are a half dozen grimy men sitting at the bar. A couple of girls in tiny shorts and tops are trying to entice them into the stripper room. Acid is behind the bar, pouring a measure of whisky into a glass. He flips the bottle in his hand and darkness flickers over his features as he sees me framed in the doorway. I guess he's seen the words *Black Orchid Killer* splashed all over the news.

"Afternoon, boss. You here to lovingly tend my wounds?" He pulls his shirt up to reveal the stitch marks and pinkish scars fading on his chest.

"Where's Zagreus?"

Acid nods over my shoulder. "In the back room."

I turn to go, but Acid comes out from behind the bar toward me.

"The day Sienna was taken..." he begins, and trails off when I glare at him. His jaw hardens and he tries again. "I never said I'm sorry. She seemed like a good kid."

I don't punch him in the face for saying her name. He can take that as a thank you, and I turn to go.

The back room of Strife is where the real work gets done. Two enormous men with tattooed faces guard the door. No one gets in unless they have a bounty mark, or if they're one of the Strife boys.

Or if they're me.

They nod respectfully as I approach and push open the double doors for me. Inside, it's another bar, but there's no jukebox music, no windows, and no women wandering around with their tits half out. The women who are in here are armed to their teeth and size me up as I walk in.

At the far side of the room, the man I came to see sits in a booth, a stack of silver bounty chips next to him and a laptop open. I slip into the seat opposite.

"Cashing in or picking up?" Zagreus asks, still typing.

"Setting."

"I don't accept new bounties in—" He glances at me, and his eyebrows shoot up when he sees who's sitting in front of him. Then a grin slides over his face. "Hey, boss. I had one pissed off hunter in here the other day. He lost five hundred thousand when his bounty bought it behind Ferragamo's new club."

Despite everything that's happened today, I find myself smiling as I remember Jax lying dead at Chiara's feet. "Your hunter had that chip so long it was a fucking antique."

"Everyone's saying that the pretty mayor's daughter shot him in the head. Is that true? She's running with the syndicate now?"

The smile drops from my face. "You want me to braid your hair and tell you who's taking me to the school dance, or shall we do some business?"

"You know I love business. Who do you want dead?"

"No one. Nicole De Luca, taken alive, and that's not negotiable. If she's found dead, no money. If she's collateral damage when the hunter goes in to take her, I'll put a bounty on that hunter. If she's injured, broken bones, head injury, psychological damage, half the bounty is forfeit."

Zagreus nods as he types. "All these conditions are going you cost you."

"The bounty is ten million."

Zagreus stops typing. "You know that the highest bounty I've ever set is three?"

Yeah, on his former friend and Cassius' best prize fighter, Lasher. That conflict of interests is one of my ongoing headaches, but I'm not thinking about that right now. "I want this done quickly."

"Who is this girl? She a friend?"

"Friend of a friend, not that it's any of your business."

Zagreus runs his thumb along his jaw and smiles. "The money's good, but a bounty set personally by Lorenzo Scava? I'm going to have a lot of hunters interested in this one. Plenty of people want a favor from you."

"They'll get money if I get Nicole, nothing more."

Zagreus picks up a chip, but I hold up my hand. "No chips. This is an open bounty."

He hesitates, tapping the chip on the table. "You know

my hunters hate stepping on each other's toes. If they all go in at once the risk of collateral damage to this girl is high."

I put my hands on the table and stand up. "Then they won't get their money, will they?"

Zagreus glares at me, anger sparking in his eyes. He and the Strife boys rule this territory for a two mile radius. The bounty room is Zagreus' personal domain. But when I'm here, I'm the fucking boss.

"Last known location?" he growls.

"Check the news. Where's Thane?"

"Upstairs. The bounty will be live when the money is in the Strife escrow."

I smirk at him and push away from the table. "Pleasure doing business with you."

Why do I get the feeling I'm never welcome when I come to Strife? And after nine years of keeping the Geaks and Blood Pack off their backs. That's gratitude for you.

I find Thane in a darkened room filled with computer equipment. The only light is from the six screens arranged three by two on the desk in front of him. He's wearing head-phones and doesn't look up when I stand next to him, but I'm sure he knows I'm there.

"Vinicius call you?"

Thane nods, still typing. The nails on one of his hands are painted black.

I stare at the screens for several minutes, but it's all reams of nonsense. I don't know if it's got anything to do with Nicole. Thane could be downloading terabytes of porn as far as I can tell.

I never know where the hell I stand with Thane. Vinicius

tells me to trust him and let him get on with things when we give him a mission, and I guess I'll have to.

"Well, call us when you find anything."

No response. Totally blank face.

"And people say I'm psycho," I mutter as I head back to my car.

THREE DAYS GO BY. Zagreus doesn't call to say that Nicole's been picked up. Salvatore's security team hasn't turned up anything except that her phone is turned off and her bank accounts haven't been touched. There's nothing of interest on the police scanners. Every time I enter a room and Chiara's there, she looks up hopefully, wanting to know if I have any news for her.

I've got jack shit.

Nicole's mutilated corpse hasn't shown up, and the clock is ticking. Our sisters' bodies were found within a few days of them disappearing. If it really is the Black Orchid Killer who's taken her, she should be turning up at any moment. There's a permanent ache in the base of my skull and I want to lose myself in a bottle of vodka.

I can't risk it. So I write. I write reams and reams in my notebook about Chiara while she's curled up on the sofa opposite me reading a book. I stare at her like a painter stares at a subject and then I rip her apart on the page. If I put it down on paper, I'm stopping it from happening for real.

It's past ten at night the following day when my phone

rings. I answer it after half a ring. Why's Thane calling me? "Thane?"

Chiara sits up on the sofa and closes her book.

His dark, flat voice comes over the line. "I couldn't reach Vinicius. I picked up a suspected 187 on the police scanners. Young. Female."

"In English."

"Murder."

Shit, shit, shit. "Where? Who?"

"Sending you a pin drop and a summary."

"Thane? Are you there?" I glance at my screen but it's blank. A moment later, it lights up with a text and I read it quickly and open the pin. It's in my territory, just two miles from here.

Fuck.

"Lorenzo, is everything all right?"

I clench my teeth, still staring at the screen. No, things are very goddamn far from all right. If Nicole's been dumped right under my nose, I won't be able to look Chiara in the eye ever again. I promised her that Salvatore and I were on this.

"No. No, it's not."

She gets up and comes over to me, taking my hand in hers. "Please tell me. It's okay."

This isn't right, that she's the one comforting me. "The cops have pulled a body out of the canal over by Bleaker."

I watch her expression closely, but she only winces slightly. "Is it—

"I don't know. I'm going to check it out."

"I'm coming with you."

"You shouldn't—"

"I'm coming," she says firmly, pushing me toward the door.

She's solid when it comes to blood and gore, but I still don't like it. I turn around and take her shoulders in my hands. "Princess. I'm not going to tell you no, but I'm going to remind you that this might be Nicole. You might see her body, and later you could wish you hadn't. Are you sure you want this?"

Chiara gazes at me, her eyes huge. Then she nods. "I'm ready. Thank you for checking, Lorenzo."

I stare at her in surprise. She's thanking me? I said something she's grateful for?

"What's wrong?" she asks.

"I, uh... Nothing, I guess. Let's go. You're going to be warm enough?" I grab one of my hoodies from the back of the sofa in case she needs it, and I feel her hand slip into mine.

I gaze down at our joined hands. My tattooed fingers threaded through her dainty ones. No one ever touches me. Holds onto me. I'm the one who takes hold of other people, right before I fuck them up.

"Lorenzo? What about you, are you going to be okay? Do you want me to call Cassius or Vinicius to meet us there?"

It's not the dead body throwing me for a loop. It's her. "You think I need a babysitter? I'm fine. Let go."

We walk downstairs hand in hand like it's normal and not really fucking weird.

It's a short drive to Bleaker and I park on a narrow bridge. A few hundred feet along the canal, there are a dozen emergency vehicles with flashing lights. I grab some binoculars from the glove box and get out of the car.

Chiara stands next to me on the bridge as I peer at the scene. I purposefully parked far away so that she wouldn't get a good look at what's happening.

Next to me, Chiara shivers.

"Go and put that hoodie on."

"I did."

"Then go and sit in the car."

"I'm fine. What can you see?"

Thane called me early enough that the body is still lying in the open. As soon as I get sight of her, my heart sinks. Her skin is wet and streaked with mud and green slime. There's something knotted around her neck and her eyes are wide and staring.

"What color is Nicole's hair?"

"Long brown hair with bangs."

"Tattoos?"

"No. Her parents would flip."

The girl on the bank of the canal was murdered, but there's nothing particularly sadistic or staged about her death that I can tell. Her hair is auburn and there are tattoos on her shoulders. I lower the binoculars. "It's not her."

Chiara breathes a little easier, but she still looks upset. We're looking at a dead girl and Nicole is still missing. "Was she murdered by the Black Orchid Killer?"

"I doubt it. Not his style. Probably a boyfriend or husband. Or pimp. This area has a load of sex workers."

"Poor thing," Chiara whispers.

We lean on the bridge, watching the murky water flow beneath us. I set down the binoculars, but with nothing to do with my hands, I start to feel jittery. I'm going to have write this out when we get home. I take out my knife and start twisting it in my fingers, watching the metal flash in the streetlight.

Chiara shudders, and I glance at her. She's watching my knife with a mixture of trepidation and disgust.

"You don't like my knife, do you?"

She shakes her head, her lips pressed tightly together. "It looks...evil."

I twist it back and forth in the light. "People are evil. This is just a tool."

"I've tried to be okay with it. The evil person was my father. But whenever I look at it, I feel my mother's pain."

I snatch the blade out of the air and the pointed tip gleams. I turn it slowly, examining the honed edge. "I bought this knife when Sienna was killed. I was going to kill the person who killed her with it. I feel good when I think of all the blood it's spilled and yet to spill. I feel better."

"Yeah, I know," she mutters, and looks away.

For me, this knife is hope.

For her, it's a reminder of the worst moment of her life.

"*Stop that*," I whisper, still staring at the knife.

"I'm not doing anything."

"That was the first thing you said to me. Your mom was freaking out. You were panicking. Your pretty face was giving everything away. I thought you were both so fucking weak."

The pretty seventeen-year-old who was given everything I wasn't, and her mom who wrapped her up in cotton wool and told her she was so special. So *perfect*. So *deserving*. While I was told I was nothing and my sister was tortured to fucking death.

How I hated Chiara the moment I laid eyes on her.

How I loved seeing her and her mom look at me in fear, the monster who dared invade their perfect life.

"Lorenzo, I don't need to be reminded that you—"

I hold the knife over the canal.

I open my hand.

And let it go.

Chiara gasps, and we watch it twist, over and over, flashing in the streetlight. I lean forward as it hits the water with a splash and disappears from view.

We look at each other. Chiara's eyes are wide with shock.

"You didn't have to do that," she whispers.

Her face is still giving everything away. Everything she feels for me is right there, and I drink it in like I'm dying of thirst.

I hook a finger into the neck of her T-shirt and pull her closer.

Chiara opens her eyes wide. "Lorenzo? What are you doing?"

I have no idea.

I don't like kissing. I never have. It just seems so pointless when you could do other things with your mouth like swear and bite and spit. Chiara's lips have entranced me ever since I had her on her back on my operating table. Plush, bitten red lips, full of fear and desire. She's had them wrapped around my cock and sucking me so hard it feels like she's trying to steal my soul. I've caught her staring at my mouth with longing and I couldn't figure out what the hell she wanted.

I slide a hand around the nape of her neck. With the red and blue emergency lights burnishing her beautiful face, I lower my head and press my mouth to hers.

For a split second I wonder if this is going to be a damp, nauseating mistake—

Then I groan.

I slant my head the other way and kiss her again. Harder. Her lips are so soft I could weep. She opens them for me and my tongue runs along hers. I have to do it again. And again. My teeth sink into her lower lip and my hungry mouth devours hers. Both our eyes are open.

"Close your eyes, princess," I say between kisses. "You're freaking me out."

"You're freaking *me* out," she says with a shaky laugh. "I thought you didn't do kisses."

I close my eyes, slant my head the other way and claim another kiss. We stand on the windswept bridge, our skin cold but our lips and tongues hot.

I take a deep breath and just hold her, my heart thudding in my chest. "I guess you've got me thinking about what's important, princess."

"If you never find out who—"

I shut her up with another brutal kiss. I've given up my knife, not my lust for vengeance. "I don't need my knife. I'll find out who killed Sienna, and I'll kill them with something else." I nip her lips with my teeth. "Don't worry, princess. I know a way or two."

15

Vinicius

When I arrive at Lorenzo's in the morning, I walk around the entire ground floor and there's no sign of Chiara. It's after eight in the morning and she's usually up by now. I'm about to head upstairs when I hear Lorenzo walking up from the basement. He looks tired, but kind of...

Glowing?

"Where's Chiara?" I ask.

"Still sleeping. We were out late at a murder scene. It wasn't Nicole," he adds quickly.

"Thane told me. Thanks for checking it out. I was in one of Cassius' poker pits because some asshole was bragging about being the Black Orchid Killer." I flex the fingers on my right hand, examining the bruises and cuts on my knuckles. "Cassius and I may have lost our tempers."

"No problem. Coffee?"

I follow Lorenzo into the kitchen and sit at the counter as he makes coffee. There's something weird about his face. Or is it his clothes? The way he's moving? I can't put my finger on it.

As he puts my cup in front of me, I'm still staring at him, eyes narrowed.

"Fucking *what*?" Lorenzo snarls.

"There's something different about you."

He opens his jacket. "I'm not armed."

"Where's your knife?"

"Got rid of it."

"What? Why?"

"Don't want it anymore."

I'm a consummate liar. I know when someone is lying to me, but as I peer at my best friend I sense that he's not lying. But he's not telling the whole truth, either.

"If you don't stop staring at me I will go and buy a new knife and stab you in the face."

I can't think of anything on this earth that would make Lorenzo throw away his knife when he bought it specifically to avenge his sister. Unless...

I fold my arms and smirk, nodding slowly. "Oh, I get it. You're in love."

He makes a face like I've just dipped my balls in his cup of coffee. "What? Fuck off."

"It's all right. We all are. We found the purest, sweetest girl in Coldlake, unleashed our blood, darkness, and horror all over her, and she embraced it all like an armful of roses."

"You talk a load of shit."

I get out my phone and dial our group chat, the one that Chiara's not in. Salvatore and Cassius pick up and I put them on speaker phone. "I'm here with Lorenzo. One question. Are you in love with Chiara?"

"I've loved her for nearly a year," Salvatore says right away.

"I only realized I loved her when I nearly made her hate me," replies Cassius.

"Lorenzo says he's not in love with her."

"Well, Lorenzo has to do things in his own time..."

"He threw away his knife for her."

Salvatore laughs. "Oh, shit. He's totally in love with her."

"Scava, are you there? Be a fucking man and admit you love her. Goodbye."

They hang up and I put my phone away. "Well?"

Lorenzo glares at me. "Well, what? How about you? Are you done lying to her?"

My smile fades. "Just because I might lie to her in the future doesn't mean I'm not in love with her."

"Sure. Whatever," Lorenzo mutters and takes a mouthful of coffee.

"Will you stop wanting to tie Chiara up? Will the desire to make her bleed and push her to her limits disappear just because you love her? What if she's not safe and you have to force her to go somewhere? You'll fucking do it to keep her alive, Lorenzo, even if it makes her hate you. Even though you love her. *Because* you love her."

Lorenzo glares at me. He knows I'm right. If it comes down to choosing between her safety and the truth? There's no fucking question.

"You'd do the same as I would, only I'd do it with words, and you'd do it with zip ties and threats."

We're finishing our coffee when my phone rings, and I see it's Thane. I put him on speaker and hold the phone between Lorenzo and me. "It's Vinicius. What's happened?"

"Another body." Thane hesitates, which makes all the hairs stand up on the back of my neck. Thane never hesitates. "I think this one's her."

Lorenzo and I exchange glances.

"Send me the location. We'll check it out."

"You can't."

"Why?"

"She was dumped right outside the mayor's house. There are roadblocks and the area is swarming with cops. The press is there. The description of the girl fits and it's the Orchid Killer MO. There's a black flower in her mouth. You've got about three seconds before the news breaks online."

"Shit." I hang up and run for the stairs, Lorenzo right behind me. Chiara's phone will be next to her bed. She could be awake and checking the news right now.

In Chiara's bedroom, she's just sitting up in bed. Lorenzo strides forward, swipes the phone from her nightstand and shoves it in his back pocket.

"Good morning, guys—hey, why did you take my phone?"

I sit down on the bed next to Chiara and take her hands. Her expression of confusion turns to fear as she sees my face. She glances at Lorenzo, and then back to me.

"Nicole's dead, isn't she?"

"We think so. I'm so sorry, kitten."

Chiara stares at me, despair bleeding into her expression. Finally, her face creases and she sobs, "But Nicole didn't do anything wrong."

Neither did our sisters. They were innocent of any crime except being connected to us. Now, the Black Orchid Killer is tormenting Chiara. "We're going to find this asshole and end him slowly. I swear it."

"Are you sure it's her? Are you certain?"

"I'm going to confirm it as soon as I can." I need pictures. If the police are automatically backing up to an online server then Thane might be able to access the photos.

Our phones buzz, and Lorenzo checks his. "The story has hit the news. Cassius and Salvatore are on their way."

"Can't we go to the scene and see for ourselves?" Chiara asks him.

Lorenzo shakes his head. "The area's locked down. If we show our faces, we'll be arrested and you'll be jumped on."

"Where was she found?"

Lorenzo doesn't want to say. Neither do I, but I finally admit, "Near your father's house."

Chiara doubles over and moans. "This is all my fault. She was killed because of me."

"Stop that." I take her shoulders and make her look at me. "Did you kidnap her? Did you kill her? This is no one's fault but the killer's."

Chiara slumps against me and sobs in my arms. I cradle her against me, and press kisses to her brow. "Kitten, I have to make a phone call, but Lorenzo will stay with you, okay?"

"Okay," she says, her voice thick with tears and misery.

As I get to my feet, Lorenzo shoots me a look of alarm.

"What do I do?" he hisses under his breath.

"Just hold her. It's not hard." I put my hands on his shoulders and shove him down next to her.

Lorenzo looks as uncomfortable and panicky as Cassius used to, but he gathers her close, grits his teeth and pats her back. A moment later, he slides a hand around the nape of her neck and tucks her head against his shoulder. Slowly, he relaxes, and I leave the two of them there, Chiara's anguished sobs following me down the stairs.

In the kitchen, I call Thane back. "Can you access the police servers to see if they've uploaded any crime scene photos yet?"

"Already did it. I'll send them to your encrypted folder." I hear typing, and then Thane adds, in a darker voice than usual, "Don't let your woman see these. It's not fucking pretty."

No chance. As I access the folder and start swiping through them, I can hear someone walking up from the basement, and then Cassius comes through the door.

"I saw the news. Is it really her? How is Chiara..." He trails off as he looks at my expression. "Are you all right?"

"I have pictures."

"Show me."

I hold out my phone. Gladly. Anything to get those blood-soaked, degrading images away from me.

Cassius swipes through a few. "What's that stuck inside her?"

I swallow hard. "A crucifix. She went to Catholic school."

"*Mio Dio,*" he mutters.

It's the same killer. It has to be the same one. The attention to detail. The cruelty. The showing off of the mutilated body.

"Who do you think is going to get the video?" Cassius asks, passing my phone back. "Nicole's father? Or us?"

I guess we'll just have to wait and see. One thing I know for certain, I'll die before I let Chiara lay eyes on either these photos or that video.

TWO DAYS LATER, I'm leaving my house when a gaunt-faced man gets out of his car and walks slowly toward me. He has the stiff-legged, shambling gait of someone in the throes of severe exhaustion.

I stand by my car, wondering if this is the worst attempt ever at a citizen's arrest. "If you want that one million dollars for turning me in, you're going to have to try harder than this."

He stops in front of me, and close up I can see his watery eyes are red and his shirt has been buttoned through the wrong holes. "I'm Carlo De Luca. You're Vinicius Angeli, aren't you?"

De Luca. This must be Nicole's father. "Yes, I'm Vinicius Angeli. I'm sorry about your daughter."

He blinks rapidly and stares past my shoulder. Poor bastard. There's nothing I can say to alleviate the full-scale horror he's living through right now, so I don't even try.

"I didn't know where else to turn. Of the four of you, you always seemed the least..."

"Crazy?" I supply with a smile.

His voice cracks. "He told me I couldn't go to the police. He has something. He wants to see me."

He. The killer? I glance around quickly. "You fucking idiot. We could be being watched right now. Get in the car."

De Luca sobs in the passenger seat as I check the rearview mirror and the cars behind us on the main road. There doesn't seem to be anyone on our tail. After a few minutes he pulls himself together.

"Where are we going?"

"Nowhere. We're driving, and you're going to tell me what you want."

"Can I see Chiara?"

My eyes narrow at the road ahead, and I say quietly, "You don't want to say her name to me, Mr. De Luca. I'll start wondering whether you mean her harm, and that won't be good for your health."

"I didn't mean—"

"Have you received a video yet?"

"What video? Why?"

No one but us and the killer knows about the videos. We never turned them over to the police and we don't tell anyone about them. "This asshole loves to gloat over people's pain. He sent us videos of the murders, but maybe that's not enough for him anymore. If he wants to see you, it's because he wants to watch you suffer."

Mr. De Luca mops at his face and takes several deep breaths. Then in an entirely different voice, he says, "I'll take that trade. He can watch me suffer, and I'll have a chance to kill him."

I glance at the man. "Are you serious?"

"That's my baby girl he tortured to death."

I get onto the freeway and merge into traffic. "All right. Tell me everything that's happened since Nicole's body was found. If you really have been contacted by the killer, then we're interested in helping you."

An hour later, I leave Mr. De Luca on a quiet street and drive to Lorenzo's. The others are already there and we're meant to be discussing what our next steps are in keeping Chiara safe, but I quickly derail that conversation and fill them in on what De Luca has told me.

"Are you saying that De Luca can get us in the same room as the killer?" Salvatore asks.

"Potentially," I reply.

Chiara grabs my arm. "We have to try. This is too important to pass up."

I gaze down at her, but don't say anything. *We* aren't doing anything, kitten.

"It could be a trap. De Luca may want us dead, or caught," Cassius points out.

"Maybe, but the man's a mess. If it's a trap then it's not going to be a very good one."

"Poor Mr. De Luca," Chiara says softly. "He wasn't a very good father, but he's a good person. He loved Nicole. I wonder if he's regretting being away for all those medical conferences now."

What De Luca will be regretting right now is ever letting his precious daughter out of his sight. It's a special kind of shame and despair knowing someone suffered and died because you weren't there to protect them.

"It could be a trap laid by the killer," Salvatore points out. "He could be betting on De Luca coming to us for help."

"If it gets us close to him, then I'll take that chance," I reply.

"It could be a trick by the cops," Lorenzo points out. "Or anyone else who isn't our fucking fan."

The talk goes around and around in circles until Chiara finally stands up and says that she's going to make coffee.

As soon as she disappears into the kitchen, I lean forward and say softly, "It could be a trap by anyone, but you all know and I know that we have to see for ourselves. It's all arranged. We're meeting De Luca at midnight. Any questions?"

They exchange glances and then one by one shake their heads.

Lorenzo leans back in his chair so that he can see into the kitchen and then turns to us. "Chiara goes to bed around eleven. If all goes to plan, we'll be able to wake her up with the news that her friend's murderer is dead."

We look at each other, wondering if someone's going to say it. That we should tell Chiara what we have planned and that she's coming with us over our dead bodies.

No takers?

Fine by me.

I get to my feet and say quietly, "I'm going. I'll meet you all out front at a quarter to midnight."

Eight hours later, I'm sitting in my car in the dark, watching Lorenzo pull out of his gates. Cassius and Salvatore are already waiting. I lead the four cars to a location near to where De Luca is meeting the killer, just inside the border of the Geaks' territory.

We gather in the shadow cast by a warehouse, all armed and dressed in black. Lorenzo and Salvatore have arranged two dozen men as backup and they're hiding in the shadows.

"Phones on silent. Text when you're in position. If you

see anyone approaching, let everyone know." I take a deep breath. "This might be our only chance. If we don't stop him now, it could be Chiara next."

The other three nod, and pull their ski masks down. "I'll take the north side. Cassius the east, Lorenzo the west, Salvatore the south. Good hunting."

We slip into the darkness on foot, each of us heading in the same direction at first and then peeling off one by one. The target location is a rundown apartment building. On the north side, there's a parking lot and a broken fence. I crouch down between two beat up cars.

A moment later, my phone vibrates.

Cassius: *I'm in position.*

The bottom drops out of my stomach when I see that he's sent the message to the chat that includes Chiara.

Salvatore: *Wrong chat, Cassius.*

Cassius: *Fuck.*

Cassius: *Fucking technology.*

Lorenzo: *Fucking grown ass man who can't send a text to the right fucking chat more like, you fucking idiot.*

"Fucking idiots pinging her phone over and over," I mutter, dropping a message in our private chat for them to shut the fuck up. But it's too late.

Chiara: *What's going on? Where are you all?*

Great, just fucking great. I type, *Kitten, we need to focus. We'll explain when we get back. Stay inside.*

Chiara: *You went without me, didn't you? To meet Nicole's dad?*

Chiara: *Tell me where you are.*

Chiara: *GUYS. I'M SERIOUS. I WILL CUT ALL YOUR*

BALLS OFF IF YOU DON'T TELL ME WHERE YOU ARE RIGHT THIS SECOND.

I take a deep breath and let it out slowly. She's going to be furious, but the best thing right now is to concentrate and get this done.

And I have no choice but to focus because someone just stepped out of the shadows just ten feet from me and is walking toward the building.

16

Chiara

I stare at my phone for several minutes, but there's no reply. I curse in frustration and run for the front door. Four of Lorenzo's armed guards are standing in the hall and their expressions are stony as I race toward them.

"Where did Lorenzo go?"

"I'm sorry, Miss Romano. We can't tell you that."

"You have to tell me. He needs me there with him. They *all* need me there." But the men are unmoved by my pleas. I type a message directly to Lorenzo.

Tell your men to bring me to you or the next time I see you, I'll stab you in the throat, just like how you taught me.

I stare at my phone, waiting for the three dots to appear. Something from Lorenzo. Anything to tell me that he's all right.

Nothing.

I turn and press my face to the wall and groan. If anything happens to them while I'm locked in here like a useless idiot, I'll never forgive myself.

For several minutes, I pace up and down, picturing all the horrible things that could be happening to them. I'm too scared even to be angry with them. There'll be time to be angry with them when they get back.

I try calling Lorenzo, and to my surprise he picks up. I put my hand over my heart and sign in relief. "Oh, thank God. Tell me where you are. Lorenzo?"

There's nothing but silence on the other end. Then I hear faint, labored breathing, as if someone in a great deal of pain or confusion is holding the phone to their ear.

"Hello? Is someone there?" Panic races through me. "Lorenzo, are you hurt? Where are you? Where are the others?"

"Chiara," says the voice on the other end. It's a husky, slurred voice, and female. Definitely female.

And familiar.

"Don't come," the unknown person says, every syllable a painful effort. "Stay...away."

"Who is this?"

"It's a..."

A jolt of electricity races through me. I know this voice, but it's impossible. It should be impossible.

I'm talking to a dead girl.

Her voice is a faint, crackly whisper. "Trap."

"Nicole?" I whisper. "Is that you? Where are you? What's happened to you?

"It's a trap."

"*Nicole!* Please tell me where you—"

There are three bleeps in quick succession and then the line cuts out. If that was Nicole, she's definitely in trouble and I need to find her. But how did she get Lorenzo's phone? I redial his number and listen to it ring.

Don't come.

It's a trap.

The Black Orchid Killer. The monster who's been tormenting them for years has found a way to get them all in one place. I picture each of them with their throats cut or a bullet in their heads and moan in panic. This can't be happening. I can't lose anyone else.

The line picks up and I say frantically, "Lorenzo? Nicole?"

"Dad," Nicole whispers.

Dad?

Or did she say *dead*?

"Is it your father? Is someone dead? Is anyone hurt? Who's with you right now?"

Her voice is so faint that I can barely hear her. She seems like she's only just clinging to consciousness.

"I'm...sorry."

Panic races through me.

"Blond man," she whispers, sucking in a frightened breath. "Scary."

Dead.

Blond.

And scary.

No, no, no. Please God, no.

Nicole's not listening to me, but I scream anyway, hoping

I can rouse her and she can take her terrifying words back. "Nicole? *Nicole.*"

There's a scuffling sound, Nicole's mutterings suddenly sound far away, like someone's ripped the phone from her hand and pressed it to their ear.

I can hear him breathing.

I grip the phone in my shaking hand. I'm listening to a murderer breathing. The man who brutally tortured and murdered four women in cold blood and tormented their brothers in the cruelest possible way.

He took from them.

And now he's taking from me.

EPILOGUE

Chiara

"Who are you?" I whisper into the phone, but there's only silence. When I pull it away from my ear, the screen is blank.

All around me, Lorenzo's guards' phones start to ping. They exchange glances, and then one of them says, "Oh, shit."

The one who seems to be in charge suddenly snaps into focus and says, "Orchid Protocol."

Then they all look at me.

"Orchid Protocol? What's Orchid Protocol?"

Without replying, the men grab me and hustle me downstairs. I try to fight them off and demand they explain themselves, but they ignore me. They barely treat me like I'm a human being. More like I'm a stubborn package that doesn't want to be delivered.

"Did Lorenzo just text you all? Is he all right?"

One of the guards opens the back door of an SUV. "Automatic message, Miss Romano. Something happened to trigger it. We have to get you out of here, now."

"What happened to trigger it? Is Lorenzo all right? *What happened to Lorenzo?*"

But they won't answer me. They push me into the SUV, shove me onto the floor and cover me with a blanket. And I thought my being kidnapped days were over.

I struggle to sit up but one of the men is holding me down. Is this really on Lorenzo's orders? Is he somewhere, bleeding out, his vital signs diminishing? Or is he dead already, just like Nicole seemed to say, and Orchid Protocol is some kind of fail-safe he set up to protect me without telling me?

We've only been driving for a few minutes when whoever's at the wheel hits the brakes. Hard. The guards swear and I hear guns being pulled out of holsters. There's the sound of doors being opened and slammed. Men shouting. Grunts of pain.

The weight on my back disappears. As I'm extricating myself from beneath the blanket, hands grab me and I'm dragged out of the car. I'm still tangled in the blanket and I can barely see anything.

"Who are you? Let me go! Lorenzo? Vinicius?"

There's a flash of silver. A flash of black. A hood is pulled over my head and I'm shoved into another vehicle by someone who's tall and strong. The floor beneath me is hard metal and two doors are slammed. I'm in a van?

I open my mouth to scream, and a hand is clamped over my mouth. I bite down on the finger and there's a mild hiss of irritation.

Irritation.

Fuck this guy. I'm more than a goddamn irritation.

I bite harder and struggle as hard as I can. As I flail, the hood slips and I see that the person holding me from behind has black nail varnish on one of his hands. A second man in front of me has a distinctive black and green skull tattoo decorating his throat.

I'm so shocked that I stop struggling.

A sarcastic voice purrs, "We have to stop meeting like this."

I picture a pair of vivid green eyes opening in a pale, blood spattered face. *You're not what I was expecting, Miss Romano.*

My mind races. If Nicole's not really dead, it was a trap after all. But not for the four men.

For me.

"It was you? All along it was you? You're sick. *You're fucking sick.*" I struggle and scream at the top of my lungs. Years of blood and pain and misery, for what? A petty struggle over a sordid corner of Coldlake? "How could you do this to Lorenzo? How could you do this to all of them? He trusted you."

I lash out with everything I have and my knuckles and heels connect with muscular legs and torsos. There are two of them and they're *strong.* I can't get free.

"I saved your life, asshole. Lorenzo saved your life. He got shot for you. All these years, Lorenzo protected you from your enemies. *He would have done anything for you.*"

"Shut her up," says a dark, deadpan voice. It must belong to the man with the black nails.

A pad of something cold and astringent is pressed over my mouth. I take a mouthful in surprise, then realize my mistake and I hold my breath.

"Sweet dreams, princess," Acid whispers in my ear.

How dare he use his boss' nickname for me. I take a breath and dizziness crashes over me. I can't take another or I'll pass out. My lungs are burning.

Please don't let any of them get hurt.

I picture each man as I struggle to stay conscious. Salvatore's ferocity. Vinicius' beauty. Cassius' severity. Lorenzo's icy resolve. They wouldn't give up if they were fighting to save me.

They would never give up.

But I can't stop myself. My lungs expand, and I draw the thick, acrid anesthetic deep inside me. I've failed. It's all over. All I'll be is a mutilated corpse and a screaming, dying girl in a video.

As black spots fill my vision, I send up a prayer.

If you're still alive, please don't watch the video, Lorenzo.

Don't any of you watch it.

Just destroy it.

And forget you ever met me.

Third Comes Vengeance (Promised in Blood, 3) is available December 8.

Pre-order now

BONUS CHAPTER

I didn't plan on any MM for the Promised in Blood *series, but two of the guys—best friends who've been through hell together, the two who weren't raised to be mafia bosses but are owning their shit alongside the others—have been getting in my head.*

And screwing.

Who am I to tell them no when it's just so hot? Please enjoy this bonus MMF chapter featuring Vinicius, Lorenzo, and Chiara, set after the canal scene when Lorenzo first kisses Chiara and sometime before the end of the book.

Thank you to my First Comes Blood *beta readers Azmira and CC for your support and encouragement. My partner is always grinning at me and saying, "You've just got to make it dirtier, don't you?" He should meet my beta readers!*

This chapter features hardcore MM content. If that ain't your jam, just skip it and I'll see you for Third Comes Vengeance *on December 8.*

Chiara

Someone's planting soft kisses up my neck. I smile, wondering if I can figure out who it is with my eyes still closed. He gets his hand beneath my T-shirt and strokes his fingers over my nipples. Barely there caresses. He wants to wake me slowly. And make me horny.

Too gentle to be Lorenzo.

Too stealthy to be Cassius.

Too patient to be Salvatore.

Definitely Vinicius.

"Salvatore," I moan, reaching arching my back and running my nails along his thigh.

Vinicius jerks his head away. "Salvatore? It's not goddamn Salvatore. It's *me*."

I dissolve into laughter, my shoulders shaking. "Of course it's not Salvatore. I was teasing you."

I roll over in bed to face him. The morning light paints Vinicius' beautiful face golden, and his eyes glow.

"Troublemaker," he says, and presses his lips to mine in a heated, open-mouthed kiss. "Good thing I forgive you. Good thing I don't want...revenge."

He suddenly digs his fingers into my ribs and tickles me. I shriek with laughter as we tussle back and forth. "Mercy. *Mercy*."

Vinicius pulls my T-shirt up and over my head. "Mercy? I'm a cold-blooded killer. I eat bullets for breakfast. I'll show you *mercy*."

He takes one of my nipples in his mouth and sucks hard, at the same time he drags my underwear down to my knees. I arch up off the bed, my clit suddenly aching to be touched.

A deep, sarcastic voice speaks over our head. "Sure, just

come in without saying hello to the man who fucking owns this house."

We look up into furious blue eyes. Lorenzo is standing over us, hands on hips. He's shirtless and wearing only jeans, and his hair is damp. His intricate tattoos stand out on his chest and throat. He surveys my naked body, with my underwear around my knees, and pins me with an accusing look, like this is all my fault. I put my thumbnail between my teeth and open my eyes wide.

I wasn't doing anything.

While he's watching, my other hand slides over my hip bone and my fingers slide into my slit.

Lorenzo's pupils dilate, and I smile slowly. He loves watching me touch myself.

Vinicius props his head on one hand and clears his throat, giving his friend a dazzling smile. "I was just saying good morning to Chiara."

"I can see that. Were you just going fill my house with the sounds of your sex while I'm downstairs working?"

Vinicius cups my breasts and squeezes my nipples. "Screw working. Come join us."

I gaze up at Lorenzo with hazy, lust-filled eyes. "Yes, join us."

He drops his knees onto the bed and leans over Vinicius to get to me. "Princess, you were already begging for mercy. Sure you can handle two of us at once?"

I twine my arms around his neck. "I can handle three of you at once, remember?"

"Fuck, so you can." Lorenzo smiles, and takes hold of my jaw in one tattooed hand and slants his mouth over mine. All the breath is stolen from my lungs.

Lorenzo's kisses are shocking. And he *bites*, sinking his teeth into my lower lip and then swiping it with his tongue. I don't think I'll ever get used to his kisses.

"Holy shit. You kissed her?" Vinicius asks. "You kiss now? When did this happen?"

"Quit making such a big deal about it," Lorenzo mutters, and kisses me again. His tongue runs along mine and he groans softly. He seems surprised all over again that he likes the sensation of his mouth against mine.

He grasps my inner thigh and squeezes, and pulls my legs open. I love the sensation of being manhandled by him.

I can feel Vinicius undressing, and I slide my hand over his naked stomach. This is the best way to get woken up. I'm such a lucky bitch.

I open my eyes and look between the two beautiful men. "I have a question. You two have obviously been up to things in the past. Who have you had a threesome with? Was it one of the bounty hunters down at Strife?"

I bet it was one of the hunters. Lorenzo's always down at Strife and Vinicius knows Thane. They probably drink down there and have the strippers and hunters crawling all over them. Gorgeous, ferocious women who would happily follow these two upstairs and let them do whatever they like.

The two men exchange glances.

"A foursome? *More?* Come on, tell me. The night we played poker, Lorenzo said he's seen the way you give head."

"He *knows* the way I give head," Vinicius replies.

"What does that—"

Instead of saying anything, Lorenzo lets go of me, grabs Vinicius and presses his mouth against the other man's in a hard, savage kiss.

Lorenzo

Vinicius breathes in sharply, and he opens his mouth beneath mine.

Ever since I kissed Chiara, I've been wondering if it would feel just as good to kiss Vinicius. His tongue flicks against mine, teasing me, inviting me deeper. I plunder his mouth with my tongue, my cock straining against my jeans.

Yeah. That's good.

Fucking delicious.

Vinicius never bugged me about not kissing him, but I knew he found it cold. I pull away, breathing hard and staring down at him.

Chiara is gazing at me in shock. "Oh, my God. Lorenzo. You're kissing...Wait, you two have had sex?"

I sit up and plant a hand on both their chests, glaring from one to the other. "Do you want to run a Q&A, or do you want to fuck?"

Vinicius smiles up at me, and touches the tip of his tongue to a pointed canine. I already know what he wants.

I turn to Chiara. "Well, princess?"

Chiara's staring up at me with wide, blue eyes. I'm braced for her to freak out or cry about me not wanting her just because I want him as well. Let's not do that, please.

"Kiss him again," she breathes. "That was so hot."

A heated smile slips over my face. Perfect. I lean down and press my mouth against Vinicius', softer this time. I don't know what's gotten into me lately, but this sort of thing doesn't seem so irritating or tedious anymore. Everything in my head is just...quieter, in a good way. I find myself lingering over the kiss, and then turn my head to capture Chiara's lips.

They're both so fucking pretty.

I alternate between kissing them while someone unbuttons my jeans and pushes them down my thighs. I feel a large hand wrapped around my cock and moan. Vinicius works me slowly up and down in his fist.

"You wet for me, princess?" I say with a heavy groan as I push her thighs apart. I take my middle and ring fingers and push them into Vinicius' mouth. He sucks on them as I pulse them in and out of him, his tongue running over me. When they're good and wet, I pull them from his lips and drive then into Chiara's cunt.

"Come on my fingers, princess. I want your first orgasm. Vinicius's going to give you the rest, so make it a good one for me."

Yeah, she's fucking wet. "Good girl," I say through gritted teeth. Vinicius has moved down the bed and taken my cock in his mouth. Heat floods my body as I look at the two of them.

"No fair," she whimpers, clutching the pillow and panting. "You're not meant to be sweet to me. I don't know what to do."

She clenches on my fingers, like that *good girl* has gone straight to her pussy. "What do you mean? I'm so fucking sweet. Watch this." I thread my fingers through Vinicius golden hair and clench it tight, then thrust deep into his throat. "Good boy."

Vinicius breathes in hard through his nose, and a drop of pre-cum appears at the end of his dick. I laugh softly and let him go.

Chiara can't tear her eyes away from the blow job that he's giving me, like it's the porniest thing she's ever witnessed. Oh yeah, Chiara's probably never watched porn. This must be the first time she's ever seen two other people have sex.

I lean down closer to her as I keep slamming my fingers into her pussy. "You're a dirty little perve, Chiara, staring right at my dick getting sucked. Nice girls don't stare. Nice girls don't gush all over bad men's fingers while they're getting finger fucked. You know what we've got here, Vinicius? A little slut who's dying to watch a man get railed."

"Shut up," she whispers, her cheeks flaming even redder, but still staring at my cock.

"He's so good at it, isn't he? Your tongue is pressing against the roof of your mouth, isn't it, princess? You wish you were sucking my cock. Don't you? *Hey.*" I tap her chin and point with two fingers into my eyes. "Look at me when you come."

Chiara's on the verge of losing it as she gazes, flustered and breathing fast, into my face.

"One day soon I'm getting my dick in here along with someone else's and we're both going to fuck your pussy at the same time. Who shall I choose? How about Cassius. Cassius' big, fat dick and mine railing you together. Will that be enough for you? You greedy bitch. You little cock slut."

Chiara gives a strangled cry and her head flies back on the pillow, and I smirk. There she goes, right on cue. Coming all over my fingers and just about squeezing them blue she's clenching so hard.

"You're so *crude*," she mutters, her back arching and her eyes still closed as she floats back down from her orgasm.

"Don't fucking enjoy it so much, then." I thrust my thumb into her mouth. Her lips close around it and she sucks. "You want a cock in your mouth?"

She nods, moving my thumb up and down.

"Perfect. Slide down there, princess, and show us what you can do. And make it good."

I push Vinicius down on his side and lay behind him. Chiara wriggles down his body and gets to work.

Vinicius drinks in the sight of her on one side and me on the other. "Finally, the adoration I deserve," he says. Chiara laughs with her mouth full and pinches his belly. "Ow!"

I left a bottle of lube in her bedside table drawer a few days ago, and I reach in and grab it. I spread lube over two of my fingers. "Princess, I want to see you sucking him real good. You never look better than when you have a cock in your mouth."

"What about me?" Vinicius asks.

I fist my hand in his golden hair and hold on tight. "What about you?" I shoot back, and press the tip of my finger against the tight ring of his ass. He never looks hotter than when he's falling apart because I'm fucking him hard. Or I thought so, until I push my finger deep inside him as Chiara sucks slowly up his cock.

Both of us pleasuring him. That's so much hotter.

And sexy.

And *pretty*. The two of them look perfect together, beautiful and radiant like personifications of the fucking dawn or something. I don't know. I'm not a poet. But I can't stop staring at them.

Vinicius groans, his eyes closing and his brows drawn

sharply together. Chiara grasps his hips and pulls him deeper.

"Fucking beautiful," I murmur, watching them, and add a second finger and pulse them in and out of Vinicius. "Both of you."

While she works her mouth up and down his length, Vinicius reaches behind himself and grasps my cock, giving me an unsteady hand job, squeezing me in pleasure more than he's stroking me.

"Kitten, your mouth feels incredible," he moans, his ass contracting around my fingers.

"Ease up down there, princess. Don't let him come yet."

"But he looks so good when he comes," she replies, and then swallows him deep again.

"If he comes, you're not getting another orgasm."

That convinces her to slow down.

Vinicius reaches off the bed and takes a small, dark bottle out of his pants, pinches off one nostril and inhales sharply.

Chiara sits up and tries to take the bottle from Vinicius, but I slap her hand away. "Not you."

"But I liked it last time."

I bet she did. For a few seconds she was high as a kite. "I told you, it was just that once."

"Is it dangerous?"

Not necessarily, but I'm her over-bearing, overprotective, asshole doctor and nothing's touching her, getting inside her, or altering her without my say so.

Besides, she doesn't need it when she's not the one getting fucked in the ass.

"It's dangerous to argue with me," I point out with a nasty smile and wrap a hand around her throat.

"Vinicius is allowed."

"Vinicius corrupted himself a long time ago."

Vinicius winks at her. "Don't worry kitten, I'll teach you all the tricks to get whatever you want out of Lorenzo."

"Someone's begging to get railed," I snarl.

He caps the bottle and throws it aside, and then glances at me over his shoulder. "Always."

God, it's been fucking weeks. I ease my fingers out of him, snatch up the lube and dump a hefty amount on my cock. "You watching, princess?" I mutter to Chiara as I rub myself up and down, getting my cock slippery.

Of course she is. She's sitting up, her eyes huge, as I massage the head of my cock into Vinicius asshole. He always holds so still. So fucking eager. I hold tight to his hips and sink into the deliciously tight ring of muscle.

Vinicius groans and presses his face into the pillow.

I give him a few shallow thrusts, and then push deeper. Chiara's mouth falls open. "Oh, my God. That looks amazing. How did you both manage to do that to me?"

"And you fucking loved it. Get beneath him, princess."

Vinicius has one hand braced against the mattress and he scoops Chiara under him. I push one of her thighs up to her shoulder, and he thrusts into her.

"Fuuuuuck," he moans, stopping after the one thrust, overcome by what we're doing.

I hold myself still and give Chiara an amused look, who's staring at me over Vinicius shoulder. *Isn't he cute? Watch this.* Making myself sound annoyed, I tell him, "Get it together, Vinicius. Are you screwing her or not?"

As Vinicius pulls back, he pushes me deeper into his ass, and then sinks into Chiara. Every slow thrust has him moaning in pleasure.

I reach into the bedside drawer and pull out the wand Salvatore used on her, and put it into Chiara's hand. "Play with your toy, princess."

She figures out the setting and gets it onto her clit. Suspiciously quickly. I bet she's been using it on herself in the middle of the night.

I thrust lazily, enjoying how the two of them are red-faced and panting. "You've been playing with that wand, haven't you?"

She nods. "I found it the other day. I was curious if I'd still like it."

"And do you?" Vinicius asks.

"I came seven times," she replies, and he laughs.

I start to thrust faster. We're a tangle of limbs and messy, delicious rhythms. "I'm fucking you both at the same time. You feel me, princess?"

She nods rapidly, whimpering. Vinicius can't even speak. His eyes are closed and I can tell from his expression that he's on another planet.

"I'm fucking him into you. That's my cock in your pussy."

She rakes her nails along my shoulder, and then Vinicius'. She kisses him, and then breaks the kiss as she comes. Loudly. She fumbles for my hand, her eyes closed, and I hold on tight. Her hand in mine. My cock in Vinicius ass. God, this is so perfect.

Vinicius is going to come in a moment and I pull him out of her. "Put that against the underside of his cock. Near the head." She's still hazy from her orgasm and I snap my fingers in her face. "Hey, I'm talking to you, princess. Do as you're told."

She blinks up at me. "God, you're so *bossy*. What, this?" Chiara asks, holding up the wand.

"Yeah. Crank it up."

She does, and Vinicius' eyes practically roll back in his head.

"I'm going to fucking nut," I say through my teeth, thrusting fast. "Are you going to make him come, princess?"

"I think—" She yelps in surprise as Vinicius suddenly spurts all over her hand and groans. Chiara grins and rubs his cum up and down his dick.

Oh, Jesus, that's hot. I need to fuck the two of them more often. I need...

I fucking need...

Fuck.

I shoot my load deep into Vinicius, vaguely aware that Chiara has pressed a hand against my belly and she's stroking me. Pleasure rolls through me, taking my body prisoner.

When I open my eyes, Chiara's smiling up at me. Vinicius has his face buried in her neck.

I stretch my arms over my head and groan. Damn, I needed that. I ease out of Vinicius, get up and head for the shower and turn it on. A moment later Chiara and Vinicius get under the hot water with me. They're both come-drunk and put their arms around me, more interested in touching me than getting clean.

"Get in the way, why don't you both," I mutter, reaching for the shampoo and squeezing some on both their heads. They let me wash them and they're both no help at all.

"You're so cute when you smile," Chiara tells me.

"Shut your face," I say, and kiss her.

Chiara takes my hand as I walk back into the bedroom and pulls me back toward the bed.

"Afraid I might run away, princess?"

"Yes," she replies, tugging me down beside her and nestling against my side.

Vinicius gets into bed on my other side, and they both wrap their arms around my belly and put their heads on my shoulders.

"I have shit to do."

"No, you don't," Vinicius replies, his eyes closed.

Fine. Five minutes, but then I'm getting back to what I was doing before I heard Chiara squealing for mercy.

I close my eyes and my body melts into the bed, warmed on either side by Chiara and Vinicius. Her fingers are still twined through mine and I squeeze her gently. A bittersweet pang goes through me, and my nerves suddenly scream at me to get up and leave. This moment's going to end anyway so I may as well end it on my terms.

I take a deep breath, and let the impulse pass.

We must fall asleep, because the next thing I know I'm being roused by someone moving against me.

Vinicius is sitting up on one elbow, gazing down at me and Chiara. She's fast asleep, drooling on my shoulder. As our eyes meet, Vinicius' expression is puzzled but pleased, and he mouths, *What are you doing?*

Falling asleep next to him. Kissing him.

For the last nine years, a part of me has been laying on my kitchen floor, a gun in one hand and bottle of vodka in the other. Waiting to kill myself. And I didn't even realize it.

I don't want that.

I don't fucking want to die.

I glance down at Chiara, and say softly, "Shall we keep her?"

Vinicius smiles and nods.

"If something happens to me—" I begin.

"Shut up." Vinicius kisses me. Next to us, I feel Chiara wake up and sleepily bury her face in my armpit as she stretches her toes. Then she sits up.

Her long hair tumbles around her naked shoulders. I smile, and my mouth stings. I slide my thumb along my lower lip. "My lip is chafed. What the hell?"

"Vinicius didn't shave this morning," Chiara explains, yawning.

I stare at her, and then at the stubble on Vinicius' chin. "You're kidding me. Kissing did this? Do you go around suffering all the time, princess? Four men kissing you must be fucking torture."

"Only if one of you hasn't shaved for about a day. Except Cassius. He has a beard, so he's soft, not prickly."

"New rule, everyone fucking shaves," I say, reaching for my phone and typing into the group chat.

Lorenzo: *Did you all know that stubble rash is a thing?*

Lorenzo: *You've just been going around kissing Chiara while you have stubble?*

Lorenzo: *It's like kissing fucking sandpaper.*

Lorenzo: *You fucking animals.*

Vinicius grabs his phone so he and Chiara can read the messages.

"Are Salvatore and Cassius going to figure out the subtext here?" Chiara asks.

"Oh, no, Vinicius. Salvatore and Cassius will know we fuck," I mutter, still typing.

Vinicius rolls his eyes. "Don't mind him. He gets sarcastic after sex. It's his way of showing that he's happy."

"You were keeping it from me, and those two are just so traditional I thought maybe they'd get judgy."

"We weren't keeping it from you. Lorenzo's had his mind on other things and I prefer to show, not tell."

"Oh, yes. I know all about your sneak attacks." Chiara scrunches her nose at him and smiles. Then she grows serious. "My heart hurts every time I think about the terrible things you've been through together. It makes me feel better to know that you had each other all this time."

"You already knew that, princess," I point out as I throw my phone aside.

"Yes, but it's different knowing that you're more than friends. You make each other feel like you make me feel, and that's lovely."

Vinicius and I exchange glances. He doesn't reply, so I don't, either. We don't want to burst her bubble. Sure, we had each other and we've always been friends, but we never lay around together like this. I never showed him any affection.

I reach out and cup his jaw, trying to convey with a look that I'm sorry. I didn't mean to be so goddamn cold all the time.

Vinicius gives me a crooked smile, and his eyes warm. He knows.

"What are you thinking about, Lorenzo?" Chiara asks.

Vinicius answers for me. "He's thinking how happy he is here with his two favorite people."

Chiara runs her fingers over my collarbone, smiling. "Is that true?"

I look between them, from Vinicius' golden eyes to Chiara's big blue ones. Their hands on my chest and tangled in my hair. Their bodies lying against mine like I feel good to them. Like I make them feel safe, not afraid.

"He's not saying no," Chiara says to Vinicius.

I shut my eyes and settle back on the pillows, gathering them closer.

Yeah. I'm not saying no.

Third Comes Vengeance (Promised in Blood, 3) is available now.

Get Third Comes Vengeance now

Thank you for reading Second Comes War! If you enjoyed this book, please consider leaving a review on Amazon and Goodreads.

I've been stolen. Paraded. Forced to vie for their crown.

Through a cruel twist of fate, the dangerous life I escaped has seized hold of me again. Three men have snatched my freedom and they're playing a twisted game, and they're the only winners.

My captors glitter like diamonds in the dark, each one more handsome and ruthless than the last. Konstantin, the scarred and heartless ringleader, and mastermind of my fate. Elyah, the demon from my past who once craved me and now covets my demise. Kirill, a bloodthirsty maniac with depraved needs who thrives on misery and mayhem.

Sixteen women are forced to compete in their twisted pageant, and one by one we're eliminated until there's only one jewel left. My captors' desire burns as hard as their cruelty, but the true torment only begins when the pageant ends.

Heavy is the crown that glitters on the winner's head.

Author's note: Contestant is a reverse harem prologue novella with Russian mafia anti-heroes. The full book Pageant contains captive themes, violence, and a Why Choose romance with ruthlessly possessive men. The story is dark, dirty, and delicious, so please read at your discretion.

You can also pre-order the full book Pageant now

ABOUT THE AUTHOR

Lilith Vincent is a steamy mafia reverse harem author who believes in living on the wild side! Why choose one when you could choose them all.

Follow Lilith Vincent for news, teasers and freebies:

Newsletter

TikTok

Instagram

Goodreads

Facebook Group

Made in the USA
Monee, IL
24 May 2022

5de8f42d-9e08-475c-90e7-9aaa817fd540R01